Down in Louisiana, they live the Southern way. Family is everything, and women are strong when they need to be and soft when they should be. And the best men are gentlemen....

Meet Jennifer Blake's LOUISIANA GENTLEMEN—all cousins in the Benedict clan.

First there was KANE, also known as Sugar Kane—'cause he's sweet as sin...with all the consequences.

Then there was LUKE, who never met a damsel in distress he didn't stop to help—whether she wanted him to or not.

Even if he weren't sheriff, ROAN would be the man to call whenever there was trouble.

Now there's CLAY—the Benedict who's always ready for anything. Good thing, too, since Janna Kerr and her daughter are about to make Clay's life very interesting....

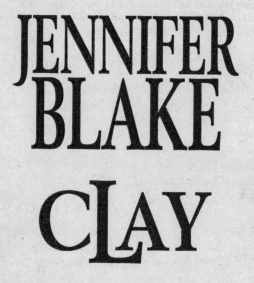

JENNIFER BLAKE

CLAY

MIRA®

MIRA®

ISBN 1-55166-819-X

CLAY

Visit us at www.mirabooks.com

Printed in U.S.A.

For Kathryn Seidick, aka romance author Kasey Michaels, with warm appreciation for sharing the trials and the triumph of her son Michael's fight against renal disease as told in her incredibly moving story "Or You Can Let Him Go." And for all signers of organ donor cards, wherever in the world they may be, for they are the truest of heroes.

1

Clay Benedict was out cold, his large frame sprawled in boneless grace on the worn linoleum of the old camp's kitchen. Janna Kerr stared down at him with her hand pressed to her mouth while one part of her brain exalted in her success and the other stood appalled by it. She had him, had Clay Benedict, the one man in the whole world that was of any use to her. The thing was done. She had turned a possible disaster into certain triumph.

It seemed too easy. So few things in her life had been easy in recent years that it made her extremely nervous.

He appeared dead, but that wasn't possible. Surely it wasn't? She'd had no time for careful measurements, however, little time for anything except finding a way to prevent him from leaving. The sedative had taken forever to kick in, so long that she'd begun to think feverishly of more desperate measures. There had been no need, after all. One moment he'd been sitting at the cheap wooden table, toying with his empty coffee cup, and the next he was toppling from his chair.

His head had hit the floor as he fell. Janna hadn't

counted on that. Moving with slow care, she knelt at his side and put out her hand as if to touch him. Then she drew it back again, closing her fist so tightly that her short, neat nails dug into her palm.

What if he was playacting? What if his eyes snapped open and he grabbed her? She was strong from years of lifting and caring for her daughter Lainey, also from wringing out yards of water-soaked dye cloth and searching the woods and fields for dye plant specimens. Still, she didn't much care for her chances in a wrestling match with the man on the floor.

He was a superior specimen of the male animal if she'd ever seen one, with whipcord muscles and the deeply tanned skin of an outdoorsman. His chest, under the blue T-shirt that matched his faded jeans, was broad and deep before it tapered into a flat waist and lean hips. Power marked his chiseled features and the firm line of his lips, though the impression was softened by the length of his lashes and the smile lines that fanned from the corners of his eyes. Even in a stupor, he appeared self-contained, invincible in his assurance of exactly who and what he was inside.

He was a Benedict. A Benedict of Turn-Coupe, Louisiana, with all the assurance verging on arrogance that went with the name.

Annoyance at the idea steeled Janna's nerves, and she reached out again to feel for the pulse in the side of his neck. The warmth of his skin was startling against her chilled fingers, and she could sense the faint prickle of his dark beard underneath it. It had been a long time since she'd actually touched a man. The act felt so intimate that it was a second before she could concentrate on the vigorous and steady beat of his jugular. She counted it for a moment, then let out a sigh and sat back on her heels.

She had Clay Benedict, all right. But what in the name of heaven was she going to do with him now that she had him?

She wouldn't need to hold him long, a week, two at the outside. She had done so much already, made all the contacts, raised the money, moved Lainey and herself into this fishing camp in the back of the beyond. Getting hold of Clay Benedict had been a last, totally unexpected boon, the spun sugar icing on the cake. It was possible that it would make the whole thing perfect.

Absolutely everything was in place now. Soon it would be over, all over.

She'd had to improvise when Clay had arrived so unexpectedly at the camp an hour ago. Denise had asked him to check on Janna and her daughter, he'd said. It made sense when she remembered how close-knit the Benedict clan was, how they looked after each other and everything else in what they considered their ordained corner of the world, the Benedict community on Horseshoe Lake and its swamp. Then had come the bad moment when he'd shown too much interest in the photos of Lainey scattered over the table where Janna had been putting them into an album. She couldn't allow that, so had been forced to act on her half-formed impulse. Now it was beginning to seem that it was meant to be.

He lay so still. The rise and fall of his chest was deep, his breathing soundless. His cleanly molded lips were parted a fraction, his hands, with their scattering of nicks and pale scars, were open and the fingers lax. It gave her an odd feeling around her heart to see him so defenseless.

She could still back out; it wasn't too late. Some excuse could be found for why Clay had passed out in her kitchen. She could let him sleep off the sedative then send him on his way. Dr. Gower might not be too happy with this substitution in the plan, after all. With so much lead-time, Clay Benedict might also figure out what was going on. Suppose he got away and moved to stop her? Buying and selling a human organ was illegal, after all, and the penalty for it wasn't light. If she actually stole one, they'd probably put her under the jailhouse instead of inside it.

That Clay would turn the key himself if he were able, Janna didn't doubt. She knew all about the strict ethics of the Benedicts—she'd heard enough about them nine years ago. They came down firmly on the side of law and order and strict moral conduct. The Benedicts, male and female, would never allow someone to be deliberately injured for their benefit, not even if it meant losing the person they loved most in the world.

Janna wasn't made that way, at least not when her daughter's life was at stake. She had Clay Benedict and she was going to keep him as long as he was useful to her.

A low groan came from the man beside her knee. He might not be quite so far gone as she'd thought. She had to make a move, and fast, if she meant to hold him.

The fishing camp had only three rooms, an L-shaped living room, dining room and kitchen combination, and two bedrooms. Space for a bathroom had been carved out of one of these, so that the other, the one facing the lake, was larger. Janna and Lainey slept in the big bedroom, since sharing a bed made it easier for Janna to get up at night with her daughter and to check on the medical equipment. The other bedroom had been turned into a workspace by pushing the ancient iron bedstead into a corner. Her workroom would be the best place, Janna thought. Anyway, it was closer. Dragging Clay Benedict that short distance should be possible if she used her leg muscles. The problem would be getting him onto the bed. She wasn't exactly petite, but heaving his hard-muscled mass around was beyond her.

His airboat also had to be considered. It was sitting in plain sight at the camp's boat dock, next to the old aluminum skiff that had come with the camp. It would be a dead giveaway if anyone came looking for its owner. What on earth was she going to do with it?

Pushing to her feet, Janna leaned over to grab first one of Clay's wrists and then the other, drawing his arms straight above her head. She flung the long, silver-blond rope of her hair behind her back, then gritted her teeth and dragged him backward, inch by slow inch out of the kitchen and down the hall. Thank God Lainey was taking her afternoon nap, she thought as she maneuvered him through the open doorway of the smaller bedroom. Not that she could keep the man hidden from such an inquisitive child, but at least Lainey needn't be upset by seeing him so obviously comatose. To satisfy her daughter, Janna was going to have to come up with some good reason for keeping him in this extreme form of time-out. Everything was black and white, wrong or right to Lainey. Janna was sometimes forced to wonder if moral codes weren't a genetic trait.

She stopped for a moment to lean on the bathroom doorjamb and pant for breath, then struggled on until she had Clay lying in the middle of the small bedroom. That was as far as she could go.

Her back muscles were on fire, her jaws ached from clenching them, and she had strain-induced spots dancing in front of her eyes. She cursed silently as she collapsed on the floor beside Clay Benedict. Leaning her back against the bed frame, she rested her head against the mattress and closed her eyes. She would think of some way to get him tied up and onto the bed in a minute. Surely she could. And would, as soon as she caught her breath.

"Janna! Janna, gal, you home?"

That call was followed immediately by the bang of the lightweight screen door that led onto the camp's back porch, also screened, then the shuffle of footsteps. Both were easily recognizable. Alligator Arty had come to visit.

She'd known her capture of Clay Benedict was too easy.

Janna put her hands over her face and pressed hard. Of course the old coot, the only person within miles of the place, would come today, now, this minute. Why not? The way her luck usually ran, he probably had the sheriff of Tunica Parish, Clay Benedict's cousin, with him as well.

"Janna? You decent? I'm comin' in."

"Be right with you," she called.

Scrambling to her feet, she moved quickly from the bedroom, closing the door behind her. The old latch didn't quite catch, for she heard the hinge creak as it swung wide again, still she didn't stop. Arty was a law unto himself, single-minded in pursuit of his own aims, with few manners, zero pretension and zilch in the way of inhibition. She wouldn't put it past him to barge in on her even if she were in the bathroom.

He stood waiting just inside the back door that opened from the screen porch into the kitchen, a wiry and tough scarecrow of a man from whom all spare flesh had been burned away by many decades of hot Southern sun. His straggly beard tickled the bib of his clean but ragged overalls, and his intent eyes were like swamp water, sometimes clear, sometimes murky, and of an odd color not blue, brown nor green but a mixture of all three. He grinned at her with appreciation while close to his chest he held his lucky fishing hat, a fedora so tattered and stained with age that it could easily date back to the forties and the last heyday of dress hats for men.

"Howdy, Janna, ma'am," he said, ducking his head in a truncated bow. "I seen Clay's Jenny as I was paddling by, and thought as how I'd come find out what was keeping him."

"You saw what?" Her brain made little sense of his words, perhaps because her nerves were jangled by the hint that he knew Clay was being detained.

"His boat. Name's Jenny, though why the devil Clay ever—but never mind that. Where's he at?"

"I really don't know what to tell you." That was the simple truth, if ever she'd spoken it.

The old man opened his eyes wide. "Tarnation, woman, he's got to be here someplace. I mean, there ain't nothing but lake and Louisiana swampland for God knows how many miles."

"Please keep your voice down. Lainey is asleep," Janna said. "All right, Clay Benedict stopped by for a second, but—"

"Why the heck would he do that, I ask you?" Arty demanded, lowering his tone a mere half decibel as he stepped toward her so she had to back up a quick pace. "He was supposed to come see about Beulah. I've been waitin' for hours but he ain't come, and Clay's a man of his word. So I set out to see if he'd run into trouble and there was his Jenny at your dock, pretty as you please. Which don't surprise me none since Clay's always had him a fine eye for a pretty lady, but I ain't got time to wait around while he sweet-talks. My Beulah's bad sick, bellowing fit to raise the dead, and he's the only one who can dose her. So where's he hid out?''

Janna lifted a brow. ''Are you suggesting something is going on that shouldn't be?''

A pained look crossed his face. ''I don't give a flying—uh, fig what's going on. I just want Clay to come out here and talk to me.''

''I told you he isn't here.''

''So I heard.'' He advanced so she was forced to back up again. ''But he's not a man to go off and leave his Jenny. I know for a fact that he loves that boat.''

''Now wait a minute,'' she began.

Arty stalked on, bearing down on her so she had to give way or get run over. ''And Clay said as how he'd be by to see Beulah today. He gave his word so I know he means to, come hell or high water. Nothing can stop him, well, nothing except maybe a fine-looking—Gawd almighty!''

He'd reached the narrow hallway and a position that would allow him to see into the spare bedroom. Janna closed her eyes that were unexpectedly filled with tears. Then she turned slowly to face the old man.

He stood in the doorway, staring from Clay Benedict stretched full-length on the floor to Janna, and then back again. The silence stretched. From the bedroom down the hall came the sound of the bedsprings as Lainey turned over. Her daughter whimpered in

her sleep, perhaps at the memory of pain, in a sound
that never failed to pierce Janna's heart.

Alligator Arty's face turned a mottled red. Jerking
his head toward Clay, he asked, "What's the matter
with him?"

What was the point in lying? She might have handled one man, but what could she do against two?
With a tight shrug, Janna said, "Doped with the barbiturates the doctor gave me so I could rest. As if I'd
dare take them without someone to look after Lainey
while I was out of it."

"Yeah." He stood ruminating a moment, his old
eyes shrewd as they rested on her face with its tear
streaks. "I see."

Possibly he did. He'd been in and out often in the
ten days or so that she and Lainey had been at the
camp. The old swamp rat was lonesome, she thought.
He'd taken a liking to Lainey, and why not? She was
sweet and loving, a precocious kid who seldom saw
a stranger. Her temporary home fascinated her, especially its backwater lore, which the old man
dredged up to entertain her. Janna didn't mind; she'd
even encouraged Arty's visits by feeding him and of-
fering to trim his hair. She was glad of anything that
kept her daughter from dwelling on the reason they
were hiding out and what was going to happen to her
when they left the swamp for Dr. Gower's medical
center.

Arty said now, "You're afraid for the little gal, that
it?"

Janna nodded. That was it, all right, and in so many ways.

"This operation you said she's gonna have ain't exactly what you'd call normal, is it?"

"Not exactly." The old man was shrewder than she had imagined. He was also accurate. Lainey had no close family member who could provide a match for a kidney donation—even Janna's tissue had proved unsuitable. Her daughter had been on the list for a cadaver kidney for more than two years, but her blood type was O, the least likely of all for a match. Still, the call for a possible donation had come twice during the intervening months. Each time, Janna had been wild with hope. Each time, Lainey's blood and lymphocyte samples had shown antibody reactions to the organs, positive indication for rejection. The disappointment, in both cases, had been devastating.

Who knew when another suitable kidney might become available? It was even possible that there would never be a cadaver match, that she had some genetic predisposition toward antibody reaction to all except the tissue of a near relative. In the meantime, her incidents of BUN and creatinine imbalance, acute peritonitis and blood pressure surges were growing more frequent. The next one could kill her. The inherent dangers were so many and severe that life expectancy for a child on dialysis was a mere sixteen years. Ten kidney patients died every day while waiting for a transplant.

The wonders of genetic engineering promised that patients like Lainey would be able to regenerate their defective kidneys one day, actually growing new, healthy ones from implanted tissue. But the technique wasn't yet perfected, and the date when it might be available was too far in the future to offer hope.

Waiting, endlessly waiting while watching her child endure the pain of intermittent peritoneal dialysis every other night of her young life had worn on Janna's nerves until she could stand it no longer. She'd picked up the phone and called the number of a doctor whose name had been whispered to her the last time that she'd waited outside the door of the pediatric critical care unit. Dr. Gower was a miracle worker, the last hope for patients like Lainey. He had been most interested in Lainey's case and certain that he could find an appropriate black market kidney for her. She only had to wait a little longer. It might not be the optimum solution, but was better than any other that was offered.

Janna was tired of waiting. Now she had a solution of her own.

"You didn't have in mind to hurt Clay, did ye?" the old man asked.

"No." Janna looked away as she spoke. It was true in principle, wasn't it? "I just…I was just going to keep him here for a little while. Until it's…over."

Arty grunted, then appeared to ruminate while staring at his hat, which he turned around and around in his hands. Finally he said, "I guess I could maybe bring Beulah over here."

She swung back to face him at the hint that he would not interfere. "Arty!"

"Now don't go making nothing of it. It ain't my business what you do, and I guess you got your reasons."

"You know…"

"Don't tell me!" he said in irascible haste. "Less I know, the better I like it. Besides, I got eyes in my head for what's going on, don't I?"

Janna was silent as she wondered just how much the old man really did see. She glanced at Clay, who seemed to have drifted into deeper slumber now, then back again to Arty.

As if in reply to the strained speculation of her gaze, he gave a curt nod. "I ain't doing this for you, but for the little gal."

"It's the same thing, really," she answered, her voice quiet. "But I don't care why you're doing it. I'm still grateful and will love you forever."

"Be a waste," he answered succinctly. "You'd do better saving that for some hunk like Clay, here. But enough palaver. You'll be needing some help with him. Might be best if he's well and truly hog-tied before he wakes up."

It seemed an excellent idea.

Janna had heavy jute string that she used in her fabric dyeing, but couldn't imagine it would be stout enough to hold a man like Clay. A diligent search turned up little else among her belongings or in the camp house. Just when she was becoming desperate, she found the veterinarian's supplies on Clay's airboat. The vials of muscle relaxants and other medical tranquilizers for large animals were tempting, but she settled instead for an armload of animal restraints. At least, that's what Arty called the bundle of nylon ropes and plastic covered steel cables and chains she showed him.

Clay used the things to immobilize Beulah and other such patients, or so Arty claimed. He had trained as a vet and actually had practiced with the local horse doctor for a time. That was before he'd abandoned that career to devote his time to rambling through the swamps with camera in hand. He'd gained a measure of fame and glory as a nature photographer the year before with publication of his coffee table book on the Tunica Parish wetlands, and was working on a second book at present. Regardless, he still saw special patients, like Beulah, from time to time. His equipment appeared to be in excellent working order, especially with the addition of a couple of padlocks and keys taken from the boathouse.

In a relatively short time, Janna and Arty had heaved Clay's inert form onto the mattress of the iron bedstead and fastened his wrists in front of him with one short length of nylon rope with end loops. While she slid a second rope around his waist to secure him to the bed frame, she asked, "You know Clay well?"

"I should smile, I do," the old man said. "Been seeing him back here in the swamp since he was a boy, him and his brothers and all his cousins—that would be Wade and Adam, and Kane, Luke and Roan, too."

"You know whether he's married then?"

The old man gave her a sly look. "Now why'd you want to know a thing like that?"

"Not the reason you're thinking," she said shortly. "I just wondered who will miss him when he doesn't come home this evening."

Arty snorted, a sound that might have meant anything. "Clay ain't married. Lives alone for the most part, says no woman could put up with his rambling around the swamp for days on end or dragging home muddy plants, sick birds or hurt things. Probably right, too."

"That's good, then."

"'Course, some folk could still get a mite perturbed if he stays gone too long."

"Such as?"

"Roan, for one. Clay's supposed to dress up in a fancy suit and stand up at the sheriff's wedding, or so he told me the other day."

Janna stiffened. "You don't mean it?"

"Big to-do, for these parts anyway," the old man said with a nod. "The sheriff went and got himself a rich wife with a lot of high-falutin' friends. They started out planning just a little bit of a wedding, but the thing's sort of snowballed on 'em. Least, that's the way I hear it."

"You think the sheriff will come looking for him then."

"Sooner or later."

"How soon?"

Arty rubbed the back of his neck as he squinted in thought. "Don't rightly know. Might be a few days, might be longer."

She could be forced to move faster with arrangements for Lainey's surgery. At the thought, she felt her nerves wind a few turns tighter. "The airboat," she said. "It's sitting out there in plain sight. I'd do something with it, but I can't leave Lainey. I don't suppose you would..."

"'Bout as well, I suppose, since I've gone this far," he said with a laconic rasp to his voice. "I can hide it over to my place."

One more problem down, Janna thought. And only a million or so more to go.

Arty attached an extra length of plastic-coated cable to the nylon rope at Clay Benedict's waist. The addition was long enough, barely, to reach to the bathroom that was just across the hall. The old man tested it for holding power, then stood staring down at the younger man for a long moment. Finally he gave a slow shake of his ragged head.

"Sorry you helped me?" Janna asked from where she stood at the foot of the bed.

"Just thinking about what's going to happen, after."

In the stress of the moment, she hadn't looked that far ahead and couldn't seem to now for the jumble of thoughts and fears and plans in her head. "I don't follow."

"I mean, when it's over, or maybe just when Clay wakes up. He ain't gonna like being tied down one bit."

No, she didn't imagine he would. Her gaze flickered to the man on the bed, his solid bulk and strong, competent hands. "You think he'll press charges, maybe for assault, kidnapping—whatever?"

Arty pursed his lips. "Might."

Dread surged through Janna. She was perfectly willing to face prosecution for the sake of her daughter, but what would she do if she had to leave her to the care of someone else while she appeared in court, or worse, served time?

"On the other hand, he might not," Arty went on.

"Meaning you think he'll be too embarrassed?"

"Wouldn't say that."

Arty's features had not relaxed. Studying the old-timer, she asked, "What, then?"

"Don't know, since Clay's not exactly like other people. He's a deep one, not easy to figure. He's also a wild one, not some lapdog you can keep on a leash, and he's tricky, especially with tools and such. Most country vets are, being as they learn early to make do with what's on hand. You'll have a job holding him, I can tell you that much. And I warn you that the devil may be in him when you let him go. Or what's worse, if he manages to get loose on his own hook."

A shiver ran over her, bone-deep and completely involuntary. Then she lifted her chin. "He won't find it easy to get away from me. And when he's finally free and in shape to get back at anyone, then I'll be far away from here."

"You'd better pray you're right," the old man said, his voice dour.

She did that, and fervently.

2

Clay awoke in ragged snatches, like hacking a path through the thick jungle of his mind. He lay still with his eyes closed while he assessed the situation. His head hurt like hell, the back of his skull felt as if it had been thumped against the floor, the inside of his mouth was like a desert and he couldn't feel his hands. He also had a strong sense of being watched.

It wasn't the best start to a morning he'd ever had. Still, he was sure it was daylight for he could see its brightness through his eyelids.

The last thing he remembered was late afternoon of the day before, and stopping to visit a few minutes with Denise's friend who had borrowed the old fishing camp. His cousin, who had escaped Turn-Coupe for the delights of New Orleans, had asked him to look in on Janna Kerr. It was likely he'd have stopped by anyway, of course, since the camp was his great-granddad's old place, and he and his two brothers shared ownership with Denise. Janna had turned out to be an Amazon almost as tall as he was with a plait of silver-blond hair as thick as his arm hanging down her back. She had stepped out to greet him as he pulled up at the rickety dock. They'd talked a few minutes, and then she'd invited him inside for a cup of coffee.

It had been terrible stuff, he remembered that clearly. He'd swallowed most of it while it was still hot because he felt it would gag a mule when it cooled, but also because he'd been brought up to be polite. In any case, he'd been too intrigued by Janna Kerr, by her dark brows and lashes in striking contrast to her pale hair and dove-gray eyes, and her calm self-possession while living in such isolation, to give it more than surface attention.

Big mistake.

God, but who'd have thought that a woman who looked like a Greek goddess come to life would slip him a Mickey? He might have been on his guard in some New Orleans dive, but not out here in the back reaches of the lake where it met the swamp. He could remember, barely, the hope and horror in the woman's face as he'd passed out at her feet. Now she had him trussed up like a Christmas turkey, or at least he assumed the restraints were her idea. The crazy thing was, he didn't know whether to kick and curse—or lie back and enjoy it.

A soft sigh feathered over his face, coming from only inches away. Clay prided himself on excellent self-control, but his eyelids snapped open; there wasn't a damn thing he could do about it.

The face so close to his was beautiful, with a del-icate oval shape surrounded by soft blond curls, smooth, fine-grained skin, rosebud mouth and silky lashes of ridiculous length surrounding the clearest, most intense blue eyes nature ever made. It also belonged to a child, a girl maybe seven years old, eight at the outside.

"You're awake," she said, a smile breaking across her face in sunny brilliance. "I'm Lainey. Who are you?"

"Lainey," he repeated. His voice sounded husky from disuse, even in his own ears. He could feel his heartbeat slowing again, and was wryly aware that its fast pace had been because he'd expected to find a very different female beside him in the bed.

"Where did you come from? You weren't here when I went to sleep."

Clay did his best to focus on the questions and other details of his surroundings, but it wasn't easy with his head pounding like a jackhammer and a small nose mere inches from his own. "I came by boat," he answered, even as he dredged his mind for the scant details Denise had given him about her tenant. "You wouldn't be Janna Kerr's daughter, would you?"

"Yes, I would. I mean, I am. She's my mama."

So much for fantasy. "And where's your dad?"

"Don't have one."

The unconcern packed into those three words held Clay silent for long seconds. "No?"

The girl plucked at the ruffle on the dress of the rag doll she carried then met his gaze. "Mama says we don't need a man, that we're better off without one."

"Then what, I wonder, does she want with me?"

he asked with irony and no real expectation of an answer.

"I wonder, too," the girl said, her tone matching his word for word. "Are you going to get up?"

Clay considered that idea a second. "I'm not sure."

Young Lainey drew back. "Why not?"

"I seem to have a problem here."

She glanced from his bound hands to the restraint at his waist, then back again. "I think maybe you could stand up, if you tried hard enough."

"Thank you for that vote of confidence," he said as he levered himself to one elbow. "But it's not as easy as it may look."

"Are you sick?"

"Not exactly." He felt a little queasy, but there seemed no point in admitting to that weakness.

"You can have breakfast with us if you're hungry. Mama's making scrambled eggs and orange juice, but no bacon. I can't have bacon."

There it was again, that matter-of-fact acceptance of another of life's major defects. Clay looked at the child more closely. Her skin was milk-white and so transparent that the veins showed beneath it. The shape of her small face was altered by puffiness at the jawline and around her eyes. In stark contrast to her sunny disposition was the impression of haggardness caused by brown-tinted half-moon shadows under her eyes, shadows that were the trademark of kidney malfunction. Her arms were thin, and in the crook of one elbow could be seen the needle mark and bruising caused by a recent blood test.

Janna Kerr's daughter was one sick little girl. Clay felt his chest tighten with sympathy even as he swallowed a rush of bile. He hated needles, hated them for himself, hated them for other people. It was the main reason he had dropped out of premed, the reason he was no longer a vet. He couldn't overcome that inborn antipathy, couldn't stand to stick even an animal, much less a person.

Shifting his gaze from the needle prick, Clay met the small girl's gaze once more. A tingling sensation moved over him then, one that was oddly familiar. He studied her features more minutely; the vivid blue eyes, the almost adult thickness of her brows, the high cheekbones. These were striking trademarks that he'd noticed before, he thought, in photographs seen briefly yesterday afternoon. Her hair was like her mother's, but the rest of her features in combination gave her a look that was oddly familiar, though he couldn't quite place it.

"Lainey! What are you doing in here?"

Janna Kerr spoke from the doorway, her voice holding equal parts of anger and concern. The small girl whirled around at the sound, the picture of guilt.

Clay put his bound hands on her arm in an instinctive gesture of reassurance. The silvery-gray eyes of the woman in the doorway widened with dismay, as if she thought he might contaminate her daughter. His temper, quiescent until that moment, flared into life.

"What's the matter?" he asked, his voice silky as

he drew Lainey closer to him. "Don't you want her to meet the man who spent the night with you?"

"You did no such thing!" The Kerr woman drew a deep breath. "Turn her loose, or I swear I'll—"

"You'll what?" he interrupted. "Make me another cup of your special coffee? Thanks, but no thanks. I believe Lainey and I will have our breakfast here, together. Unless, of course, you'd like to explain to me what the hell you meant by—I mean, why the heck you decided to keep me around?"

Her gaze flickered, perhaps in reaction to his obvious reluctance to use profanity in front of her daughter. Then her chin came up and she advanced a step into the small room. "I don't have to tell you anything. You will let my daughter go this instant, or I swear I'll make you extremely sorry."

"Mama..." Lainey began, a small frown between her eyes.

"I'm sorry already, lady. If I'd known Denise had let a crazy woman have this camp, I'd never have come anywhere near it. And I can promise I'll be out of your hair and your life in two seconds if you'll just let me up from here."

"You'll leave when I say so and not before," she answered. Hard on the words, she swooped down on Lainey, caught her around the waist and snatched her up.

"Don't! Mama, wait!"

Clay could have held on, could have turned it into a tug-of-war, but it wasn't in him to injure the little girl in any way. The instant she cried out, he let her go. Then he watched with his lips set in a grim line as Janna backed away with her to the door.

"You hurt me, Mama," Lainey wailed.

"I'm sorry, honey, so sorry, but I had to get you away."

Voice abrupt, Clay asked, "What's wrong with her?"

Janna stopped as if she'd hit a stone wall. "Nothing's wrong with her."

"I know better," he insisted. "I've got eyes, not to mention a bit of medical training."

"Then maybe you should tell me the problem."

"Renal disease, at a guess. Is it hereditary?"

"Certainly not," she answered with a catch in her voice.

"The result of a virus or some other illness, then. How far advanced?"

"That's none of your business."

"She's a sick kid from what I can see."

The blood receded slowly from Janna Kerr's face. "You see too much," she answered, then closed her lips in a tight line, as if she'd said more than she'd intended.

"So why is she way out here at an old fishing camp without modern conveniences beyond running water, a working bathroom and electricity?" He watched her, his eyes narrowed.

"My work requires that I travel to out-of-the way places for short periods of time and she has to go with me. Besides, I have a cell phone. Not that it's any of your concern."

"Your work?"

"As a fabric designer. I also hand-dye fabrics with natural dyes on commission." She stared at him with a defiant look in her gray eyes, also a flash of something that might have been extra awareness.

"Right," he answered without inflection, letting that one laconic word stand as his comment on the value of her job versus her child's life. "I don't suppose that's my concern, either. But what definitely is my business is why I'm here. Is there an explanation you'd like to make, or do I just deduce that you have kinky habits?"

"You wish," she said with a derisive twist of her expressive mouth, though her creamy-smooth skin turned all the colors of a sunset sky.

"You mean you don't want me for a sex slave?" His tone was limpid, but his gaze was as heated as he could make it when he surveyed her slowly from head to heels. She was magnificent; there was no other word for it. As full-figured as the Venus de Milo, round where a woman should be round, flat where she should be flat, she was an armful of paradise with enough muscle and sinew to make a long rainy afternoon spent on a mattress a backbreaking, mind-blowing experience. The tingling sensation below his belt buckle was fair warning that he needed distraction from that particular image.

"It's nothing like that!"

"What's a sex slave, Mama?"

"You're absolutely positive?" Purring insinuation, that was the ticket, Clay thought, as long as he could ignore the too-inquisitive frowns from the little one. "And here I was all set to tell you that you wasted whatever narcotic you slipped me. All you had to do was ask."

"As if I would!"

"Mama?"

"Then what the hel—heck do you want with me?" He sat up on the side of bed as he spoke. That too-fast movement threatened to turn his intimidating growl into a croak, since it gave him a strong urge to throw up. Swallowing down that sick feeling did nothing for his temper.

"I want you quiet, immobile and where you can do no harm for the next few days," she told him with a lift of her chin.

"And why is that? If it's money you're after, I have to tell you that book authors don't count too high in the celebrity and money sweepstakes. You should have chosen a rock star."

"I don't want money."

"What then?" In his frustration, he jerked the restraint that held his wrists so hard that it jangled the old iron bedstead, though with little other effect.

"You'll see."

Her tone held such confidence that he went quietly ballistic. Voice taut with promise, he said, "You're playing with fire, lady."

"My privilege," she answered with a wintry smile. She swung to go.

"Wait!"

She turned back with one brow arched in inquiry.

Clay hesitated. Finally he asked, "Do I know you? Have I done something to you, something I don't know about, to get on your bad side?"

"We never met before yesterday afternoon."

The words she used were precise yet he caught a glimpse of some secret intent in the depths of her eyes that was more than a little disturbing. "You're sure?"

"Positive."

"Then why do I feel as if—" He stopped, not quite sure what he meant to say.

"What?" she asked, her gaze steady, though the hot color returned slowly to her face.

"Never mind." He frowned to cover that moment of uncharacteristic indecision, as he asked again, "Why? What do you want with me?"

"You'll find out. Eventually."

"That's not good enough."

"Sorry."

She wasn't; he could see it in her eyes, in the steely set of her mouth and the way she stood. She had a reason behind what she'd done all right, and it wasn't trivial. The question was whether he would survive it. Voice tight, he said, "Fine. So who else is here with you?"

"What makes you think there's anyone else?"

"I didn't get here from the kitchen on my own two feet, and I can't see you managing it by yourself."

"You're right. I had help, a friend who will be back again this morning."

"An accomplice. I might have known."

Her lips curled at one corner. "I don't know that I'd call him that."

"What then? I know he isn't your husband because your daughter says she has no father. What is he then? Pal? Lover? Significant other? Or maybe pimp?"

Her face congealed for a long second, becoming as hard as marble. Then she gave a short, winded laugh. "Nice try, Clay Benedict. But if you think the prospect of slapping your head off will make me come close enough to be grabbed, you're mistaken."

He shrugged. "Doesn't hurt to give it a shot. But you know who I am? I mean, beyond my name?"

"Sure. You're Denise's cousin, one of the so-called 'Bad Benedicts' of Turn-Coupe. She told me all about you."

"And you're positive you don't have a grudge against me?" His voice was flat with disbelief.

"I assure you that neither Lainey nor I have ever laid eyes on you before, or you on us. We have no past between us. And when this is over we'll never see each other again so we also have no future." Spinning on her heel, she ushered Lainey from the room. She closed the door behind them both.

"That's what you think, lady," Clay muttered to himself as he lay back on the pillow and closed his eyes. "That's what you think."

He tried to nap in an attempt to overcome the headache throbbing between his temples. It couldn't be done. Anger and irritation, bafflement and intrigue chased themselves around in his brain until he was dizzy with them. Step by miserable step, Clay went back over the previous afternoon in his mind one more time.

He had set out to answer a call from Arty about his precious Beulah and also to swing by and check on Denise's friend as a favor his cousin. With these two errands out of the way, he'd planned to catch the last of the daylight over the backwater beyond Arty's place where the egrets roosted, since low-hanging dust clouds in the west promised good sunset color.

Janna had opened the door to his knock. He'd been so taken with her face and form and quiet voice that he was inside before he knew it, though that was the last thing he'd intended. He'd sat down at the kitchen table near the door, glancing over an album and a couple of scattered packets of photos that she'd been working on. His interest was not unnatural given his line of work, but Janna had snatched up the album and pictures as if they held state secrets. He'd drank the coffee she served, talking of this and that to be sociable. Then the world went dark.

What in God's name was going on here? Was Janna really involved with whoever had put him in this bed? Was the guy her accomplice, and were the two of them using the camp for drug smuggling or something equally illicit? He didn't know, and the puzzle, as well as being unable to see what he was up against, was making him nuts.

Giving up all thought of sleep, he lay staring around him, at the amateurishly plastered walls, yellowed ceiling and cheap curtains that hung at the win-

dows. A rough wooden table on the far side of the
room was stacked with books, drawing pads and
sheaves of papers. Next to them were brushes and
pens stuck upright in pottery jars, while white plastic
buckets sat under the tabletop. The air smelled of
musty, unused bedding, plaster dust and the faint odor
of pine oil cleaner mingled with turpentine and other
caustic chemicals.

The old place was run-down, in need of renovation;
he hadn't realized. Built by his great-granddad back
in the early fifties as a retreat from female company,
it had been refurbished by Denise's dad as a family
camp. Denise seldom came near it anymore. He himself had hardly been there, either, not since his
brother had died.

That thought triggered the memory of the strange
sensation he'd noticed so fleetingly as he talked to
both Janna and Lainey Kerr. It was one he hadn't felt
in a long time, a tenuous connection, almost like
shared thought waves, which he'd known with only
one person: Matt, his identical twin. That sensation
was almost more unsettling than all the rest.

Abruptly he lifted his lashes to stare at the yellowed ceiling tiles above him while a picture formed
and grew clear in his mind.

That was it.

Lainey's eyes were the key. Staring into their intense blue lit with interest and laughter had been like
reliving the staring games he'd played with his twin
when they were kids.

Or like staring into the mirror.

No. It couldn't be. Clay took a strangled breath, held it, then let it out again. No, impossible.

He had no yard children, had never been in a situation so fraught with uncontrolled passion that he'd forgotten protection. He'd been careful, he damn well knew he'd been careful. Besides, he was as positive that he'd never before laid eyes on Lainey's mother as she was that she'd never met him.

That left a few other Benedicts unaccounted for.

Yet Matt had not been the kind of man who would abandon responsibility for whatever he might do, either by accident or on purpose. If he'd fathered a baby by a woman like Janna, Clay was certain, then both mother and child would be members of the Benedict clan today; that was all there was to it. The same could be said for his other brothers, Adam and Wade. All four of them had heard a thousand lectures on the perfidy of women who, like their mother, trapped men into marriage with this oldest trick in the book. It had made them several notches beyond wary of female wiles. No, it had to be something else.

It should be, but was it? Was it really?

Two weeks before he'd died, Matt had rhapsodized about some glorious female. He'd been cock-eyed in lust, if not in love, but had laughed in his brother's face when Clay had demanded to meet the woman of Matt's dreams. He'd bring her home to Turn-Coupe when his ring was on her finger, he'd said, and not before. His and Clay's tastes in women were too much alike; he didn't intend to risk his twin cutting him out. He'd bring her home, Matt had promised, the next time he came home in his two-week-on, two-week-off cycle with his job as a driller on an offshore oil platform. He'd be sure about her then.

Thirteen days later, the oil platform Matt worked on had blown out then exploded in flames. The fire had burned for weeks. They never saw him again.

Nine years ago, that had been. Nine long years during which hardly a day passed that Clay didn't feel the loss. It was like having an arm or a leg chopped off, some part of him so necessary yet taken for granted that it was difficult to believe it could be gone, almost impossible to function without it.

Was Janna the woman Matt had described? Could that and the mental closeness of a twin be the reason he felt he should know both her and her daughter? Was it remotely possible?

Janna was in the kitchen for he could hear her moving around and clattering dishes in the sink. He considered getting up and standing in the doorway to watch, or maybe to test if the cable attached to his waist reached that far. It was too much effort. He preferred to lie back and rest his hands on his chest while he figured out whether he was going to make his break for freedom before or after he found out what the woman in the next room wanted from him.

He couldn't concentrate for the sound of her voice as she talked to Lainey. The melodious cadences played across his nerves, plucking them like the strings of a harp. He was aware of her movement from one place to the other and of her passing moods from affection to remonstrance to indulgent laughter.

The prattle of the little girl was a high grace note weaving in and around the main instrument's theme, enhancing it until the music seemed to be a part of a distant dream.

"Well, doggone it, Clay, you so danged comfy that it's too much trouble to even try to get loose?"

Clay opened his eyes and turned his head on his pillow to stare at the swamp-thing apparition standing in the bedroom door. His energy was at such a low ebb from his narcotic hangover and the bump on the back of his head that he had only a single profane and highly descriptive name for Alligator Arty.

"Now, now," the old buzzard said with a delighted grin.

"Traitor," he insisted.

"Figured it all out, have ye?"

"It suddenly stands to reason," he answered, his voice tight. "Why else would she let you in, after all?"

"Well, don't get het up. I know you've got reason to be testy, but it ain't no use calling names."

"I guess you're going to tell me you aren't responsible for these?" Clay indicated his makeshift shackles.

"As to that, the little lady was in a bind. What could I do except give her a hand? You'd have done the same." He looked over his shoulder, as if to make sure Janna wasn't following on his heels. "Anyway, I thought it might not be a bad idea for you to hang around a bit."

Clay lifted a satirical brow. "As a prisoner?"

"Oh, come on, boy. When did it get to be such a hardship to loll around in the bed of a woman like—" He broke off, clearing his throat with a choking rasp as Lainey appeared.

The little girl had a rope in her hand that she was holding so her fingers were white at the knuckles. Her eyes were as round as dinner plates and she walked with care and frequent looks back over her shoulder. Waddling behind her was a behemoth, a monster so moss-backed and clumsy that its progress was little more than a jerky crawl on the slick linoleum, and its arms and legs appeared as jackknifed as the joints of an overweight spider. It looked around with a frozen grin of such maniacal pleasure on its face that it was hard to say whether it was delighted with being allowed inside or merely judging the assorted legs within reach for breakfast possibilities.

"Jeez," Clay exclaimed. "You've brought Beulah?"

"You can't go to her, so she had to come to you. It's her belly, doc. Something she et."

"Or somebody?"

The old man gave him an indignant scowl. "You know good and well she wouldn't hurt a flea."

"Maybe," Clay said, relenting somewhat. "But how the heck do you expect me to look at her while lying flat of my back?"

Lainey spoke up then in piping tones. "I think Beulah swallowed a clock, like in Peter Pan."

Clay smiled at the earnest look on her face because

he couldn't help it. "Probably, and would like my arm as dessert."

The child gave him a scathing look. "Alligators don't eat people parts except in movies, where they don't know any better."

"And how do you know that?"

"Arty told me. He tells me lots of stuff."

"Is that so?" Clay lifted a brow at the old swamp rat who had left out the essential fact that though alligators seldom attacked large living mammals such as human beings, they had no compunction about eating anything that was thoroughly dead. "And what else has he been telling you and your mama?"

"That they need looking after," Arty said simply.

Arty was a dubious protector, Clay thought, though he didn't say so. Few knew the swamp better, and he was a lot tougher and sharper than he looked, but he was erratic in his habits. He sometimes disappeared for days or weeks as he tended his whiskey still during the summer or ran his trapping lines in winter. He was the last of a vanishing breed, a man who eked a living out of the swamps. Once there had been thousands like him in the state, particularly around the marshes farther south. They'd had a fair return for their hard, wet work while fur prices were high, but that ended with the decline of furs as fashion accessories. Now they could hardly give skins away if they got them, and the nutria and muskrats and minks were increasing in such numbers that they were overrunning the wetlands. The nutria especially, being imports from South America instead of native animals, were destroying the vegetation, leaving only holes of water.

Aloud, Clay said, "So now Beulah needs my expertise. If you'll just release my hands, I'll take a look at her."

"No!"

That command came from Janna as she strode through the door and placed herself between Arty and the bed. She crossed her arms over her chest.

"Come on," Clay said as anger rose inside him. "This has gone on long enough, don't you think?"

"You can treat Beulah from where you are or not at all."

"Now wait a minute," Arty began.

"I mean it." She didn't even look at the old trapper.

"Let me go. Now," Clay said in his most commanding voice. "This isn't funny anymore."

"I don't think so." Janna stared at him, her gray eyes hard. "And it never was funny to me."

"Be reasonable, woman," Arty told her. "This ain't no desperado you're dealing with here."

"Any man can be desperate when he's pushed far enough," she declared.

"Dang it all…"

"You heard me."

"I'll still need the use of my hands," Clay said, his voice tight.

"You can manage." Janna stood unflinching, her shoulders as straight as the line of her mouth.

Arty looked at Clay and cocked a brow in silent

inquiry. It was plain that his old friend was torn, half inclined to switch his allegiance for the sake of his pet. Clay was tempted to encourage him just to see how Janna Kerr would handle it. However, Beulah chose that moment to let out a grunt that made him take a closer look at her.

"Uh-oh," he said. "I think Lainey may be right, more or less."

The others looked down at the alligator. Beulah stared back at them with her rictus grin while waving her tail back and forth in slow sweeps with a back draft powerful enough to drag dust bunnies from under the bed.

Janna met his gaze again. "You're joking, right?"

"Not exactly. I'd say she's about to give birth to several dozen little Beulahs. That's if somebody will take her home and leave her alone so she can build herself a nice mud nest in a quiet place."

"It ain't possible," Arty protested.

Clay tipped his head in a warning look toward Lainey who was following their every word with rapt attention. "Positive, are you?"

"It's late in the season, but there was that one night when I heard a lot of bellowing…" He scratched his beard thoughtfully, then slapped his battered hat back on his mostly bald head. "I sure hope you're right."

So did Clay. Heaven help him if he was wrong and Arty's precious alligator died. The old coot would probably wash his hands of Clay and let Janna Kerr do whatever she wanted with her prisoner.

"I'd get a move on if I were you," he said to Arty,

"unless you want alligator eggs scattered from hel—Hades to breakfast."

"Beulah is going to have babies?" Lainey inquired.

"Lay eggs," Janna said shortly. "It's not the same thing."

"Is, too," Lainey said. "I saw it on television." She turned to Arty. "Can I go with you and watch?"

"No!" Janna said.

"No!" Clay said at the same time, and wasn't at all surprised when the girl's mother turned a look of astonishment on him. Lifting a shoulder, he said, "I only meant that Beulah might object to an audience. It's no place for a grown-up, much less a child."

"I'm not a child," Lainey declared, frowning at him.

Clearly he needed to mend his fences with Lainey if he wanted her as an ally, Clay thought. "No, you're a girl who's smart enough to see that a female wild animal—which is what Beulah is in spite of being Arty's pet—can be dangerous when it comes to taking care of its young. She could hurt you if you get in her way."

"Exactly," Janna agreed. "Like all mothers."

Clay, caught by something in her voice, met her eyes then. What he saw there sent a warning tingle down his spine. And he wondered, suddenly, if he could possibly be caught between Janna Kerr and something she wanted for her daughter.

3

Janna stood at the kitchen window, watching the stately progress of a great blue heron as it stalked along the lakeshore in search of an afternoon snack. Beyond the water bird, the lake's surface shifted with gentle wind currents, dazzling the eyes with countless sequin gleams. Majestic cypress trees standing knee-deep in the water draped the narrow apron of land in front of the camp with their green shade and broke the view into sections. They were like giant bars, closing her in with her prisoner.

What had she done?

The act that had seemed absolutely necessary, almost preordained, the evening before had a crazed, unreal feeling in the light of another day. She didn't know what she'd been thinking, wasn't sure she'd thought at all, but only acted on instinct. Three years of constant fear and responsibility, added to long days and nights of caring for her daughter, making sure she took her medication, overseeing her home dialysis and trying to make a living while getting by with little sleep and almost no relief, had finally caught up with her. Something had snapped.

Janna closed her eyes and took a slow, deep breath

against the tight band of nerves around her chest. What was she going to do? What? She was getting in deeper and deeper, going ever more wrong. She knew it, but seemed unable to stop. Sometimes, especially in the darkest hours of the night, it seemed that nothing she'd ever done had turned out right, with the exception of refusing to give up her daughter for adoption.

She'd fallen in love at the wrong time and been too carried away to keep from getting pregnant. She'd failed to tell Lainey's father she might be going to have a baby so he'd died without knowing. She'd somehow allowed her daughter to get sick, hadn't realized her illness was more than the usual childhood head cold so that infection and fever destroyed her kidney function. She had abandoned hope of obtaining a kidney for her through normal channels and opted for an underhanded alternative. And now she'd drugged and tied up the one man most likely to destroy her, and Lainey with her, if he found out just who Janna was and what she was doing.

Regardless, Janna wasn't sure there was anything she could have done differently. She'd followed her heart, always. She'd loved her daughter and cared for her the best she could. She'd tried so hard to make the right decisions, especially in the past few weeks. Clay showing up had been a shock, yet too perfect an opportunity to pass up; it was as if she had conjured him out of thin air, or else some higher power had delivered him to her. Not that she was particularly superstitious or religious, or even aware of feeling that way at the time. No, she'd simply moved as in a dream to keep Clay Benedict at the camp where he was needed.

The idea of introducing her daughter to the Benedicts had been at the back of Janna's mind when she'd first contacted Denise about staying at the camp. Second thoughts had hit her almost immediately. They were far too upstanding and law-abiding to risk bringing them into the present situation. What if they not only refused to help, but once they learned about Dr. Gower, moved to stop the surgery? What if they tried to take Lainey from her as Matt's father had threatened the one time she'd spoken to him?

The reason she'd decided to come in the end, was that Denise had said she could have the old place rent-free. Passing up the offer was not something Janna could afford. Her time at the camp would be limited after all, she'd thought; with any luck she would be gone without the Benedicts ever knowing she'd been near them.

So much for that idea.

What in the name of heaven was she going to do with Clay Benedict? Second thoughts about what she intended plagued her, but she was terrified of releasing him. Suppose Arty was right? If Benedict decided to make her pay for holding him, if he had her arrested for assault, what would become of Lainey? It was dangerous to keep the man but she couldn't let him go.

A quiet sound came from down the hall behind her. She stood listening. It was Lainey laughing. She must be awake from the afternoon nap she took every day, and either playing with the raccoon that Arty had brought her last week or had put one of her cartoon movies in her video player. Janna was turning her attention back to the window when she heard a chuckle in a husky and much too male baritone.

She felt her heart jar in her chest. Whirling around, she ran from the kitchen. The door of the extra bedroom was closed. She shoved it open so hard that it banged against the wall, then plunged inside.

Lainey sat on the bed beside Clay Benedict just as she had earlier, curled up within the circle of his bound arms while he propped his back against the headboard. She was smoothing with her small fingers at the red ridges that marked his arms where the restraint held them. As the pair looked up, her daughter's expression was tinged with guilt, but that of the man who held her mirrored unadulterated mockery.

"I thought I told you to stay out of here, young lady," Janna said in grim reprimand.

"He was lonesome, Mama. I asked him if he was and he said yes."

"That isn't your problem. Come here at once." Janna moved a cautious step nearer the bed.

Her daughter frowned as she watched her. "It's all right, you don't have to grab me again. We're only talking. I don't see what's wrong with talking."

She wouldn't of course. Lainey had never met a stranger in her life. In spite of all Janna could do, she struck up conversations with people in the hallway of their apartment building, in grocery stores, while waiting in line at movie theaters, everywhere. She was especially drawn to men of all ages, which was how they had become so friendly with old Alligator Arty in such a short while. It was easy to see that she missed a male influence in her life. She'd even been asking about her father more often in the past few months, but Clay Benedict was not an acceptable substitute.

Falling back on the ageless ploy of parents, Janna said, "Mr. Benedict has better things to do than play with you."

"He's not doing anything. Besides, he likes kids."

"He told you that, too, I suppose?" The glance she gave the man in the bed was tight-lipped and accusing, though she might as well not have bothered for all the impression it made.

"Yes, he did. And I told him he looks just like my daddy."

"She sure did," Clay drawled, his gaze steady and more than a little quizzical.

Janna felt light-headed for an instant. Grasping at the first excuse that came to mind, she said shortly, "It doesn't mean a thing. She thinks every reasonably good-looking man looks like him."

His lips curved in a diabolical smile. "Should I be flattered?"

"I was not implying that I considered you handsome!"

"No? Too bad, I think I could get used to being in your bed." Clay gathered Lainey a little closer, and she nestled against his chest as if she'd been doing it all her life.

"You're not. I sleep with my daughter." The words were meant to be scathing, but had a fraught sound instead. She could feel the color returning to her face along with added heat.

"An arrangement that could be changed." He craned his neck a bit to give her daughter a conspiratorial wink. "We'd let your Mama join us, wouldn't we? She might like it, don't you think?"

"I expect so," Lainey said, her small face serious. "She loves to cuddle."

"Does she now? Me, too. I wonder what else…but never mind. Time enough for that later."

"Not likely!" Janna corrected with some force. "I told you there was nothing personal about why you're here."

"So you did," he answered, his gaze bright, "but I don't have to believe it."

He was trying to get to her, perhaps to entice her closer out of anger, or even attraction, so that he could get his hands on her. He'd wait a long time before she did anything that stupid; still she needed to get Lainey out of his clutches.

"Come on, honey. I have a lot of work to do, and you can help me."

Lainey sat up straight. "Can I dye fabric?"

"If you want." It was Lainey's favorite part of Janna's job. She loved to put the lengths of fabric into the various dye batches and watch the colors seep into them. She was actually pretty good at judging shades and hues, and had an instinctive feel for color harmonies.

"Isn't this your studio?" Clay asked with a nod toward her table and other supplies.

"I work on designs here. The dyeing is messy and requires ventilation. It's done outside."

"You make a living at it, it's not just a hobby?"

The need to restrict information about her warred with the pride in her work, and lost. "You could say that. My current project is a summer collection for a large manufacturer. Next summer, of course."

"Designs on cloth."

"Woven goods of pure cotton, primarily for quilting. I do a lot of patterns from nature."

"Like the thing you have on, I guess."

She stared at him a second, surprised that he'd noticed. Her dress was a draped and rather artistic garment that she'd put together herself, sewing it from fabric she'd designed and dyed in fluid shades of teal and purple like water reflections. Sewing was a necessity rather than a hobby. She couldn't afford to waste finished fabric. "It was an experiment. I like to see how the designs and colors are going to work on the cloth itself."

He tipped his head as he allowed his gaze to slide from her breasts down over the flat surface of her abdomen. "Reminds me of the lake just before dark."

"Observant of you." Her voice was flat.

"My mother is an artist. I guess I'm used to looking at things from a different perspective." He paused, then asked, "So you're staying here for the inspiration?"

The words were so offhand that she almost missed the significance behind them, might have if she hadn't been half expecting some kind of interrogation. With a noncommittal smile, she answered, "Why not?"

He let that challenge pass as he glanced around the room once more. "Anyway, don't let me chase you out of your studio."

"You aren't. I just choose to work elsewhere."

"Because I'm too much of a distraction."

"Not at all.

"Maybe you're just afraid of what else Lainey might tell me."

His tone and his gaze were dulcet with suggestion. She chose to ignore both as she said, "She really has nothing to tell."

"You might as well work here, then, hadn't you? It will be more convenient with all your supplies around you, not to mention cooler for Lainey."

He was right about the last. The two window units that cooled the camp—one in the kitchen and one in the larger bedroom—were working overtime. It would be stifling outside. "We can set up the dye baths now, I suppose, then work on the fabric later this evening."

"Or work tomorrow and play today."

Play. She'd almost forgotten what the word meant. Not that Lainey lacked for attention. They read together, watched video movies together, cooked together, took walks together. They were together constantly, in fact. But the reading was primarily for home schooling, the movies were to distract Lainey during medical procedures, the cooking was to encourage her daughter's interest in food despite her restricted diet and the exercise was because the doctors prescribed it. Little of what they did was for simple pleasure. Which wasn't precisely a new thought, though it seemed much drearier now than in the past.

"I don't have time for fun and games," she said curtly.

Clay tipped his head. "What about Lainey?"

What indeed? If Janna's plan worked out, her daughter would have all the time in the world for being a child. If not, oh, if not, then playing would be ended forever, for both of them.

She gave Clay Benedict a straight look. "Why are you so determined to keep me...keep us in here?"

His smile was all high-voltage charm. "Maybe Lainey's right, maybe I'm lonesome."

She doubted it, but was painfully aware that her daughter could be in need of company other than her mother's and had perhaps projected her feelings onto Clay. In any case, Janna thought, it might be just as well to stay where she could keep an eye on the man. She distrusted his docility so far. She'd thought earlier that he was recovering from the hefty dose of barbiturates she'd given him, but that should have worn off. Some kind of violent protest or attempt to escape would be normal, surely, but it hadn't materialized. Either he meant to lull her into false security, or else was remaining quiescent for reasons of his own. And she wasn't sure which prospect made her more nervous.

"I've changed my mind, Mama," Lainey said. "I'd rather stay with Clay."

"Oh, honey, I don't think…"

"I'm not going to hurt her," Clay said. "I wouldn't do that."

She met his gaze and was lost for long seconds in its rich blue depths. Honesty and integrity seemed to swirl there, along with steadfast promise. Could she believe him? Did she dare? He wasn't the person breaking the law here, after all, but only a man who had been going about his business until she had way-laid him.

Abruptly Janna pulled herself up short. No matter what Clay was like, she didn't dare leave Lainey alone with him.

"Are you sure you don't want to help with the dye baths?" she asked her daughter in coaxing tones.

Lainey shook her head. "Not right now."

"All right then. Maybe we'll wait until the morning, after all."

Janna skirted the bed, staying well out of reach of any sudden lunge in her direction. Moving behind her worktable, she leafed through drawings, laid out watercolor pans and brushes, picked up a soft lead pencil and put it back down again as she tried to gather her concentration. She mixed watercolors and doodled on cold-pressed paper, hoping something would appear from the shapes she brushed across it. Nothing did, except swaths of blue that were, she realized, the exact color of Clay Benedict's eyes.

Abandoning that effort, she tried to depict a series of small, jewel-green tree frogs like one she'd seen that morning, but their eyes kept turning blue and far too knowing. She rinsed the green and blue from her palette and replaced it with lavender, but the resulting sketch of a water hyacinth appeared overblown and sinister, as if it might be hiding something poisonous behind its curving, sensuous leaves.

She had far less immunity to distraction than she would have thought. So little, in fact, that she had to leave the room to make lemonade for them all in order to regain focus. Not that it did much good.

She told herself that her snatched glances toward the reclining man were to keep tabs on what he was doing and to make sure Lainey was all right. They had nothing to do with the well-shaped planes of his face, the chiseled line of his lips, the smoldering power of his gaze or the way his hair waved over his ears. Certainly there was no correlation between them and the way her attention wandered from the strong line of his throat as he swallowed his sweet-tart lemon drink to the firm muscles of his long legs outlined by his jeans. And none of these things had any bearing whatever on the fact that she accidentally rinsed her paintbrush in her lemonade glass instead of her water jar.

After a time, Janna was able to persuade Lainey to climb down from the bed and come paint with her. Her daughter dragged her feet as she ambled over, but was soon engrossed in form and color. With the tip of her tongue protruding from one corner of her mouth in concentration, she managed a credible portrait of Beulah complete with sharp teeth in a grinning snout and bulging stomach. When she presented it to Clay for his approval, he seemed suitably impressed. That sent the girl back to the drawing table to try even harder. While Lainey held the attention of the man on the bed, Janna was actually able to get a little work done.

"I wish I had my camera."

She glanced up at that comment, realizing in the same moment that it had been almost a half hour since anyone had spoken. "What on earth for?"

"The two of you make a great picture together. Lainey is like a miniature of you, you know."

Janna gave him a suspicious stare. "We're almost nothing alike."

"Same hair, same face shape, same frown of concentration." He waited, as if daring her to disagree.

"I don't stick my tongue out when I draw," she said, her voice cool.

"Mama!"

"No, you bite your bottom lip. Did you know that?"

She did, but only because it sometimes became chapped in the winter. Instead of answering, she said, "What you're really telling me, I suppose, is that you're bored."

His smile was brief. "I've had more scintillating days."

"I can imagine."

"Can you?" He stretched, making himself more comfortable in the bed. "Now just what do you see me doing. And where?"

That was something he'd never know. "If you're serious about the camera, you can have it. Arty brought it inside before he took the airboat away."

"Considerate of him."

"I think he was afraid the bag with your equipment might be stolen."

"Theft on top of kidnapping? What is the neighborhood coming to?" The irony faded from his voice as he added, "Where did he take Jenny?"

"I've no idea. Somewhere safe."

"And out of sight?"

She sent him a cool glance.

Lainey piped up then. "Mr. Arty took it to his house, I'll bet. He has lots of junk there."

"Good guess, punkin," Clay said with a wry smile. "First place I'll look when I get away from here."

The girl's eyes widened, then she threw down her brush and ran to climb back up on the bed. "You're not going yet, are you?"

"Don't worry, honey," Janna said in acid-tinged sweetness. "He'll be with us a little longer."

The look he sent her held the heat of anger and some other dark, fathomless emotion that kicked her heart into a higher rhythm. She held it as long as she could, then she put down her brush with deliberation and went to retrieve his camera.

"What about the bag?" Clay inquired when she handed it over from a safe distance.

"You didn't mention it."

"My extra film, lens, filters and so on, are in it."

She tipped her head. "And that's all? No wire cutters or handy dandy file?"

"Maybe a tool kit," he said with the lift of one shoulder.

"I noticed."

"You could take it out."

"Later," she answered in dry tones, meaning much later, when she'd had a chance to see what other goodies he had stashed away for emergencies. She turned away without waiting for an answer. Her prisoner made no other protest, but she could feel his gaze burning into her back.

Lainey abandoned all thought of art to sit enthralled while Clay took off the lens cap of his camera, checked and cleaned it, then fiddled with its settings. He shot a few frames of the girl with her drawings, making her laugh with his droll comments so she smiled gaily for the lens. It crossed Janna's mind that Clay was doing his best to beguile her daughter, and was obviously succeeding. A moment later, she dismissed that idea; he had no one else to talk to, after all. Regardless, Janna kept a close watch on the pair. That was until she noticed that her watercolors were beginning to dry in their palette wells. She returned to work with ostentatious dedication then.

Time slipped past. Janna was only marginally

aware of the two on the bed as Clay explained F-stops and exposures and lighting as if Lainey were eighteen instead of eight. After one whispered consultation, Lainey left the room, returning shortly with three or four unopened film canisters held tightly to her chest. Clay reloaded his camera while Lainey bombarded him with questions about what he did with the empty canisters. When they began to discuss their use as doll dishes, Janna tuned out the pair completely.

The next time she looked, Lainey was giggling helplessly as she tried to keep possession of the two empty canisters she'd stolen away from their owner, while Clay tickled her ribs and tummy to make her release them.

"Stop!" Janna cried. She threw down her brush and palette with a splattering clatter, and ran around the end of her worktable. "Don't do that! She can't—"

Suddenly Lainey's laughter became a high scream followed by gulping sobs. She dropped the canisters on the bed as she clapped her arms around her middle.

Consternation sprang into Clay's face. He caught the girl's shoulders. "What is it?" he inquired in low urgency. "Where do you hurt?"

Janna hit him like a whirlwind, shoving so hard that he was thrown backward away from her daughter. Reaching for Lainey, she pulled her into her arms and dropped onto the bed, holding her daughter close while searching her abdomen for signs of blood.

"What's wrong?" Clay demanded as he came upright again with the coiling of hard muscles. "What did I do wrong?"

"Stomach catheter," Janna snapped. "For dialysis. If you've pulled it out—"

"She'll have to go to a hospital," he finished for her as he turned white around the mouth. "I should have realized."

"Exactly."

"No hospital," Lainey sobbed. "No sticks. Please, please, no more sticks yet."

Sticks. It was the word for injections that she'd picked up from the nurses who came at her with syringes in their hands. "Now there's going to be a little stick," they'd say, and they were right in their way. But administering little sticks day after day, thousands of little sticks, was considered heinous torture in some societies.

The plastic tubing showed no sign of leakage that Janna could see, no bloodstains coming through the gauze pads that covered the eternally raw incision. The discovery triggered rage instead of relief. She turned it on the man beside her. "Why in hell did you start a roughhouse game? Did you want to kill her?"

"I'm sorry. She seemed so near normal that I forgot."

"She has renal disease, you know that."

"Yes, but…"

"End stage renal disease." The words were bald; still she let them stand.

"End stage..."

His voice trailed to a halt while sick comprehension rose in his eyes. He needed no other explanation, Janna saw. He understood that no simple drug or procedure was ever going to restore Lainey to the health and ordinary kidney function of a normal child. She wasn't normal, would never be normal again in that respect for as long as she lived.

As long as she lived. Which might not be long if some chance virus, imbalance of the different chemical reactions in her body or other disaster caused a sudden emergency episode. It had happened before, the infection of the stomach lining, the sudden spike in blood pressure, the excess fluid around the heart. And so it would continue for crisis after crisis, until something went so terribly wrong that Lainey failed to recover. Or until she had a transplant.

"She's really that sick," Clay said, the words harsh.

Janna only looked at him as she rocked her daughter in her arms.

"Then why is she way-the-hell out here in the middle of nowhere instead of close to a first-class medical center?"

That was the nightmare question that Janna lived with from one second to the next. It was the one thing she couldn't change or control, the enormous chance that she was taking for the sake of a better life for her daughter. That Clay had dragged this weakness in her plan ruthlessly into the open brought her anger surging back again. "I'm taking care of my daughter the best way I know how, just as I've taken care of her from the minute she was born,'' she told him, her voice shaking. "You're in no position to know or understand, can't conceive of everything I've been through, everything we've been through together. Lainey's health and what I choose to do about it is none of your business, not now, not ever.''

He watched her for a long moment while cogent thought raced behind his eyes. Then he asked softly, ''Are you sure?''

"Of course I'm sure!'' She was proud of the certainty in her tone, though she couldn't prevent the shiver that ran down her back.

"I'm not. In fact, I have to wonder if it doesn't have something to do with the reason I'm here.''

"That's the most ridiculous thing I've ever heard.'' She was able, barely, to keep the tremor from her voice. Lainey, perhaps sensing the undercurrents between the two adults, had subsided to only an occasional hiccuping sob as she watched their exchange from the shelter of her mother's arms.

"Then why am I still at the camp?''

Clay held her gaze, his own so intense it was as if he willed her to tell him the truth. And he almost got it, would have if there hadn't been so much at stake. Trying for a low laugh, Janna looked away from him. ''I thought you had that all figured out.''

"Meaning?''

"You were positive I had designs on your body.''

He eased away from her, putting his shoulders to

the wall beside the bed. "Are you saying I was right?"

Men could always be distracted by sex or the promise of it, couldn't they? Janna hoped that bit of common knowledge was true. Choosing her words with care because of Lainey, she said, "I'm a single mother who hasn't had a decent relationship since well before my daughter was born. This camp is isolated and we're alone here. Would it be such a bad thing?"

"Possibly not, if I believed it." His words were grim.

"What's so hard to believe? You're an amazingly attractive man."

"But not," he said with precision, "an idiot."

"You don't think I'm attracted to you?"

"I think drugging a man and tying him to a bed for the sake of a so-called relationship is going too far. I think any kind of affair that involves force is no affair at all. I think you're much too gorgeous to have to coerce a man into doing what you want. I think the only reason you haven't had a man is that you didn't want one."

He wasn't stupid at all, which was a real shame since it required something more drastic of her. With a tight smile, she said, "Maybe the word relationship was a bit much. Maybe what I want from you is more basic. Involvement is something I don't need. All I really require is..."

"Intimate bodily contact."

"Exactly." She was grateful to him for providing that nongraphic phrase since she'd been stuck for one.

"How about what I require?"

"I thought the big deal with men was that they are able to separate love and lust?"

"Some can, some can't, and some prefer not to reduce the attraction between the sexes to that kind of self-serving rationale."

A knot of unreasonable regret formed in her throat as she stared at him. Still she tilted her head, summoning a smile as provocative as she could make it as she tightened her grasp on her daughter. "And just where do you fall in there?"

"Guess," he said, his gaze straight.

"You said earlier that all I had to do was ask. Suppose I'm asking?"

"I make love to you and then I'm free to go. Is that it?"

"I didn't say that."

"No, you didn't, did you? So what's to keep me from using my greater strength to compel my release if I ever take you in my arms."

The goose bumps that rippled over her skin had little to do with his suggestion and everything to do with the mental image created by his choice of words. Still, it was a reminder of the danger she'd forgotten in her concern for her daughter. There was absolutely nothing to keep him from tackling her now, this instant. What was stopping him? Guilt? Concern for Lainey? Or was it the suggestion she'd just made? Whichever it was, it seemed best to pretend she was oblivious in the hope that it would continue until she was out of reach again.

On a strained laugh, she quipped, "Starvation, since I'm the cook?"

The answering movement of his lips was grim yet undeniably amused. "It could be worth the chance."

It could indeed, Janna thought as her gaze caught on the slow curve of his mouth that deepened the smile brackets on either side and she felt the spiraling heat at the center of her being caused by his words. Could she risk it, risk making love to Clay Benedict? Could she bring herself to use sex to distract him from what she really wanted or possibly even to gain it without risking his life?

It seemed that she might have to try.

4

The direction of her thoughts was so uncomfortable that Janna slid Lainey off her lap, getting ready to rise to her feet. Clay put out his bound hands to catch her arm, his grasp warm and firm. She paused, meeting the fathomless dark blue of his gaze. Seconds passed while Lainey stood staring from one to the other with a puzzled frown between her eyes.

Clay glanced at the girl then released Janna with an abrupt movement and settled back until his shoulders touched the wall again. The expression on his face promised that next time he would not be so lenient.

Janna let out the breath she'd been holding. She had her answer, she thought; it was Lainey's presence that had saved her. Clay Benedict was reluctant to resort to violence in front of a child, perhaps, or was afraid of hurting the girl again if she should be caught between the two of them. Janna appreciated that consideration, but almost wished he'd not shown it. She didn't want to like him or admire his values, didn't want to feel the slightest regret for what she was doing to him.

In a pretense at composure, she said, "It's about

coffee time for me, I think, my answer to the midaf-ternoon slump. Care for a cup?''

"I'm not exactly slumping since this isn't my normal level of activity," he answered. "But then, I don't get up at night to check on…things."

"You heard." It was not a question.

"At one this morning, and again at four," he answered, his gaze level. "I wondered. But not anymore."

She looked away, moving toward the door. "Yes, well. Is that a no to the coffee then?"

"As much as I love it, ordinarily, I may have to pass on yours."

She looked back, saw the wary distaste in his face. Comprehension brought the heat of a flush. With a grimace, she said, "No additives this time, I promise."

"Not even for convenience?"

He meant because it would make it easier to hold him, she thought. "It's a great temptation, but maybe I can resist."

"That's what they all say."

"Would you believe that I prefer you awake?" If he could resort to double meanings, then so could she, in spite of the flush that refused to go away.

He made a sound that might have meant anything, but his gaze didn't leave hers.

"Well?"

"I take mine black."

"I remember," she said, and gave him a grave

look over her shoulder before she moved from the room and down the hall toward the kitchen.

She was still nervous about leaving Lainey with Clay, but not as much as before. She was fast coming to think that Clay Benedict represented a more invidious threat. He was learning everything there was to know about her, would soon know enough to destroy her. The question was whether she could do what she needed before that time came.

Janna put the kettle on and fresh grounds in the coffeepot, then leaned against the cabinet with her arms crossed over her chest as she waited for the water to boil. A minute later, her daughter's footsteps sounded in the hall, then Lainey appeared in the kitchen.

"Clay's hungry, Mama," she announced.

"He had breakfast."

"I know, but he's bigger than we are. Can he have one of my special cookies with his coffee?"

Lainey's diet restrictions made anything sweet a scarce commodity in her life. That she felt inclined to share one of her favorite chocolate-chip cookies with the man in the spare room was a sign of great favor. Janna smiled at her daughter. "I don't see why not, though I suppose that means you get one, too?"

"Just one," her daughter agreed, her face solemn.

Janna opened the jar and doled out the two cookies, then watched as Lainey skipped off down the hall. After a moment, she could hear the two in the other room discussing the various merits of chocolate chips, coconut and peanut butter as cookie ingredients. The murmur of their voices continued, barely heard above the boiling of the kettle, but it sounded as if Clay might be using Lainey's diet as an opening to ask more questions about her condition.

Janna closed her eyes a second then turned to pour the water in the pot, then take down mugs and remove the half-and-half that she used in her coffee from the refrigerator. As she lined them up on the cabinet, she heard Clay make some comment followed by Lainey's delighted giggle. Clay joined in, his laugh so rich and deep that it seemed to vibrate in the air. Suddenly memory flooded over Janna of another day, another man and another moment of transient pleasure. It sent a wave of wistful nostalgia over her, though she had trouble bringing the man's face into exact focus.

No. She wouldn't think about Lainey's father; it had been years since she'd allowed herself that luxury. For a long time, it had been too painful. Afterward, she'd been too busy, too determined to make a living for herself and her daughter, too dedicated to making certain that nothing ever hurt like that again.

It hadn't, either, not until Lainey got sick. Then nothing else mattered. Nothing.

As the coffee finished dripping, Janna filled the mugs and added cream to one, then picked both up and started toward the spare room. She was almost to the door when she heard her daughter from inside as she spoke to Clay. Voice serious, she was saying, "Sharing is important. My mama says so."

"Absolutely," Clay answered. "Mine always told me that only people with no heart refuse to share."

"My heart is all right."

"Yes, I know, punkin. It was nice of you to share your cookies."

"I was just wondering."

"What?"

Clay's voice sounded wary to Janna, which brought a crooked smile to her lips. It showed he was beginning to take the measure of her daughter. But then she stopped breathing as she heard what Lainey said next.

"Would you mind sharing a kidney with me? I mean, I know I'm only little, but a grown-up kidney would be all right because the doctor said so. Mama would do it, but her blood is all wrong. I'd only need one, so you'd be okay and not get sick like me. We would both be fine and stay alive a long time. It wouldn't hurt so much, really. We could even be in the same hospital room, if you wanted. When it was over, there'd be no more mean nurses and doctors who think they know how you feel but don't, and no more weird machines."

Janna gripped the coffee mugs she held until her fingers hurt, but she scarcely felt it for the hard knot of tears in her throat and the squeezing sensation in her chest. She had kept little from Lainey about the progress of her disease, had always answered her questions as truthfully and completely as she was able. Still, she hadn't realized exactly how much her daughter understood of what she'd been told.

Now she knew.

She also suspected that the plea hidden behind her daughter's oh-so-reasonable words was destined to go unanswered, just as her own appeal to the Benedicts years ago had received no reply; it could be no other way. But Lainey's mother would not fail her, not now, not ever. Standing there with her eyes pressed shut, Janna vowed to do whatever it took to save her daughter. And to hell with what it cost or who got hurt.

In the spare room, Clay was quiet. Then he cleared his throat with a rasp. When he spoke, his voice was carefully neutral. "My blood might be all wrong, too."

"I know," Lainey agreed, "but I thought it might be right because your eyes are like mine."

"I'm not sure that matters. And I'm not at all certain your mother would like this idea of yours."

"Yes, she would. I heard her tell Nona that she was desperate to find a kidney for me because she couldn't stand to lose me."

"Nona?"

"My grandma. She lives in Mississippi with my grandpa. She goes to church a lot and prays all the time. But she made Mama mad when she said that God would let me get well if that was what he wanted."

"What did your mama say to that?"

"That God might expect her to do something to help instead of just sitting around wringing her hands. So Nona said she didn't want a thing to do with it, and Mama said that was all right, that she'd handle it by herself.''

"She's a strong woman, your mama."

"I know. But sometimes she cries when she thinks I can't see her."

It was a second before Clay answered, then he said, "Does she, punkin?"

"She doesn't have anybody now, and she gets tired. But mostly, she's afraid."

"Me, too, sweet thing. I don't like sticks much more than you do."

"You don't?" Lainey was quiet a minute. "It would only be a few. When it was over, there wouldn't be anymore, or at least not too many."

"I see." Clay's voice sounded husky.

"But that's not what scares my mama."

"What does, do you think?" Something more than mere curiosity shaded his tone.

"What's going to happen. To me, I mean. If you were at the hospital, too, maybe you could hold her hand when they put me under and tell her that I'm going to be all right."

"I...see what you mean. But I just don't know if I can be there."

That sounded like a polite refusal to Janna. It was no great surprise, since Clay barely knew them and, so far as she was aware, had no idea of their connection to his family. Even if she took the risk of telling him, it seemed doubtful the knowledge would weigh against his resentment at being held prisoner. At least she was saved the trouble of putting the question to him herself, something she'd considered as she lay awake the night before.

The little talk in the spare room had gone on long enough, she thought. Blinking swiftly to remove any trace of tears, she pasted a cheerful smile on her face then pushed inside.

"Here we are," she said as she handed a mug to Clay, making certain that he could catch the handle with his bound right hand. "I see the cookies are gone. Would you like juice, Lainey?"

The girl frowned as if interrupted in a matter of extreme importance, which it was to her, of course. As she caught sight of her mother's face, however, she made no protest but folded her arms across her chest and pressed her lips together. When Janna offered the juice again, she only stared at the floor and kicked her feet back and forth where she dangled them off the edge of the bed.

It was impossible to say anything to soothe or reassure Lainey without showing that she'd overheard the discussion with Clay. That was the last thing Janna wanted, since it could bring on questions she had no intention of answering. She'd try later to make her daughter understand that she didn't have to worry about a transplant or her mother, but all she could do for now was gloss over the situation and hope for the best.

Sighing, she looked away from the child's small, pinched face. Her gaze met that of the man on the bed almost by accident. She expected to see derision there, or even censure, but found an unnerving sympathy instead.

It was later that night, after she'd put Lainey to bed with all the usual sterile procedures and medications then made ready for bed herself, that she remembered the camera bag. She'd promised Clay he could have it once she'd checked it. It would help keep him entertained, perhaps, and she might also wind up with some of the shots of Lainey. She had relatively few pictures of her daughter other than a couple of sets done during discount store specials; there had been little money for such things in the early days and no time in the past three years. Flinging a cotton robe around the T-shirt and underpants that she wore for sleeping, she left the bedroom and padded into the kitchen and dining room in her bare feet.

The camera bag, a duffel-like affair of black nylon, was heavy when she picked it up. Setting it on the table, she unzipped it and pulled it open. Inside were two other cameras, along with dozens more rolls of film, an assortment of lenses and filters, a couple of collapsible tripods, a thermos and an insulated food bag holding stale sandwiches, a lightweight rain poncho and the tool kit she'd noticed earlier. Every item was tucked into its own pocket or strap. In his profession, at least, Clay Benedict appeared to be a neat, methodical man. It didn't quite go with her impression of him as a devil-may-care charmer more interested in zipping around the swamp taking pictures than in actual work, but she supposed that everyone had different aspects to their personality. Removing the tool kit, she hefted the bag to one shoulder and walked back down the hall to the spare bedroom.

Clay looked up as she entered, then tossed aside the magazine he was reading, one on watercolor that he must have taken from her worktable. With his gaze on his equipment, he said, "Such service. I could get used to it."

"Don't," she recommended briefly as she tossed the bag onto the bed. "It's not going to last."

"Does that mean you're letting me go?"

The look she sent him was caustic as she stepped back well out of reach then turned toward the door again.

"Wait," he said quickly. "Stay a while."

"It's late. I need to get a little sleep."

"Before Lainey wakes up again?"

Her nod was brief.

"So you'll just leave me shut up, going out of my mind lying here with nothing to do except talk to myself."

"Sorry."

"I'll bet you are. The least you can do is tell me the point of it. What is it you want? Ransom maybe, so you can afford a kidney transplant?"

"What makes you think that?"

"Logic, also something Lainey said. Though I'd think you could get help from some charitable association or government agency."

"No such luck," she said in flippant tones. "So how much do you think you're worth?"

"Not as much as you may think. Anyway, who's going to take care of your daughter if you wind up in prison?"

"I'll worry about that later. For now, I've got all that I can handle."

"Including putting her life in jeopardy for the sake of your career?"

His gaze was hard, and Janna would swear there was real anger in his voice. She said, "We have to live. But how nice of you to be concerned, especially when you know nothing about it."

"I know enough to understand that you're risking her life by being out here. What in hell are you thinking?"

Her smile was grim. "Maybe that's why you're here, to help take care of her."

"You're joking."

"Why? You have medical stuff in your vet's kit."

"I'm not a medical doctor!"

"You'll do in a pinch," she assured him with all the confidence she could muster.

"You're crazy."

She thought he was trying to keep his voice down to avoid waking Lainey, which only made the frustration in his tone more apparent. "Well, there you have it, the explanation for everything."

He stared at her, his gaze penetrating. "I don't think so," he said finally. "I think you've got something up your sleeve. I'm not sure what it is, but it seems to me that it has you running scared. You're jumpy and on edge and ready to hit out at anyone

and everyone who comes too close. Fine, but don't
be surprised if they hit back.''

"I take it that's a warning?"

"Take it any way you want."

With a lift of her chin, she said, "If this is your
idea of witty conversation to relieve your boredom,
I'll pass. Good night."

She swung toward the door so quickly that her
loosely tied housecoat swirled open. Clutching at it,
she bent her head while she sought the ends of the
tie that held it together. Behind her, there came a soft,
slithering noise. A warning tingle zipped along her
nerves. Her head came up.

He was on her before she could move, whipping
an arm around her waist, shoving her against the wall
beside the open door. Her cheek scraped against the
plaster. Her breath was forced from her in a rush. A
second later, she was jerked around so her back was
to the hard surface. He grabbed her right wrist and
pinned it beside the turn of her neck with his left hand
while the hard ridge of his right arm, which was
bound to it, pressed into the softness of her breasts.

"Now," he said softly, his warm breath brushing
over her cheek and tickling her ear. "Let's see if this
improves my communication skills."

Janna gave a small moan that had nothing to do
with pain or fear, but was from pure chagrin that
she'd let herself be lulled into complacency by his
quiescence, compassion and handsome grin. It had
been stupid of her to go near him. It had also been
idiotic to forget that he had slack in the cable that
held him, and dumb to think that he wouldn't attempt

to escape because he'd shown no sign of it. It had been criminally half-witted, as well, to forget that he could react with violence simply because he'd refrained until now.

He drew back a fraction, searching her face with his gaze. What he saw must have satisfied him for the tension in his features relaxed a fraction. "All right, end of game," he said grim purpose. "Where are the keys to the damn padlocks?"

She swallowed convulsively as she tried to think. That wasn't an easy task with his hard body flattened against hers. His heat surrounded her. She could feel his heartbeat against her breast. One firm, muscular thigh was jammed between her legs, holding her with insistent pressure that did nothing for her mental processes. With a catch in her voice, she said, "I don't have it."

"Wrong answer. Try again."

"I mean it." The feel of his weight, the hint of heated maleness against her thigh, unsettled her. Alarm ran along her nerves. Grasping a fistful of his shirt with her free left hand, she tried to push him away. He shifted slightly to increase the rigid pressure of his hold. As the air left her lungs, she was still again.

"I'm not playing games," he informed her with deadly quiet. "I feel for you and your daughter, but I have better things to do than lie around this camp at your pleasure. Get these damn ropes off me or you'll regret it."

The hard edge in his voice was a strong indication that there was more to Clay Benedict than met the eye. He was capable of being extremely unpleasant if pushed. Regardless, she could not make herself believe that he would hurt her. The man who had let her sit within arm's reach that afternoon without lifting a finger because he didn't want to frighten a little girl didn't fit the profile. That was fortunate since she really didn't have the keys but had left them in the pocket of the dress she had discarded before taking her shower.

Voice quiet, she said, "Let me go. I can't help you."

"I think you can," he insisted. "Shall we see who's right?"

He made an abortive movement with his left hand, as if he would lower it, had forgotten that he could not. Cursing impatiently under his breath he gave the wound ropes another irritated jerk that gained a centimeter or two of slack. Then he moved both hands in a lightning swift gesture that skimmed along her side, brushed the fullness of her breast near her armpit on first one side and then the other. Leaning back slightly to allow space between their bodies, he smoothed his palm down to the pocket of her light-weight robe that lay directly over her pubic bone.

She had been frisked in his search for the keys. Clay Benedict had put his hands on her—still had them there—while she stood in stunned disbelief, without protest or resistance. Voice acid with self-disdain, she asked, "Find what you were looking for?"

He didn't remove his hand. The tensile warmth of his fingers so close to the apex of her body created an electric charge inside her that increased as he spread his fingers wider. A slow grin tilted his lips before he answered, "Not yet."

"I told you, I don't have the keys."

He shook his head, his eyes bright and faintly mocking as he watched her. "Ah, but there you're wrong. What you have may be the key to the whole thing."

She saw it coming. Lifting her hands in swift defense, she tried to push him away. He blocked the effort, snatching her wrist again and using his left elbow to pin her shoulder. Then holding her wide gaze, he lowered his head until his lips touched hers.

She was outraged, of course she was. She despised being overpowered, couldn't believe it was happening, feared where it might be leading. And yet his lips were tender, the brush of them a light, teasing arousal of long dormant senses. A drugged sensation flowed along her veins. Her heart thudded against her ribs and she felt as if the center of her being was melting like warm caramel.

He flicked the line where their lips joined with his tongue and she tasted his sweetness, his intense, unique flavor. Janna held her breath. She wanted to flow into him and around him, to pull him closer until their bodies merged and he filled the innermost depths of her being, which had been empty for so long, so terribly long.

It came to her, as she stood motionless in his arms, that she had nothing to lose by cooperating. Hadn't she considered using sex to help her daughter? Yet the feelings he aroused were so startling that they brought fear in their wake. She couldn't afford to let anyone get that close to her. She had to step back and think, had to make certain it was the right thing before she got in so deep that she couldn't get out again.

In sudden fearful decisiveness, she wrenched her mouth from his and brought her knee up hard between his spread legs. He felt the movement, tried to turn away, but didn't quite make it. Snatching a strangled breath, he bent at the waist. Janna yanked free of his lax grasp and whirled toward the door. Seconds later, she was safe on the other side.

She didn't stop there, but ran the few short steps to her bedroom, well beyond the reach of the cable that held Clay Benedict. Closing that door behind her, she locked it then leaned against it. She clamped her hands to her mouth as if she could stifle her hard breathing with them or hold her dread and dismay inside.

How badly had she hurt him? Did he need help? Should she risk asking or let it go?

She wasn't cut out for this sort of excitement. Her heart threatened to bang its way out of her chest and she was shaking all over. She was really afraid that she couldn't do any of this, wasn't coldhearted enough or capable of that much deception.

And yet she must be. Somehow, someway, she must.

5

Clay was awake long before daylight. He spent some time working at the bonds on his hands since it was clear that nothing short of using Lainey as a hostage was going to force Janna to release him, and that wasn't an option. Arty had done a good job, but Clay was able to loosen the ropes a bit. He might have done more if he'd been ready to leave the camp—he'd discovered during the night that Janna had failed to take the folding combination tool from his pocket, one he'd carried so long that it was polished from wear. It had a handy item that he'd used to pick locks before. But he wasn't ready to go just yet. Close contact with Janna last night had put a new light on his confinement. They had unfinished business between them that would be best settled here.

Nonetheless, the forced inactivity was beginning to get to him. He paced up and down at the end of his cable for some minutes, then ran through a series of exercises to limber his stiff muscles. A strong need for a cup of hot coffee plagued him, but he could think of no way to get it short of shouting for Janna. He didn't want to do that since he was well aware that she'd had another hard night with Lainey. It struck him as exquisitely funny, this concern with her rest when she was so indifferent to his comfort or convenience, but he couldn't help it.

He was checking out the file folders on her drawing table, which she also used for a desk, when the door eased open. A small blond head appeared around the edge. Lainey's gamine grin brightened her features as she saw that he was up. Sliding into the room, she came toward him. She was wearing short pajamas and carrying a piece of paper of some kind in her hand.

"What are you doing?" she asked.

"Nothing. Wishing I had somebody to talk to or something to do."

"You can talk to me." She came to his side and took his hand. "It might be better than touching Mama's drawing things. She doesn't like it, and I'm not allowed. Nobody's allowed."

"She'll get mad, huh?" That wasn't a great worry, though Clay frowned to show he recognized the seriousness of it to the little girl.

"Very mad. It's how she makes a living for us, you know."

"Right."

"Besides, I have something to show you."

She tugged him back over to the bed as she spoke, and Clay allowed himself to be led since it seemed she was trying to keep him out of trouble. As he sat on the side of the mattress, he asked, "What is it?"

She didn't answer but only thrust the paper she held toward him. He took it automatically while his gaze remained on her small face. The circles under her eyes were darker this morning, he thought, and her cheeks a little puffier. He shook his head a little before glancing down at the paper.

Clay lost his breath. He forgot to blink for so long that his eyes began to burn. The grip of his thumb and forefinger tightened until both were numb.

What he held was a photograph. It was one he had taken himself nearly fifteen years before, when he'd first begun to mess around with a camera while in college. The dark-haired young man he'd captured was in the prime of life, staring into the lens with bright sea-blue eyes and a cocksure grin.

"See?" Lainey said as she leaned on his knee to peer at the photo. "I told you that you look like my daddy."

He did, exactly like him in fact. The man in the picture was Clay's brother who had been dead for nine impossibly long years. It was his twin Matt whom he still missed every single day of his life.

"Where did you get this?" Clay asked in a voice that sounded hoarse even in his own ears.

"It's Mama's. She's had it a long time, since before I was born."

"How do you know this is your father?"

"She told me so." The child looked up at him as if she thought him incredibly dense. "She knows because she's my mama."

"Did she tell you anything else?"

"She said he's dead, that he died before I was born. But I thought..."

Clay glanced at her. "What, punkin?"

She studied him, her wide blue gaze searching his face. "I thought she might be wrong about that part. I thought maybe that's why we came here, why she got you and tied you up."

Lainey thought she might be his daughter, regardless of what she'd been told. It was impossible. The photo was proof enough, but more than that if he'd ever made love to Janna, he'd damn well remember it.

Matt, Lainey's father. Suspicion of it was one thing, but acceptance was something else altogether. Matt had been a happy-go-lucky type who loved women and appreciated the fact that they loved him, but he'd never been irresponsible.

A distant memory flashed through Clay's mind of his father ranting about women who led men on, then used pregnancy to force them into marriage. The old man had been rabid on the subject since he'd not only been caught that way himself but left with four boys to bring up alone after their mother deserted him. But Clay, who had heard a slightly different version of the tale from their mother, had let the warning go in one ear and out the other. Matt had surely done the same. No, there had to be something more to this story.

"Sorry, sweet pea," he said, quietly. "Any man would be proud to have you for a daughter, but I'm not your dad."

"But you look like the man in the picture," Lainey argued with inescapable logic.

"He was my twin."

"Does my mama know that?" Her eyes were huge as she waited for his answer.

"I'm sure she does."

The child sighed, then eased around to sit on the mattress beside him. "I was 'fraid so, because Mama knows a lot. But I thought she might be wrong about you, and it didn't hurt to ask."

It did hurt, however, Clay thought. It hurt him to see her disappointment, and also to think of what he might have done to help her and Janna if he'd had the right. It hurt to be forced to turn his mind to the problem of why Janna would keep such a vital piece of information as Lainey's birth a secret from his family—and also what that might have to do with why she was holding him.

Clay put down the photo then reached for his camera, as he so often did when trying to work something out in his mind. Lifting it, one-handed, from its bag beside the bed, he adjusted the focus then snapped a quick close-up of Lainey. She made a face at him and he caught that, too, as well as the nose-wrinkling grin that followed.

Even as he clicked off the shots, his mind registered the details of the small features he saw through the camera's viewfinder. By degrees, he realized what it was about her that had seemed so familiar that first morning. Lainey looked like a feminized version of him and his brothers in their childhood pictures. Her wide gaze, broad forehead, high cheekbones and determined chin were the same. Some things were different—the fine, silver-blond hair, small, straight nose

and beautifully shaped mouth had been inherited
from her mother. Still, she definitely had the look of
a Benedict. The little old ladies of Turn-Coupe who
could trace family resemblance through endless generations would have pegged her in a second.

"Lainey, honey, time for breakfast."

He hadn't noticed Janna's arrival in his preoccupation. Lowering the camera, he gave her a narrow,
assessing look. A flush rose to her hairline and she
lifted her chin while flinging her long, silvery braid
over her shoulder in a gesture he was fast coming to
anticipate. Her gray eyes held defiance, as if she half
expected him to make some snide comment about the
night before. He might have, too, if Lainey had not
been present, or if he didn't have other things on his
mind. Such as how to make her admit that Lainey
shared his bloodline.

He wasn't ready to confront Janna without giving
more thought to the problem, however. With a
smooth gesture, he palmed the picture of Matt, then
put his arm around Lainey. The girl glanced up at
him with wide-eyed consideration that let him know
she'd noticed his action. Still, she said nothing, and
Clay hugged her briefly, aware again of an odd sense
of closeness to the small girl.

"Come along now," Janna said to Lainey with a
quick, imperative gesture. "You need your shower,
then we'll make your favorite buckwheat pancakes."

Pancakes of any kind would be a treat for a kid in
Lainey's condition, with those made with buckwheat
flour more acceptable than the normal variety. It was

a bribe, pure and simple, also a good indicator of how much Janna needed to get her daughter away from him. She was so certain that he'd use Lainey against her, it seemed, was perhaps even more nervous of it after the night before.

"Relax," he told her. "She's all right."

"Is she really?" The tone of her voice was a great deal more belligerent than the look in her eyes.

"I don't make war on children."

She was bright and she was quick. "Only on adult women then? I'll remember that." Spinning around, she headed for the kitchen without waiting for a reply.

The pancakes, no larger than beverage coasters and served with warm applesauce, were delicious, and so was the hot, spicy sausage that came with them. Lainey insisted on eating hers in Clay's room, and Janna didn't argue. Instead she brought her plate to her worktable as if compelled to remain on guard.

It wasn't a particularly comfortable meal. When they were done, Janna gathered the dishes and took them back to the kitchen. Then she rejoined him and Lainey, working on a series of water bird studies while Clay showed her daughter a few more points about handling a camera.

He was framing a shot of the girl as she sat cross-legged on the bed, squinting through an extra lens so her eye looked as round and bulbous as a frog's, when a small sound from Janna caught his attention. He glanced over to see her watching them with her face set and tears making a silver shimmer in her eyes. He paused, while slow anger rose inside him.

"What is it now?" he demanded. "I'm not doing anything to her."

"No. It's just that…" She made a helpless gesture from his camera to Lainey, as if her throat was too tight for speech.

Clay stared at her in perplexity. He glanced at his camera, then to Lainey. "What?"

"Photographs are so permanent. I mean, compared to the people in them."

Clay watched her for a second longer. Then it came to him that while he had been simply fooling around, playing with the girl to pass the time, in Janna's eyes he was recording images of a child so ill that each day could be her last. He snapped the shot of Lainey with grim concentration. Afterward, he didn't spare the film. If Janna noticed, however, she made no further comment.

It was some time later that he got to his feet and moved to where he could see what she was doing. Studying the blue heron taking shape under her watercolor brush, he said, "You're good, darned good."

"And you would know." So unimpressed was she by his compliment that she didn't even look up.

"I grew up with artists. My mother has a studio and gallery down in New Orleans, in the old warehouse district."

That got her attention. "She paints? Would I have heard of her?"

Clay gave the name, different because his mother

had abandoned Benedict in favor of her maiden name after the divorce. It was marginally amusing to see respect for it rising in Janna's eyes. "She's a traditionalist, of course," he continued with a shrug, "known for her bird studies in pastels as well as watercolors of French Quarter scenes."

"And you paint with film."

It was exactly the way he thought of his camera work. He tried not to be gratified that she saw it, but knew he was fighting a losing battle. Purely as cover, he said, "My mom would tell you that your blue heron should have a patch of coral pink at the top of its wings. I have a close-up showing the right color, I think. It's in my bag if you'd like to see it."

"I... Yes, that would be good. Thank you."

He thought it probably pained her to say the words, but he'd seen enough of her work to understand that her professionalism would demand correct details. Rummaging in the side pocket of his bag, he produced several heron studies, as well as a sheaf of prints showing other swamp denizens. It was good for his ego to watch her sort through them with care and attention.

Finally she looked up. "These are for your next book, I suppose?"

He stared at her then tipped his head in ascent. "You know I've done one already?"

For an answer, she pulled a copy of the coffee table-size volume with his face on the dust jacket from a shelf under the table. "I've been using it as a reference."

He gave a slow shake of his head. "Amazing."

"That I bothered or that I know you're the author?"

"Either one. Or both."

"I came here partly because of this book." She looked down at the heavy volume, rubbing her hand across the slick front cover with its depiction of a pair of white cranes with orange tinted wings in flight against a sunset sky.

"Partly?"

She ignored the question as she went on. "I fell in love with the watery world you portrayed. Since I was in need of fresh inspiration, this area seemed to offer good possibilities. Of course it helped that I knew Denise."

"Of course." The words held a certain irony since there was nothing at all cut-and-dried about it as far as he could see. "How is that, by the way? She doesn't lend this old camp to just anybody."

"School," she said briefly.

That could mean anything since Denise's grandfather had moved away from Turn-Coupe during World War II when he'd gone down to Houma to work in the shipyards. Somehow, that branch of the Benedicts had only ever returned for fishing trips to the camp. But it happened that Houma was a jumping-off point for crews heading out to the offshore drilling platforms. Matt had often stayed overnight with Denise and her family when he'd gone in and out on his rotating two-week shift.

"Denise was always talking about the lake and the

swamp and the summer vacations her family took up here to the old camp with long days of fishing and swimming, reading and being lazy, and hanging out with all her cousins. She even invited me to come here with her once.''

"It's a grand place if you have the eyes to see it,'' he answered. "A lot of people think of it as hot, snakey and mosquito-ridden, which it can be, of course. But it's also still and peaceful, more than a little exotic, and endlessly life giving. It's the habitat, permanent or migratory, for hundreds of different kinds of fish, bird and animal life, and home to plants as tiny as floating duckweed or big as skyscraping cypress trees.''

"You love it,'' she said in quiet discovery.

He lifted a shoulder. "Crazy, but there you are.''

"I don't think it's crazy at all.'' She paused, veiling her expression with her lashes. Finally she asked, "I don't suppose you'd know anything about dye plants for blue color that might grow here?''

"Dye plants?''

"I make hand-dyed fabrics with native materials on commission for a specialty house, as well as designing. Natural dyes are never the same because so many variables go into making them, including degrees of color material within the plant matter itself. Fabrics dyed by hand with natural dye stuffs are one of a kind, always unique.''

"And more expensive because of it?''

Her smile was cool. "As you say, but also a lot of work to produce.''

"Why do these plants have to make blue dye?"

"It's the rarest of all colors from natural dyes. You can find material to create infinite shades of green, yellow, brown or even red, but only a handful of plants give a truly blue hue."

"Such as false indigo or maybe black elderberries?"

She stared at him a long moment. "You know something about it."

"A bit. I tried tanning and decorating my own leather as a teenager, like a Native American."

"I have indigo and elderberries, at least in their dried state. I was hoping for something better, or more rare."

"You asked Arty, I suppose?"

Her smile was almost whimsical. "Critters are more his thing than plants, to hear him tell it. He said that the man I needed was you."

At that auspicious turn of phrase, Clay swung his head around to meet her gray gaze. And suddenly he was awash in the same heated craving that he had battled for half the night: the need to feel her softness and warmth against him once more, the urge to free her hair and spread it out around and over her like a shimmering veil. The primal inclination to bury himself in her and be lost in soft, velvet wonder.

For the barest portion of a second, he wondered if he was being wooed, if possibly she had decided that she required a bed partner, if not a sex slave, after all. She seemed that approachable, that sweetly vulnerable.

Then reality kicked in and he had to question where she could be headed with such a come-on. Also what she would ask of him once she had him where she wanted him.

He needed a distraction and needed it badly, for himself if not for her. Deliberately, he asked, "Ever hear of a plant called Aphrodite's Cup?"

Her gaze was open, receptive. "I've come across it once or twice in old books. Extinct, isn't it?"

"Not quite. The color it makes is almost indescribable, not a true blue but rather an aqua. The color is darker than that, however, more blue than teal, but more green than turquoise, and with just a smidgen of purple in it."

"It sounds breathtaking."

"The French were wild about it during Louisiana's colonial days, in the early 1700s, because it blended so well with all the soft grays and corals that were fashionable then. That's a major reason why it's almost nonexistent now. The old French settlers called the dye they made from it *couleur de l'amour*, the Color of Love."

She stared at him a long moment, her gaze searching his, before she asked, "You're kidding me, right?"

"Would I do that?"

"With pleasure, I'm sure."

She had him there. Turning away from her, he said over his shoulder, "Fine. Then I guess you don't want to hear any more."

"You're saying you can really take me to this plant?"

"Maybe."

"If I'll let you go, I suppose." Her tone was jaundiced.

"It's going to be hard doing it while shut up in here. Turn me loose and I'll take you anywhere you want."

She opened her mouth to answer but was forestalled by the slamming of a door.

"Janna? Janna, gal! You home?"

Saved by good old Arty, Clay thought. Saved from doing or saying something fatally stupid, or stupidly fatal, like telling Janna Kerr that he'd take her any way he could get her. He had been that close to forgetting where he was and how he had come to be there. Not to mention what he was beginning to fear that she wanted from him.

It was possible Janna felt the same relief, for she got to her feet and moved swiftly from the room on her way to the back door. "Here, Arty," she called. "Come on in!"

She didn't return. Clay could hear that old reprobate, Alligator Arty, jawing with her in the kitchen. From the little he could catch, it appeared that Arty had come around to check on Janna and Lainey, and also to bring a meal of live crawfish for the raccoon that he'd given Lainey. The crustaceans were a favorite of this friendly little critter that he'd found wandering around lost, or so he claimed. Clay didn't doubt the food preference a bit, though he suspected that the animal had actually been caught in one of Arty's traps.

The old humbug also hinted broadly that it was getting on toward lunchtime and he wouldn't say no to an invitation. So familiar with Janna and Lainey's routine was he that it was obvious he'd been making himself at home at the camp. Knowing Arty, Clay was sure that he'd helped out around the place by way of thanks; he was of a generation that didn't believe in taking without giving in return.

At the same time, the idea of Arty hanging around made Clay a little uneasy. The old guy was a salt-of-the-earth type, but even his best friend couldn't call him more than half housebroken. Hearing him ask how the prisoner was holding up, so he was forced to realize that Arty still had no intention of helping him, did nothing for his misgivings. That was the problem with small places like the camp house; it was too easy to overhear more than was comfortable.

"It's about time you showed your ugly face in here," he said when Arty finally stopped gossiping and stepped back to the bedroom to pay his respects.

"Now don't get yourself all riled up, boy. It ain't as if you was going anywhere."

"Thanks to you."

"I told you how that was," Arty protested in aggrieved tones.

"So you did, which doesn't make it right. You owe me."

"I brought you some clothes, didn't I?" The old trapper waved the overstuffed paper bag that he carried. "Sneaked in the back window at your place to get hold of them, just so you wouldn't have to go nekkid. What more you want?"

Clay would be glad to have a change or two of underwear, if nothing else, was even grateful that Arty—or was it Janna?—had thought of it. Still, he was too much of a Benedict to like the idea of someone entering his home while he was away. His voice hard, he said, "Thank you very much. But don't do it again."

Arty gave him a wry look. "Ain't you in a stinking mood?"

"Wouldn't you be?" Since that required no answer, Clay went on without pause. "Tell me something. You ever hear Janna say anything about a kidney transplant for Lainey?"

Arty rubbed at the bristling beard on his face. "Can't say as I have. But I ain't bad to get into people's business."

That was an understatement. Arty seldom asked questions of any kind, mainly because he didn't intend to answer any himself. "She's never mentioned any kind of connection to the Benedicts?"

"Family tie, you mean? What makes you ask?"

"Just a thought." He shrugged as if it didn't matter, since it was obvious that Arty knew little, if anything. To change the subject, he asked, "How's Beulah?"

"Still off her feed. She don't look right to me, either. I'll be keeping her up close, one way and another. There's bad doings in the swamp just now."

"Meaning?"

"Found a floater this morning. Young guy not much more than a teenager. Caught on a tree limb at the edge of the main channel. Been dead a couple of days."

Dead bodies were known as floaters in the lexicon of swamp and river dwellers. Clay asked, "You found him?"

Arty gave a morose nod. "Called Roan, of course. He came out."

"Drowning victim, I suppose?" Clay felt his stomach muscles clench as he waited for the answer.

"Kilt, or butchered would be more like it. Poor kid had his heart, liver and lights taken, all sliced out clean as a whistle."

Clay stared at the old man for a grim moment before he asked. "What about his kidneys?"

"Nobody mentioned them parts, but I guess it's possible. Word is he was a drug-user, needle tracks on his arms and all that. Still, he was just a boy, maybe fifteen or so. God, but don't it make you pea-green to think of some creep doing such a thing to a young'un with his whole life ahead of him? I mean, it's bad enough, all them poor, deluded souls over in the Philippines or China selling body parts for a new start in life, but to have somebody just up and take them." The old man shook his shaggy head so his hat brim flopped. "If somebody's selling people pieces, there ought to be a law agin it."

"There is. Traffic in human organs is illegal in the United States, has been for years." Clay spoke almost at random as his brain worked on another problem altogether.

"You don't say."

"It's a felony that can cost you up to five years in prison and a fine of fifty thousand dollars." Clay had come across that particular tidbit a while back when a man offered his kidney for sale on an Internet auction site. Bidding had reached almost six million before being halted by the site owners. Human organs were a valuable commodity.

"Well, thank the good Lord that the law finally got it right for a change." Arty scratched meditatively at his beard. "But why else would anybody cut up the boy that way?"

"Being illegal doesn't mean organs aren't harvested."

Arty grimaced at the terminology. "Wasn't there some tale about a college kid during Mardi Gras who partied too hearty down on Bourbon Street and woke up in a hotel bathtub minus a kidney?"

"No connection," Clay answered. "That one's an urban legend, one of those grisly rumors that take on a life of their own because they sound so plausible. The removal of a kidney is a complicated process requiring a skilled surgical team and first-rate medical facilities. It's not something you want to try in a hotel room."

Arty lifted a bushy gray brow. "That's only if the guy with the knife cares whether the patient lives or dies, wouldn't you say?"

"Maybe. But it also assumes that having the kidney remain healthy long enough to be transplanted would be a good thing. It wouldn't last an hour without the special handling found only in a designated hospital setting."

"So where does that leave this body from the lake? You think somebody snatched the organs at some hospital and dumped the kid here to get rid of him?"

"Makes the most sense that way."

"Well, damn 'em to hell then," Arty growled.

Clay agreed completely. It sickened him to think of his swamp being used as a dumping ground. Death came often within its watery precincts, but it was a natural and unpremeditated ending, a part of the life cycle of all living things. It wasn't obscene and vicious and designed to benefit somebody's pocketbook. It didn't pollute the pure, clean air or perpetuate the idea of Louisiana's wetlands as places of lurid evil.

All the same, Arty's vehemence struck Clay as unusual. He'd known the old swamp rat for years, respected his knowledge of the place he called home, but had few illusions about him. Arty had never cared two cents for environmental issues and liked animals, in the main, much more than people of any age. He hadn't been a saint as a young man, from all accounts, and growing older had done little to improve him.

Abruptly Arty said, "Roan asked about you while he was at my place, wanted to know if I'd seen anything of you lately."

"I suppose you told him no."

"Had to, didn't I? Couldn't have him coming around here upsetting Janna and Lainey."

"Upsetting?"

"By talking about this boy that was cut to pieces. Janna's scared enough out here already. Anyway, it's not the kind of thing you talk about around women-folk."

"I hate to break it to you, Arty, my man, but fe-males aren't like they used to be. I doubt Janna will appreciate being kept in the dark. But that isn't a big concern at the moment."

"Meaning?"

"What about me?"

Arty grunted. "You're all right, ain't you?"

"For now, but what about later?"

"Later?"

Clay stared at the old man. He was deliberately acting obtuse, he thought. The question was why? Was his concern strictly for Janna and Lainey, or did he have reasons of his own?

Neither answer held much comfort.

6

He was waiting when Janna walked down the steps from the screen porch for a brief stroll to the lake's edge. She didn't see him, had no idea he was there until he moved from the darkness into the dim patch of light that fell from inside the house.

"Dr. Gower!" She stood perfectly still, her wide gaze on the physician's slender yet wiry form, his thinning, precision-cut hair and skin mottled by sun exposure during his favorite sport of bass fishing.

"Why the surprise, my dear?" he inquired with a touch of stringency. "You did contact the office?"

She had, of course; it seemed expedient after her encounter with Clay the night before. Still, her surprise was real. She'd seen the nephrologist and surgical specialist professionally, but never at the camp. It was his nurse, Anita Fenton, who came to take blood samples and pick up the installment payments for the impending surgery. A buxom woman with fading red hair and crooked teeth, Nurse Fenton worshiped the doctor and had apparently been with him for years. Actually trained as a physician's assistant, she took much of the workload from Dr. Gower's shoulders so he could spend time on his humanitarian pursuits like his free clinic for the underprivileged, as well as the transplants. Her extra effort in making house calls was designed to protect Lainey from unnecessary exposure to illness that might jeopardize the transplant operation, and also to prevent multiple office visits that could tip off observers to the clandestine activity carried out behind the medical center's charitable facade.

"I wasn't expecting a visit," Janna said after a moment, "only a return call from you or Nurse Fenton when you found the time."

"I assumed the situation was urgent or you would not have risked communication. We both know how unwise it is to speak about sensitive matters over a cell phone."

"I was careful with what I said, I promise. But I needed to let you know that I may have located a relative donor for Lainey."

"Really." The doctor did not appear impressed.

"I thought you'd be pleased, since it means we might not have to wait for a cadaver organ."

"Yes, certainly. It does present problems with security. The fewer people who know about the surgery, the better. You've discussed donation with this relative?"

She gave a definite shake of her head. "I thought I should check with your office first. It seemed that you or Nurse Fenton might do a better job of explaining the process and its benefits."

"Really, Janna." The surgeon's voice was pained.

"I'm sorry if you've made the trip for nothing. As

I said, I only expected to talk about it with Nurse Fenton.''

"She had other obligations," he said, his tone distracted. "I decided to combine this visit with a few hours of scouting the lake for the bass tournament this weekend. At least, I suppose that will be held in spite of yesterday's unpleasantness?''

"Unpleasantness?''

"Some kind of drowning accident. It was on the news." Dr. Gower waved a narrow hand in a dismissive gesture. "But we seem to have a more important problem here. You have a man inside with you. Who is he, a boyfriend or live-in lover?''

The question was so unexpected that she was thrown off balance. "What?''

"I heard a male voice as I approached the house, so naturally I investigated. The view through the curtain wasn't the best, but the gentleman appeared quite comfortably installed in your bed.''

Janna stared at Lainey's doctor. Meticulous in his speech and manners, he always appeared rigorously clean, an excellent quality in his profession. She'd never seen him anything less than formally dressed, and often wondered if he changed to casual wear or got dirty while fishing. He'd been agreeable to Janna in a distant fashion on Lainey's initial visits, but his primary attention had been for her daughter. Certainly he'd shown little personal curiosity before tonight. Her amazement was in her voice as she said, "You were spying on me.''

"Not at all," Gower answered, shifting his gaze

away from her. "It was a simple precaution. I needed to know if you were alone. Since you weren't, I was forced to wait for a chance to speak to you, not the best use of my time."

"I'm sorry, but I didn't realize..."

"That isn't the point. May I remind you, my dear, that the instructions you were given to isolate your daughter, abandon contact with family and friends and restrict your movements, were designed to protect us all."

"I know that."

"Sexual activity is important to human health. No one understands this better than I do," he went on with scarcely a pause. "Still, you must control your libido under the present circumstances. I'm afraid that your private life will have to wait."

"The circumstances have nothing to do with my private life!" Janna declared in rising anger. In fact, she had no private life as this man understood it.

"No, but who you permit to know about our association may be extremely important, since it could jeopardize everything. I thought I had impressed upon you the need to be discreet."

To reassure him on that point would be easy. All she had to do was open her mouth and tell him that the man inside was the prospective relative donor, and that he was helpless to prevent the removal of a kidney. She couldn't do it. Something inside her, some reaction to the doctor's scolding tone, some simple instinct or internal prohibition, prevented the words from forming. Moreover, she wasn't so sure

Clay was that defenseless. His response was bound to be violent, in spite of his bonds, if Dr. Gower or anyone else came at him with a sedative-filled syringe. It would require at least two people to subdue him for transport to the medical center, and possibly more. Why that hadn't occurred to her before she didn't know, since it was so obvious. She hated the idea of witnessing it, much less being a part of it.

Another factor was the doctor's obvious reluctance to accept a kidney from a source other than the one used by the center. What that meant was unclear. She didn't know—and wasn't sure she wanted to know— the exact black market conditions that provided the kidneys he implanted. She suspected that they were obtained from accident victims who had never meant to be organ donors, or perhaps other cadavers in an organ-theft ring based in some big city hospital. Another possibility was that they were taken from living donors, third world citizens desperate enough to exchange a kidney for a ticket to a new life, or drug addicts willing to sell one for the price of a few weeks or months of fixes. Such possibilities haunted her waking hours, and were another reason she'd acted so recklessly where Clay was concerned. He was not only a good candidate for blood and tissue match, but he was obviously healthy so she need have no fear that either he or Lainey would be put at more risk than they could stand. The guilt she must live with over taking a kidney would be the same, but the potential benefits much greater.

Or so she'd thought before the time had actually

come to turn Clay over to Dr. Gower. "The longer we have to wait, Lainey and I, the more risk we all face," Janna said at last. "That's one advantage of this relative donor. Arrangements could be made almost immediately instead of depending on location of a compatible cadaver kidney."

"That's no longer true."

"What do you mean?"

"I didn't come here tonight solely because of your call or even the tournament. I have news, as well, the news you've been waiting so long to hear."

A fatalistic acceptance descended on Janna. "You have a compatible kidney now? It's ready for Lainey?"

The doctor smiled a little, though he didn't answer directly. "How is the dear child? Well, I hope? No setbacks, no little illness that might make surgery problematical?"

"Nothing. If you'd like to take a look at her..."

"That won't be possible under the circumstances."

"No, of course not." She put her hand out to touch his arm under the smooth sleeve of his shirt. "I just— you are saying what I think, aren't you?"

"We've been promised a kidney." Gower's face softened and he covered her cool fingers with his own.

Maybe this was better. Maybe it would cause fewer problems in the end. "Promised?"

"Soon. Anita will be in touch. That is the good news. The bad news, I'm afraid, is that the price has gone up."

It was a moment before the last words penetrated. "Gone up? But I made the final payment last week, as agreed."

"I'm sorry. Anita insists that it's necessary, and she handles financial matters for me, you know. You have to realize that it's getting more and more difficult to arrange these things."

"Yes, but still."

"Your daughter isn't my only transplant patient. I do my best to help everyone possible, in spite of heavy expenses—complicated delivery and preservation procedures for the precious kidneys, payoffs, security personnel, that sort of thing. The money must be found to take care of them."

She believed that he was sincere; it was there in his face and voice. She'd liked Dr. Gower well enough on the occasions when he had seen Lainey, and respected what he was trying to do for those who had nowhere else to turn. She'd often wondered what caused him to set up his transplant facility down near the Projects, whether it was pure altruism as Anita Fenton maintained, or alcohol, drugs, maybe even the lure of huge fees in the form of cash that he didn't have to share with the IRS. He'd given her a cut-rate price at first because he was drawn to Lainey, she thought. Some of the patients to whom she whispered about such things during Lainey's legitimate treatments had mentioned sums well over a hundred thousand for the clandestine transplant procedure. No price was too high for her daughter's life, but Janna wondered now if the low initial price hadn't been a fraud, if she wasn't being manipulated by her own desperation.

As firmly as she was able, she said, "I don't think I can pay more."

"You must, for your daughter's sake. It will be an additional thirty percent."

Thirty percent.

Thirty percent more. Thirty percent in addition to the amount she'd scraped together by selling nearly everything she owned, borrowing from every institution that would lend her a cent and every person that she knew. Voice flat, she said, "I can't."

"I think you can if you try hard enough. You have three days before Anita comes to collect it."

"Please," she said, hating the necessity for begging but driven to it. "I really can't rake up another penny. There's just no one left to ask."

"Try your male guest," Dr. Gower recommended with a slight twist of his lips. "I will be surprised if he refuses you."

"You don't know him," she said tightly, "or the situation."

"No, but I know you. In his shoes, I'd find it difficult to say no to anything you wanted from me."

She glanced at the doctor, met his dark gaze that was only an inch above her own. Stillness settled between them, and she had the unwelcome impression that he might be waiting for her to make a different, more personal appeal. The idea was disconcerting. Had it always been there or only surfaced because of the presence of a man in her home, her bed? Had she been oblivious before in her concentration on Lainey, but was aware now because of the sexual undercurrents between her and Clay? Or was the whole thing a figment of her overwrought imagination?

"I'll see what I can do," she said, turning her gaze toward the darkly glittering lake.

"Good." Dr. Gower stepped away from her. "As I said, you'll be hearing from Anita."

He moved off quietly into the night. Janna heard the crunch of his footsteps on the gravel driveway that led to the road. Long seconds ticked past, then from some distance away came the sound of a powerful car engine starting. It purred away into the night and all was quiet again.

A shiver ran over Janna and she clasped her arms around her waist. Everything was going wrong, or so it seemed. She wasn't sure where or how it had begun, but there was no apparent end to it.

Several things today had been odd, as she thought back on them, beginning with Arty's visit. He hadn't been his usual, irascibly humorous self. He had avoided her gaze much of the time, and when he couldn't, she thought she saw condemnation in his watery eyes. He'd visited with Clay far longer than with her or Lainey, and the two men had talked in voices too low to hear. Clay had been silent, almost morose, when the old swamp rat had gone, so that she missed his lazy grin and suggestive banter. On top of that, there had been an unusual amount of activity out on the lake, with the sound of boats zipping up and down the main channel and waves lapping around the dock like surf. Regardless, Clay had not mentioned the commotion or even seemed to notice it.

Lifting her head, she stared up through the feathery branches of a big cypress at the quarter moon that floated overhead. God, but what was she going to do? This was a judgment on her; to get so close to being able to save Lainey and then have the chance snatched away.

Not for the first time, she wondered if it was really for Lainey's sake that she was so determined to pursue this illegal transplant surgery. Was it actually her daughter she was trying to save, or was it her own selfish need that was so important, the need to hold on to the only thing that made her life worthwhile? In the end, was she only trying to save herself?

She didn't know. She really didn't, and she was too tired from being wrapped up in the day-to-day emergencies of caring for Lainey to work it out. The only thing she knew was that she couldn't stop. She was in too deep, with too much at stake.

Janna moved back up onto the screen porch. The raccoon Arty had brought for Lainey was curled up in a ball in the corner of its homemade cage. Janna sat down beside him and stroked his soft fur through an opening between the wooden bars. The little critter had turned out to be as tame and mischievous as a kitten. Clay and Lainey had put their heads together and named him Ringo in honor of the stripes that ringed his tail. Janna had misgivings about the germs and infections that might be introduced by such a pet, but Clay had assured her that she was worrying for nothing. She hoped he was right, since Lainey had grown attached to the fur ball. If the truth were known, even she was developing a fondness for him.

Money, she had to have more money.

Her parents had loaned her a sizable sum already, though they objected on moral grounds and because they were horrified at the risk she was taking. They were nearing retirement age, however, and could part with no more, at least not comfortably. If she asked again for help with Lainey, they would try to talk her into coming back home where she'd be smothered and lectured and coaxed into resignation until both she and her daughter might well die from loss of hope.

Janna couldn't go back. She was grateful beyond words to them for letting her return home while she was pregnant, and for helping with the baby while she completed her degree in art at Mississippi State. She knew it hadn't been easy for them, knew also that they loved her and Lainey. But they didn't understand her distrust of male promises or her need for independence. They felt she should have accepted the first marriage proposal that came her way and become a stay-at-home wife and mother with her fabric designing as a nice little hobby.

Arty had become a good friend. She appreciated his visits in this out of the way spot, and was grateful for the few times when he'd entertained Lainey so she could work. But as valuable as his presence had become, there were limits to what she could or would expect from him, even if he had it to offer.

Dr. Gower thought she should turn to Clay. Now there was a joke. Ask for help from the man she'd drugged and tied to a bed, then kneed in his most vulnerable spot when he attempted to break free? He would help all right, help send her straight to jail.

And yet, Clay belonged to the Benedict clan, a family of influence, community standing and a certain amount of wealth. Of all the people she knew, he came closest to having the means to solve her problem. All she had to do was overcome his Benedict sense of right and wrong.

Clay was attracted to her. She knew that without conceit or any special sense of favor. It was purely physical, a chemical reaction with little emotion behind it. Could she soothe his wounded ego over being held captive by her? Was it remotely possible that she could convince him he was at the camp because she'd been so overwhelmed by instant desire that she couldn't bear to let him leave?

Sex as a bribe again. Why did that keep presenting itself as such a compelling alternative? Maybe Dr. Gower was right about her libido.

Janna squeezed her eyes tight and leaned forward to put her face in her hands. She was strung out so far past exhaustion that the most incredible things seemed not only logical but also inevitable.

How had she come to this? She'd thought never to make love except as an honest expression of deep emotion. It was abhorrent to even think of that kind of closeness, the orchestration of such intimacy, in any other way. How could she manage it without losing some portion of her pride and self-respect? Or, as far as that went, without getting hurt in the process?

It was impossible. She just couldn't do it.

Could she?

It was a half hour later when she got to her feet with weary effort and went back inside. She checked on Lainey to make certain that everything was proceeding normally with her dialysis, and that she was still asleep. Afterward, Janna showered for the night, noting as she did so that Clay had used her absence to take his own bath. He was a self-sufficient man she'd discovered, more than capable of looking after himself, entertaining himself. It was a good thing, because she had little time for the task.

If he'd been a different kind of man, he could have made it harder for her, she thought. Thankfully he wasn't, or hadn't been so far. That was worrisome, she had to admit. From the things Arty had told her, she'd expected more fireworks. What did that mean, if anything?

She brushed her teeth and pulled on her sleep T-shirt. Picking up her discarded clothes, she left the bathroom. Her long hair was caught inside the shirt's neckline, and she bent her head forward as she dragged it free. Some slight sound, or brief movement at the periphery of vision, snatched at her attention. When she glanced up, she was mere inches away from a half-naked, male body.

She stumbled, inhaling sharply, as she came to a halt.

"Careful," Clay said as he put out his hand to catch her arm. "I didn't mean to get in your way."

There was a faint huskiness in his drawled words that brought moist heat to Janna's face. She thought his every fingerprint must be seared into the skin of her arm. He was wearing only a pair of sleep shorts in a fabric that had the drape of silk but might be polyester, she noticed before hurriedly raising her gaze higher.

"My fault," she said as she stepped back. "I wasn't looking."

"Had other things on your mind, did you? Such as whatever you were talking about with your late-night visitor?"

She might have known he'd have the hearing of a wolf on the hunt. "I must have been talking to myself," she replied over her shoulder as she continued toward her bedroom and tossed her discarded clothes into the basket of dirty laundry just inside the door.

"Your testosterone level has climbed since dinner then. Sounded like a man to me."

"You're imagining things."

Voice soft, he said, "Don't play me for a fool, Janna."

She met his dark blue gaze across the space that divided them. It was cold and piercing in the dim light of the cheap overhead fixture, so that she felt suddenly chilled. It seemed there was nothing he didn't know or couldn't guess about her, that it was useless to try to hide anything from him. The impulse to tell him everything and ask for his help rose inside her with such strength that holding it back almost choked her.

She had to say something, do something to convince him that things were at least seminormal. Slipping past him again, she walked into the kitchen as she said, "I wouldn't dream of playing you at all. I'm having a glass of wine. Want one?"

He lifted a brow as he let his gaze travel from the top of her head, down the shining length of her hair, which trailed over her back like a damp shawl, to the pink toes of her bare feet. "Sure," he said, lifting a shoulder. "Why not?"

She busied herself taking the wine from the refrigerator and finding a couple of tumblers, since there were no wineglasses. After pouring the wine, she turned to hand a tumbler to Clay.

He swirled the ruby liquid in his glass, watching it stain the thick sides. Without looking up, he asked, "So who was it out there just now? Maybe a contact for a drug drop?"

She laughed with a harsh sound of strained nerves. "You don't give up, do you?"

"It doesn't pay. So was the guy a dealer?"

"Do I really look like a drug pusher?"

"You could be a go-between. Artistic types are known for a certain friendliness toward alternate lifestyles, and they can usually use the money."

"Thank you for your concern, but I haven't reached that level yet."

"No?" He paused, then said deliberately, "Must have been your contact for an illegal kidney then."

Shock washed over Janna. She couldn't speak for a second, couldn't move. She had to clench her teeth to stop their chattering and break eye contact before she could recover her composure. "That's ridiculous."

"Is it? I thought maybe it was the reason you decided to knock me out, because I got in the way somehow. Though I have to wonder who you were protecting by it, Lainey, yourself, your supplier...or maybe me?"

Outside, a breeze off the lake whispered through the trees and made the swing on the porch creak on its chains. An odd, surreal sensation gripped Janna. Almost without volition, she asked, "Why would you think any such thing?"

"It all adds up, the secrecy, your isolation out here with a sick child who is obviously the center of your life, the serious nature of her illness. Then there's the fact that Lainey expects to have major surgery soon."

Janna had heard Lainey ask Clay about a kidney, of course. The connection was fairly obvious, when all was said and done. "And what if you're right?"

"If I am, you must be crazier than I thought."

She turned slowly to face him again. Her voice as she spoke was uneven, and as breathless as if she'd been running a race. "Maybe I am, but some things do that to you. Things such as watching your child scream every time blood is drawn, or hearing her beg not to be taken in for the tests she must have to save her life. Watching her try to smile because she doesn't want the nurses to get mad at her so they pull and shove her and make her hurt. Cleaning her blood with dialysis every other night, and trying desperately to keep a sterile field for the treatments in spite of interruptions by ringing phones, someone at the door, or accidents caused by clumsiness from lack of sleep. Reading the numbers every week, knowing that they are rising and that each degree upward means your child is that much closer to dying. Going wild with hope and joy at the news that a kidney is available, only to crash when you learn that it's incompatible. Being terrified that you can't afford whatever it will take to make her well, or at least well enough to lead a seminormal life.''

"Don't.''

It was a request, harsh yet polite, as he took a step toward her. Still she couldn't stop now that she'd begun. "Then there are the little problems, like making certain that she never loses her favorite toy because letting her hold it is the only way to keep her from crying. Doing your best not to cause her pain like everyone else, but knowing you must. Listening to her cry anyway when it hurts too much.''

"Janna, please stop,'' he said again, his voice husky and his face set as he reached with bound hands to brush the cool flesh of her arm.

She paid scant attention as she began a slow rocking motion where she stood. Voice trembling now, she went on in a rush, "I have to be the mean mama always, you know, have to say no to everything she loves. To tell her, no, she can't go swimming because it might cause infection in her peritoneal incision. No, she can't have cake and ice cream and potato chips because every bite she takes should be nutritious. No, she can't play with the other children because she might get a virus that she can't fight or that would make surgery impossible at the chosen time. No, she can't go outside because it's too hot or too cold or too windy or too wet. No, she can't run because she might fall and hurt herself. No, no, no, always no.''

Clay released her long enough to take the tumbler from her shaking hand and set it on the nearby stovetop along with his own. Then he pulled her against him, lifting his arms over her head and settling her into the circle made by his fettered wrists. It was only as her face came in contact with his bare shoulder that she realized she was crying, the tears running in hot, wet streams down her face and neck to pool in the hollow of her throat. He drew her closer with gentle care, and that very gentleness snapped what was left of her self-control.

With a strangled sob, Janna put her arms around his waist above his harness and held on tight while her chest heaved with difficult breaths and all the endless, useless pain tore at her heart. He smoothed his hand up and down her back and whispered curses and other things she couldn't quite hear. He brushed his jaw against her temple in an aimless caress, and when her tears still ran, pressed a kiss to her forehead and the tear-streaked corner of her eye in the kind of passionless caress reserved for grieving children.

Feeling it, accepting the benediction of its intent, Janna found a degree of self-restraint. Lifting one hand, she caught the sleeve of her oversize sleep shirt and wiped her face. Then she leaned back a little in the circle of Clay's arms and raised her wet eyes to search his face.

He was watching her, his own gaze shuttered behind his lashes. They stood perfectly still while time stretched to match the slow and heavy beating of their hearts. Her breasts were pressed to the hard planes of his chest; her pelvis met and fit his in perfect alignment. His breath feathered her cheek, and it seemed she could feel his gaze on her skin like the touch of blue-hot steel. She couldn't move, couldn't step away for the imprisoning hold of his arms. And she wasn't sure she wanted to try.

He dipped his head a fraction, then paused. She parted her lips for a swift intake of air. Did he move again, or did she? She wasn't sure, couldn't tell, but an instant later his mouth was on hers.

7

The touch of his lips was warm and tender and tasted of wine and desire mingled with her own salt tears. It filled Janna's senses, setting off a rising tide of pure, rich pleasure. She breathed deep, inhaling his scent, which acted like an aphrodisiac so her nipples tightened, pressing more firmly against him. In some dim corner of her mind was a vagrant gratitude that he had made it unnecessary for her to carry out her half-planned seduction, but it was short-lived, banished by unexpected, unimagined wonder.

He was perfect, the absolute match for her every curve and hollow, like a lock and key or the last piece of a puzzle. The brush of his bare thighs against hers, the slight abrasion of the dark hair along their muscled length, was an enticement to move closer. She complied in mindless instinct, until only a few threads of white knitted cotton separated them.

And then there was nothing except endless, aching space as he released her in an abrupt movement.

Lifting his arms up and over her head, he stepped away until his back was against the white metal of the refrigerator. With the fingers of his bound hands lightly meshed and held in front of him at the level of his crotch, he slumped against it with his ankles crossed. In tones as devoid of emotion as his face, he said, "Sorry."

So was she, sorry that he had stopped, sorry that she was caught without a glib rejoinder to assuage her pride, sorry she could not pass off the incident as one without meaning. Frustration, both physical and mental, clouded her mind until all she could think of was how he could appear so unmoved.

"I just meant to offer a handy shoulder," he went on with the brief flicker of a smile. "Anything else seems like a bad idea under the circumstances."

"Yes," she said in mechanical agreement. Immediately afterward, she wondered why he hadn't taken advantage of her moment of weakness to force her to release him. He could have, she knew; she'd felt his strength of body and will. True, she still carried no padlock keys on her, but that obstacle could have been overcome if he'd been prepared to be cruel. Was she being lulled into complacency? Did he have some idea of taking her and Lainey hostage when he made his bid for escape so he could turn them over to the authorities? Or could Clay Benedict possibly have a concealed agenda that involved remaining at the camp?

Janna opened her mouth to put the questions to him, then closed it again. Some things it was just as well not to know, she thought, especially when they couldn't be changed.

She moved away from him and down the hall. He didn't offer to stop her. At the door of her bedroom, she looked back to find him following her movements with intent concentration. In quiet appreciation, she said, ''Thanks for the shoulder.''

He didn't reply. She closed the door quietly behind her then stepped to the bed. Easing down beside Lainey, she flung an arm over her eyes. After a long while, her breathing and her heartbeat slowed and she was reasonably calm again.

She couldn't sleep. The problem of the extra money chased itself in her head. Anxiety over the doctor's odd manner set her nerves on edge. The mystery of Clay's patient, watchful quiescence, like that of the stalking wolf she'd named him before, plagued her. Unappeased desire, held at bay for years, clamored in her blood along with the new knowledge of how easily the man in the next room could satisfy it.

She was going crazy. Nothing was working out as it should. And the consequences, should things go completely wrong, would not be simply the embarrassment and inconvenience of a prison sentence for her, but death for her daughter.

The only consolation Janna could find, as she lay staring into the darkness, was the occasional protesting squeak of cheap bedsprings from Clay's room. For all his appearance of control, he was as restless as she was.

The following day was a nightmare. The problems began at six in the morning with the arrival of the propane gas truck to replenish the camp's supply. Janna heard it coming, but didn't know what it was until she'd rolled out of bed and gone to look out the window. By the time she'd pulled on her clothes, the delivery driver was already out of his vehicle and stringing hose toward the aboveground tank located at the back corner of the house.

Janna grabbed her purse then headed outside. On her way, she pulled the door of Clay's room shut. It would be much better if he slept through the visit, though she didn't depend on it. Her mind raced as she tried to concoct a tale that would explain his captivity should he make it known. The only thing she could come up with, however, was too embarrassing for words.

Denise had requested the delivery, it seemed; she was afraid the tank was low. The gas man, Mike, was a cousin on her mother's side of the family, a detail Janna heard with resignation. She remembered Denise complaining that getting away with anything in Tunica Parish, where Turn-Coupe was located, was impossible since some relative always caught her.

Cousin Mike was a talkative sort, with a tall, skinny frame, sandy hair and an engaging grin. Working with easy competence, he advised Janna about the best bass fishing on the lake while delving into her and Denise's history together. He also told her about his baby girl who was the same age as the recent arrival of another of Denise's cousin's, Kane, mentioned the latest book out by Luke's wife, romance writer April Halstead, and described the big to-do with the sheriff's upcoming wedding. Janna let him talk because she figured he'd be less attentive to what was going on inside the camp that way. Not that there'd been much to worry about up to that moment, since the propane truck itself made a considerable racket.

So centered were her thoughts on this problem that she almost missed his change of subject. Then the tail end of what he'd said snatched her attention. Swinging back to face him, she asked, "What? What did you say?"

"Kid was found floating in the swamp. Awful, don't you think?" Cousin Mike gave a doleful shake of his head. "I really feel for his people, having to live with what happened, wondering what he saw or knew before he died, or if he was dead before they sliced him up."

"Please." The word was stifled as Janna put her hand to her mouth.

"Sorry, but it gets to me that there are people who can actually kill a kid like that for his body parts. But I guess that's the point, isn't it? If he hadn't been young and healthy, they wouldn't have bothered with him."

Sickness rose inside Janna. She'd done enough research, seen enough photos of organ transplant surgery, to have much too vivid an idea of the wounds inflicted by it. Beyond that image, however, was a specter too terrible to allow even a small place in her mind.

Her voice faint in her own ears, she asked, "Do things like this happen often around here?"

"Lord, no! First time that I know of."

"And they haven't found the person responsible?"

"They haven't even identified the kid. I mean, he'd been in the water for a while. I expect whoever did it thought the turtles and alligators would take care of him."

She drew a hissing breath, even as she shook her head.

"Sorry," Cousin Mike said again. "But you can bet they're pulling out all the stops looking for the creep who did it. Roan doesn't cotton to things like this happening in his jurisdiction—that's Sheriff Roan Benedict, you know? And the list of suspects can't be that long."

"You don't think it was someone from around here?"

The gas man checked the tank's gauge, then began to remove the hose. "My money is on the crime bosses down around Baton Rouge and New Orleans. I mean, it's not that far, and they've used our swamp for their dumping ground before."

"I'd think it would take someone with medical knowledge," she observed, almost to herself.

"Could be, maybe a doc that had his license pulled, med. school dropout, surgical nurse who's seen one too many botched operations, and so on." He shrugged. "Doesn't have to be, though."

"Meaning?"

"Lots of folks in this part of the country know a thing or two about butchering. Hunters, trappers and farmers cut up meat all the time. You don't do that without learning where all the important bits are located.''

"I see your point," she said, her voice constricted in her throat.

He lifted his head, gazing around at the camp and the lake beyond. Then he asked, "You seen anything of old Alligator Arty since you've been here?"

"He came by." It had become second nature to be cautious.

"Might want to watch out for him. He has a record, you know. Not that I'm saying he had anything to do with this deal."

"A criminal record, you mean?"

"Spent almost twenty years in the pen at Angola for taking his hunting knife to a man who got too friendly with his wife. Cut his throat for him, pretty as you please, and left him back in the swamp for 'gator bait.''

"I can't believe it," she said with a slow shake of her head.

"Weird old coot, keeps to himself. Never hurt anybody else that I ever heard, but you never can tell."

"What about his wife?"

"Divorced him, of course, moved clean out of the country. Told people she was afraid of what he'd do when he got out of prison."

"I'm surprised he didn't get the death penalty," she said.

"Jury only gave him twenty because they thought he had cause for being riled, I guess. Which is probably the same reason the wife hightailed it. Anyway,

I'd watch out for Arty. Well, and for any other strangers hanging around."

"Yes. Yes, I will." She rubbed her hands up and down her arms as goose bumps rippled over her skin.

"Yeah, gives me the willies, too," Denise's cousin said with sympathy as he eyed her quick movement. "I mean, what kind of fiend could do that sort of thing?"

"Exactly." Even as the agreement left her mouth, Janna wondered what this plain working man would think of her if he knew she could have some remote involvement with the incident.

At that moment, she heard a sound from the direction of the house. She glanced around in time to see Lainey standing at the bedroom window with Clay like a shadow only a few paces behind her. The angle of the house created glare on the glass that kept them from being plainly seen, still Janna moved to block Cousin Mike's view as he straightened and turned back in the direction of his truck. "How much do I owe you for the gas?" she asked, raising her voice a little to cover any more attention-drawing noises.

"Don't worry about it. Denise said put it on her account."

"I pay my own way," Janna insisted. "Just tell me how much."

"Can't do it." The sandy haired man shook his head as he disconnected the hose and began to stow it away. "You and Denise will have to settle it between you. I only do what I'm told." He gave her a droll smile. "So, you going to be here long?"

His curiosity, as idle as it might be, set off alarm bells inside Janna. "Not really," she answered in dismissive tones. "But thanks for bringing the gas, anyway."

"My pleasure, ma'am." He hesitated as if he'd like to say more, but apparently thought better of it. Touching a finger to his cap in a farewell salute, he turned and climbed into his truck. Moments later, the heavy vehicle rumbled down the gravel road.

Janna didn't move again for long minutes, but stood staring blindly at the drifting cloud of dust that had been left behind.

Dear God, but was it truly possible that the kidney Lainey was to receive had been cut from the body of the dead boy? As horrifying as the idea might be, it defied reason to think otherwise. Or did it?

A kidney was viable outside the body for less than 72 hours, and that was under controlled conditions with specialized machinery sending pulses of preserving fluid through it at regular intervals. Dr. Gower had said the kidney for Lainey would be ready within the week, not immediately. The time frame did not match. The death of the boy found in the swamp could not be on her conscience, then.

No, it couldn't, but what about when the specified time arrived? Might someone else be destined to die to insure that Lainey lived?

Jana had never dreamed anything like this might take place. The implication had always been that the process of harvesting organs outside the system was unethical and the profit from it illegal, but that was all. It wasn't supposed to be lethal.

A hard knot gathered in her chest, threatening to choke her. She felt trapped, caught in something inescapable. What was she going to do? What?

How long she might have stood there, she didn't know. She was recalled to a sense of where she was and what she had to do by Lainey knocking on the window behind her. She turned and tried to smile at her daughter, though the effort felt cramped and unnatural and she could barely see for the rainbow prisms of the tears that pooled in her eyes. Focusing on Clay Benedict was so impossible that she didn't even try. Bending her head as if watching her step, she wiped under her lashes with the edge of her hand and turned back toward the house.

Lainey had been trying to attract her attention because there was a call on her cell phone. Janna took the unit from her and spoke into it with caution since Clay was standing in the doorway down the hall.

It was Denise on the other end. She was just checking, she said, wondering if the gas had been delivered as promised, if the air conditioners were keeping the place cool enough, also how Janna was making out so far without malls and supermarkets. Satisfied on all these points, she finally said, "So. Anything exciting happening that I should know about?"

"Same old, same old," Janna told her as casually as she could manage.

"Really." Her friend's voice carried a note that made the muscles in the back of Janna's neck tighten.

"More or less."

"Having Clay on the premises isn't unusual?"

Janna closed her eyes. "Lainey told you, I suppose."

"Bless her little heart," Denise said with wry cheer. "At least she seems to be enjoying his company. But he must have been there a while."

Janna did not like the suggestive tone of Denise's voice. She could just picture her, the dark eyes, glossy, perfectly coiffed black hair and red, red lips that made the very image of New Orleans sophistication and suspicion. "It isn't what you think," she said with some asperity. "He only came by to check on the camp."

"And he's still hanging around?"

There was no way Janna could explain, since Denise thought her whole purpose in using the camp was the designs for her new fabric line. The two of them had been close at one time, before Matt died, but then Janna had returned to Mississippi and completed her education there. She had only told Denise about Lainey's renal problem when she contacted her concerning the camp weeks ago. Even so, she hadn't divulged its severity.

"We've...seen quite a bit of him," she said in as casual a tone as she could manage.

Denise was quiet a long moment. "He knows about Lainey then?"

"No! Not yet."

"How intriguing. So tell me, are you two involved?"

Janna glanced in the direction of her workroom. She could hear Lainey talking to Ringo, but Clay stood with his arms folded over his chest and one shoulder propped on the door facing. Holding his gaze, she answered, "Hardly."

"Too bad," Denise said with dissatisfaction. "I wish…"

"What?"

"Clay is so like Matt. The same looks, same lethal charm, same love of life…"

"I noticed," Janna answered, profoundly glad Clay could not hear his cousin.

"Oh, honey, I'm sorry. I didn't mean it like that."

Janna couldn't let her go on. "I know what you meant."

"I doubt it. I realize Matt's dad threatened you years ago, and understand why you've never wanted me to act as go-between for the family. Still, I've always wished you could get to know them, especially Clay."

"No." It was now clear to Janna why Denise had sent her handsome cousin to check on her in the first place.

"But it would be so perfect, I mean really."

"It wouldn't be perfect," she corrected with iron in her voice, "it would be obscene. I have no use for a replica of Lainey's father."

At a soft sound behind her, she turned to look down the hall again. The doorway to the spare bedroom was now empty.

"What?" Denise asked in her ear. "What did you say?"

"Nothing. I have to go."

"Think about it. Think about what's best for Lainey," Denise said in haste, as if afraid she might be cut off.

"I am."

"I mean it."

"So do I," Janna said, and punched the button to end the call.

The day wore on. Janna cleared the breakfast dishes, played tea party with Lainey using the plastic film containers Clay had given her, which were fast becoming a sizable collection, and ran a load of clothes through the ancient combination washer and dryer that sat in a corner of the bathroom. Folding Clay's T-shirts and shorts seemed an oddly intimate task, one triggering a myriad of less than comfortable reactions. They were sophomoric, she knew, but that didn't make them go away.

That he'd overheard what she'd said to Denise concerned her. How he had taken it, exactly, she didn't know; he'd remained in his room all morning and she hadn't ventured inside it. It wasn't just the unfortunate slip of her tongue that bothered her, of course, but her recent discoveries. It crossed her mind to wonder if Clay knew about the body found in the lake, and if that might not have colored his reactions. It would explain a great deal.

The only way he could have discovered that, of course, was if Arty had told him. She wasn't sure why the old swamp man would let Clay in on something so important while leaving her in ignorance, but she supposed past friendship might account for it. That was, of course, unless he and Clay had put their heads together and determined that it was best not to mention the situation because she could be implicated in it. The conclusion was logical, in all fairness. The problem was that she didn't feel like being fair.

There was another possibility; the two men could have something to hide themselves. Both of them spent their time in the swamp and knew it well. Who better to dispose of a body in its backwaters?

Janna stopped with her hands clutched on a pair of Clay's briefs and closed her eyes. Why did she have to endure this soul-searching over a fairly common medical procedure necessary to save her daughter? It was as if something was trying to tell her that what she was doing was wrong, but how could she accept that when the only other option, waiting for a legal kidney, was as potentially lethal as it was uncertain?

"That might be more rewarding if those were occupied."

Clay's drawl, dry yet layered with implication, came from the bathroom doorway. Janna knew immediately what he meant, recognized that she had been mindlessly kneading the warm cotton of his briefs that were folded with the crotch in the front. She drew back the briefs and tossed them at his chest. "For that crack," she said with disdain, "you can fold your own underwear."

"I could take care of all my laundry if I was free."

"Fat chance."

He gave her a sultry look from under his lashes. "You're sure? You might find other advantages."

It was a relief to find that he hadn't been sulking, though why she should care was something she had no intention of examining. "Forget it," she said succinctly as she picked up the laundry basket.

"You're a hard woman, Janna Kerr."

"Aren't I just?" The smile she gave him was as brittle as her voice as she slid past him into the hall. She could feel his gaze on her as she walked away, but she didn't look back.

Lunch was a simple meal of baked chicken breast strips, rolls and a fresh green salad. While Janna prepared it, Lainey wandered back to be with Clay again, and the mingled bass and treble of their voices made Janna feel left out, almost excluded from some secret society. She placed the salads on a tray, along with bottled dressing, crackers and tall glasses of iced tea, and then carried everything back to join them.

Lainey and Clay had been playing with Ringo, and the little raccoon lay curled in her lap. With a significant glance at the ball of fur, Janna said, "Time to eat, sweetheart. Run wash your hands."

Her daughter gave her a querulous glance. "Oh, Mama."

"Mind your mother, punkin," Clay said quietly.

Lainey met his steady blue gaze for a second. Something she saw there apparently convinced her it was useless to argue, for she heaved a sigh, then set Ringo aside and got to her feet. She took a couple of steps toward the door, then turned back. "Clay needs to wash his hands, too, Mama, only he can't very well. Besides, his fingers are all purple. Can't you untie him for just a little while?"

For no reason that she could think of, Janna flushed. Lainey had adapted to Clay's presence so easily, in the way children often accepted changes in their lives, that she'd assumed her daughter thought nothing of his captivity. She'd been wrong. "I really don't think so," she began.

"He won't do anything except eat, will you, Mr. Clay?" Her small features mirrored earnest concern as she searched his face.

"No," he answered with grave deliberation. "I don't think I will."

"Cross your heart and hope to die?"

The pledge was an extremely serious one to Lainey, Janna knew. She thought that Clay realized it as well for a crooked smile came and went at one corner of his mouth as he held the child's gaze. Still, he sketched a quick cross over the proper spot on his T-shirt-clad chest before he repeated with a slightly dryer note in his voice, "Promise."

Lainey looked at Janna again. "See?"

Janna thought she must really be losing it, because she did think the arrangement seemed reasonable. Denise had said Clay would not resort to violence, and he had offered none so far, in spite of several opportunities. He'd failed, in fact, to take advantage of the most blatant intimacy. The look in his eyes as he'd given his word left little doubt that he meant to keep it. The only question that remained was what else he might have in mind?

If he meant to exercise his charm on her as suggested, well, what of it? It was unlikely to get him anywhere. And if he had a little more freedom to pursue his aim, there should be even less need for violence.

"All right," she said.

"You'll do it?" Lainey's face shone as if lit from within, and she clapped her hands as she jumped up and down.

"While you go wash your hands," Janna told her then ushered her toward the bathroom as she went to find the key to his wrist padlock.

When she returned with it, she seated herself on the bed beside Clay. She held a hand out toward him, and he laid his bound wrists across her palm.

"You sure you know what you're doing?" he asked, his voice low and deep.

"I know I'm taking a chance, if that's what you mean." She removed the lock, then plucked at the knotted ropes, finally going to her desk and returning with a slender paintbrush to use as a prying tool. As the ropes loosened and she began to unwind them, she saw that Lainey was right; his fingers did have a purplish cast.

Watching her, Clay drawled, "You like living dangerously, is that it?"

"I don't know that I'd put it that way." She risked a quick glance at him, and was caught by the heat in the dark blue depths of his eyes. For long seconds, neither of them spoke, then he seemed to notice that his hands were free. Clasping one wrist, he rubbed at the marks.

"So what do I say now?" he asked. "Thanks?"

She lifted a shoulder by way of an answer, her gaze still on his hands. They were well made, strong, brown from the sun, and with long, aristocratic fingers. Watching them gave her a taut feeling in her lower abdomen that was a vivid reminder of the night before. It was difficult not to reach out to help him soothe the rope indentations as she'd seen her daughter do once before. As her gaze focused on his wrists, however, she noticed that they were marked not only by redness, but by the raw scrapes of new injuries.

"You've hurt yourself," she said, shocked into inanity.

"It's what happens when you're trying to escape," he answered, the words tinged with irony. "Of course, you can always kiss it and make it better if it really bothers you."

"I don't think so," she said at once, though she had to wonder if his arch suggestion hadn't been designed as a distraction. The only reason for it that came to mind was male reluctance to talk about his failure.

"So what made you decide to take this chance?"

"Misplaced concern, no doubt." She got to her feet without obvious haste, stepping to where she'd left the lunch tray on her worktable.

"The point being?"

"Maybe I feel sorry for you?"

"Or maybe you're sorry you started the whole thing?" He swung his feet off the bed and rose to his full height.

"Could be." Janna's throat tightened. Funny that she hadn't realized just how tall and broad he was before, or quite how knee-knocking powerful was the aura of charisma that surrounded him. She wouldn't let him know how nervous he made her, however, not if it killed her.

"Let me know when you're sure," he advised in quiet irony, "and I'll tell you how I feel about it." He didn't wait for her comment, but moved from the room and across the hall. A moment later, Janna heard him talking to Lainey above the sound of running water.

She felt as if she'd lit a firecracker and there had been no explosion. Could Clay have just hinted that he had no objection to being at the camp? What reason could he possibly have for such a thing? She stared at the food on her plate as she tried to work it out in her mind, but finally shook her head in defeat.

The raccoon, deserted by both its playmates, shimmied down the folds of the bedspread that was pushed to the foot of the bed and waddled over to Janna. She took a piece of lettuce from one of the salad bowls and bent to offer it. Ringo accepted it in his handlike paws, but didn't seem too impressed with it. While she watched, he took it to his water dish at the foot of the bed and proceeded to give it a good dunking.

Even as Janna smiled at the raccoon's antics, doubt about her release of Clay grew in her mind. She had thought before that what she'd done to him was all wrong. Now she was forced to wonder if she had compounded the error by allowing him the use of his hands.

Clay returned with Lainey and the meal progressed. The two staged a race to see who could finish their salad first. It was a ploy by Clay to encourage her daughter to take in healthy calories, she thought. She'd like to believe that he had some ulterior motive, but it seemed too natural and spontaneous, as if he was used to kids, used to taking an interest in their welfare. It was that Benedict clan thing again more than likely, where all children were looked on as part of one big family, therefore tended, protected and cherished by all.

Clay's sudden attack came in the form of a question, one that caught her off guard. "Did you mention me to your visitor last night?"

She pushed away her salad bowl and sipped her tea to give herself time to gather her scattered thoughts, but there was really only one answer. "I didn't, not that it makes any difference. He saw you."

"How was that?"

"How do you think?" Janna glanced at Lainey who was taking advantage of their distraction to sneak an extra roll from the plate.

"I doubt he was happy. Did he have any suggestion for what to do about me?"

"It didn't come up, since he seemed to think you had some right to be here."

"But you set him straight?"

"It was none of his business."

"No?"

Clay's gaze was so intent that it rattled her. "Anyway, there wasn't time. His main reason for coming was to tell me that he'd need…"

"What?" he asked as her voice trailed away.

"It doesn't matter."

"I think it does." Clay tilted his head, his gaze penetrating. "Let's see. Could it be he needs— money?"

"How did you know?"

"Call it a guess," he said with irony.

Was it really, or did he know more than he was admitting? "It's my problem and I'll solve it." To change the subject, she went on, "Speaking of finances, I've been thinking about the dye plant you mentioned. Are you sure you know where to find it?"

"Positive." He transferred his attention to his plate as he forked a bite of chicken.

"You're bluffing. Aphrodite's Cup and its *couleur de l'amour* doesn't exist, hasn't for a hundred years."

"Wrong." He handed the raccoon that had climbed up to his knee a tidbit of meat, a treat that seemed much more to Ringo's taste than lettuce.

"What would it take to get you to show me where it grows?" Janna wanted that color and the dye plant that made it. She could feel her creative energy rising at the mere thought but there was more to it than that. An idea had come to her as she made lunch, her subconscious generating visions of designs even as she arranged chicken and lettuce. It seemed that this special shade of blue, and the fabric series that she could develop for it, would be enough to gain a new contract from the company with which she worked. The promise of it might be enough to persuade her banker to increase her outstanding loan to cover Dr. Gower's new demand. That would at least return to her the choice between the two unpalatable options facing her for Lainey's surgery: using Dr. Gower's cadaver kidney or coercing Clay.

Then there was Lainey herself. She loved blue in all its shades and hues, and it seemed that helping with the dye might serve to wean her away from her growing dependence on Clay's company. That would ease the niggling worry Janna was beginning to feel about how Lainey was going to react when he vanished from her life. In short, it seemed that if she could just find the Aphrodite's Cup, everything might be all right.

Clay watched her, his gaze unreadable. Finally he countered, "How much do you need? That is, how many plants, approximately? It takes whole fields of indigo, I think, to produce a pound of dye. I'm assuming it would be the same with Aphrodite's Cup."

"I'm not sure, since I don't know how the dye is extracted. Making indigo is a long drawn-out process that includes fermentation in outdoor vats, but it might be possible to boil the stems or roots of Aphrodite's Cup. I'd need only a few plants at first, for a test."

"But maybe a lot more afterward," he said.

"I wouldn't want to harvest it to extinction, if that's what you're thinking. Should the plants turn out to have commercial application, then cultivation would have to be arranged."

He searched her face, his gaze straight. At last he said, "I'll think about it."

"But you said you could get it!"

"I never said I would," he replied, unrepentant.

In other words, he meant to keep his swamp secrets to himself, or else use them as some kind of bargaining chip, Janna thought. She should have known. "Fine," she said, her voice hard. "I'll find the damn plant myself if I have to search the swamp inch by inch."

What he might have answered, she didn't know. They were interrupted by the sound of a boat, a sizable craft from the roar of its motor. It was traveling at a steady pace, but with the caution of a driver who knew the lake and had sense enough to be wary of underwater obstacles. It seemed to be heading straight for the camp.

Janna left the bedroom, closing the door behind her. In the kitchen, she moved to the front windows and lifted a slat of the blinds that covered them. The boat was almost at the dock. It was white and shining, a fast cruiser with a spotlight and antennas decorating the front, and a man in uniform and wearing dark shades behind the console. On its side was an insignia. She couldn't make it out at first; then the boat turned broadside to her as it eased to a stop.

Janna's breath caught in her throat as the letters jumped into focus: Tunica Parish Sheriff's Department.

8

Clay had a passion for boats, had lived with them all his life, since his family home, Grand Point, was on the lake. They were to him what hot rods were to some men, and he had owned more than a few. He'd also helped work on the bass rigs, pontoon boats, houseboats and other assorted craft belonging to his cousins, Kane, Luke and Roan. It was no task at all, then, for him to recognize the sound of the cruiser maintained by the Parish Sheriff's Office because the lake and its swamp or the river bordered so much of its jurisdiction. Roan's controlled style of piloting was easy to distinguish as well. It appeared that his cousin was paying an official visit.

As the motor rumbled into silence, and then Janna's footsteps left the porch on her way down to the dock, he said to Lainey, "Look's like your mom's got company. Wonder who it can be?"

The girl wrinkled her nose in a grimace. "Probably that red-haired nurse. I hope she doesn't stay long."

"Nurse?"

"She comes to take my blood, but she was here not long ago."

"Not time for more sticks, then?" he asked with as much sympathy as curiosity.

The girl shook her head so quickly that her hair fell into her face. "Not yet."

"That why you don't like her, because she always sticks you?"

"Sort of," Lainey agreed, though she kept her gaze on Ringo. "But mostly, she's not very nice. She doesn't smile in her eyes. And she gives me orders like she's my boss, and doesn't always tell me before there's going to be a stick. I don't like the way she talks to Mama, either."

Clay reached to push the shiny blond hair, so like her mother's, behind the girl's ear and away from her face. "She talks mean to your mom?"

Lainey hunched a shoulder. "She just sounds like she's mad all the time, like maybe she doesn't like coming here."

"You're a bright girl," Clay said, his voice dry.

Lainey flashed a smile then that told him she had the potential to become an accomplished flirt in a few years.

"But it might not be the nurse coming to see you," he said. "Don't you want to find out for sure?"

Her face turned serious as she glanced at the cable that held him then returned her gaze to his face. "You want to know, huh?"

"Could be," he answered carefully.

"Okay." Gathering up Ringo, her rag doll and the handful of film canisters that had become her favorite toys, she headed out the door. "Be right back."

As soon as the screen door slammed shut, Clay, giving thanks for the free use of his hands, performed a little magic on the padlock that fastened his waist ropes with the folding tool from his pocket. Sliding off the bed, then, he padded barefoot from the room and down the hall. In the kitchen, he stepped behind the table to the window that looked out onto the screened porch and the lake beyond. With care, he lifted a louver of its blind just enough to see out.

The visitor was Roan, all right, standing at ease with his Stetson under one arm and both the star of his badge and his sandy hair glinting in the hot sunlight. A scowl drew his brows together so his forehead pleated into grooves.

Janna's back was to Clay, but he saw her make the age-old gesture with arms open and palms upturned that signified lack of knowledge for whatever query Roan had put to her. A tight grin curled one corner of Clay's mouth as he noted his cousin's ambivalence, as if the sheriff didn't know whether to believe her or call her a liar to her face. At least he was undecided enough that he made no move toward barging into the camp, which had been Clay's first concern.

Lainey, he saw, had taken up a position on the concrete steps that led up to the porch. She was setting out a tea party in front of her doll and her raccoon, using the film canisters. Ringo, bored with the proceedings, batted a canister around until it tumbled down the steps and rolled along the dirt walkway to stop just inches from the toe of Roan's boot.

The sheriff bent and picked up the plastic cylinder. He stared at it for a second, then glanced toward Lainey's sizable collection. Putting a finger inside the film container, he stood twirling it around in idle preoccupation, dividing his gaze between the facade of the camp and Janna as he talked to her. She shook her head again, a movement that somehow managed to convey regret. Roan slipped the cylinder off his finger in a show of one-handed dexterity, then tossed it back onto the porch step beside Lainey. Seconds later, he replaced his hat, tugged it down over his eyes in a polite gesture of farewell, then turned away.

Clay didn't know whether to laugh or curse. He wasn't ready to give up the cozy nest he'd made for himself, but it was just a little sobering to see how easily an attractive female could hoodwink the law.

The sheriff backed his boat away from the dock at idling speed, then pushed the cruiser into a takeoff that churned up a wide wave as he swooped into the turn. Seconds later, he straightened on a course that would take him back to Turn-Coupe. When Clay saw Janna turn toward the house, he made tracks back to his room. By the time she returned with Lainey, he was reclining like a sultan on his couch while properly restrained once more.

"So," he said, pretending to stifle a yawn. "What was the excitement all about?"

"Someone looking for you."

Strain sounded in her voice. The visit from the law worried her, Clay thought. "Anyone I know?"

"All right, it was your cousin, the sheriff." She

didn't look at him as she spoke, but began to pick up the plates and glasses they'd been using, stacking them together.

"Nice of him to be concerned," Clay commented in dry tones.

"It wasn't just that. It seems you had an appointment to be fitted for a tux as a groomsman in his wedding, one you missed. He doesn't consider your nonappearance to be like you. So when does this wedding take place?"

"A month and three days from now." He waited to see how that time limit affected her. Her lips tightened but nothing more, which led him to think that she could have a shorter time frame of her own. That bothered him. It bothered him a lot.

"A big event, is it?" she asked finally.

"Wedding of the year for Tunica Parish. That's saying something, since my cousin Luke caused a fair splash earlier in the summer. He married romance author April Halstead, you know."

"What's so important about it?"

"It involves the sheriff, for one thing, but the woman he's marrying is East Coast high society."

"Funny you didn't mention this little arrangement before."

"You didn't ask. I thought my agenda made no difference to you. Or is it just that it never occurred to you that I might have a life?"

The look on her face told him that she'd thought that exactly, or else that she'd considered photography his life in the way that work often consumed men. If the latter, then she wouldn't have been that far from the truth.

"Arty mentioned the wedding," she said, "but didn't know about this fitting, I suppose. The sheriff said he intends to make sure you show up for the ceremony, and that I should remind you if I see you."

Good old Roan, Clay thought. He suspected something was going on or he'd never have given her a message. "I haven't forgotten."

She glanced around the room, apparently searching for some missing dish since she leaned over a moment later to retrieve the glass that he'd set on the floor beside the bed. When she straightened again, she said, "I'm sorry that I made you miss your appointment."

"No problem. I expect Roan ordered the tux in his size since we're a close match."

"Well, that's all right then." She put the glass she held on top of the other dishes then turned away.

At the tart sound of her voice, it struck him that he'd brushed off her apology as though it didn't matter, as if he considered it mere form, which he had. It seemed she'd meant it, after all. Something was riding her, he thought. Her face looked drawn, and the dark shadows of sleeplessness lay under her eyes.

"If you're *really* sorry," he said to her retreating back, "you could always let me go."

She turned at the door to give him a dirty look. "I'm not that sorry."

"I thought not," he told her, but she seemed not to hear. His smile was crooked as he watched the enticing curves of her backside whisk out of the room.

They passed the remainder of the day in a fair degree of peace. Lainey acted like a buffer and convenient means of communication between them, since they spent more time talking to, and through, her than they did to each other. She was an intelligent child, Clay thought. She knew something was going on between him and her mama. Sometimes she looked at them with the same exasperation that she turned on Ringo when the dumb critter tried to eat her crayons, as if he should know better than to do things that weren't good for him.

In the middle of the afternoon, after Lainey had rested, Janna put the girl in the ancient aluminum boat that had been tied up to the dock for as long as Clay could remember. She paddled off in the general direction of Arty's place. She didn't tell him where she was going or when she'd be back, but Clay suspected that she was going to look for dye plants, particularly, the Aphrodite's Cup.

He had to admire her initiative, even if he was a victim of it. He also didn't mind watching the way she wielded a boat paddle, the grace and strength in the lines of her body as she dipped and swayed with the motion. She was quite a woman, taking care of her daughter on her own, creating her fabrics out of no more than color and imagination, willing to brave snakes and alligators to get what she wanted. Willing to go to any lengths to protect and preserve the things she loved.

Regardless, it bothered him that she was going out virtually alone this afternoon The lake and its swamplands were vast and deep, a labyrinthine network of multibranching channels shaded by tall cypress trees, of interconnected sloughs and small creeks and stretches of marshlands where saw grass grew in water only inches deep. It was easy to get lost if you didn't know it, and sometimes hard to be found again.

Added to that was the dumping of the dead boy. It might be a fluke, or it might not. Until they found out one way or the other, poking around the back reaches of the lake wasn't the smartest thing to do.

He should have warned her or at least tried to prevent her from going, Clay thought. Not that he'd known what she meant to do up until it was too late. Anyway, he had no right to tell her anything, couldn't without revealing what he knew. He comforted himself with the knowledge that there would be other fishermen and boaters on the lake. And of course, if she was mixed up in whatever was going on with the snatched organs, then she was in no danger anyway.

The urge to go after her, no matter what, was so strong that Clay could taste it. Whether he wanted to stop her or to help her find what she needed, he really couldn't say. Either one was too stupid too contemplate. She wouldn't appreciate his interference. To her he was the enemy, someone who already stood in her way.

The hours stretched. The camp seemed so empty with only Ringo for company. A dozen times, Clay thought of just leaving, letting Janna come back to find the place deserted. What kept him from it, he wasn't sure. Dark suspicion, maybe, curiosity without a doubt; concern for Lainey, certainly. Added to these was the need to see this thing through to the end. And on top of everything else, like cherry on a sundae, was the prospect of just retribution. Whatever the reason, it constrained him much more than rope and padlock.

It was funny, but he missed television in spite of the fact that he seldom watched anything except nature shows. He needed mindless entertainment of some kind, both to pass the time and also to provide a distraction. He had far too much time to think now that he was unable to watch Janna work or play with Lainey and Ringo. Some of his thoughts weren't that comfortable.

He kept coming back to the fact that Lainey was Matt's daughter and wondering how much his and Matt's family history had to do with the fact that Janna was a single mother. Their father had been a throwback in many ways, with the typical Benedict faults of stiff-necked pride and insularity carried to the extreme. A conservative to the bone, he thought in absolutes, was fast to take offense and slow to forget. Any man who wasn't with him was against him, and those who held opposing political and religious views were not only dead wrong but also terminally stupid. How he'd ever gotten involved with their mother, an unrepentant hippie with liberal views and a fascination with every offbeat idea or belief system that came along, was a mystery. Maybe it was the attraction of opposites, but it had been inevitable that the relationship would go bad. That it had started off on the wrong foot with marriage vows exchanged in haste because of pregnancy had only put the seal of doom on it. All Clay could think was that there had been a strong sexual component in there some-where, one that had served to produce four boys, Adam and Wade, Matt and himself, before it faded.

Clay loved his mother dearly, but even he had to admit that she wasn't the easiest of women. Her idea of the truth was colored by her needs of the moment. Her attention span was about two milliseconds long, and her sense of responsibility had never been partic-ularly active, especially when it came to her sons. She'd allowed her ex-husband to claim custody while she went off to Greece or Tibet. Not that they had minded, since they'd much preferred running wild in the swamp with their cousins. In spite of her faults, however, their mother was sweet-natured, generous beyond accounting and spectacularly talented. In short, she was an artist. They'd all loved her without reserve and protected her against every criticism, and still did.

It was interesting that Janna also had an artistic background. How much had that shaped Matt's at-traction to her? he wondered. And what influence had it exerted on the fact that Lainey had never been le-gally recognized as a Benedict? Had Matt been ner-vous about bringing another creative female home to

Grand Point? Had he been afraid of what their father would say or how he would treat her?

Ironically the problem would not have lasted. Their old man had died of prostate cancer almost four years ago. It was, not incidentally, about the same time that Clay had left veterinary medicine and taken up nature photography full-time rather then treating it as a hobby. It was also when he'd really become reacquainted with his mother.

The longer he stayed around Janna and Lainey, the more certain he became that this family history had some bearing on why Janna had drugged him. Every passing hour made it clearer what she might have to gain.

Who better to provide a kidney than another Benedict? Who better, indeed, than a man who was an exact genetic match to Lainey's father? Janna would be fully aware that a donor kidney from a close relative match would have a ninety percent survival rate during the first year, with seventy percent over a five-year period. An unmatched kidney, on the other hand, was more likely to be rejected immediately or, even if retained, have less than a fifty percent chance of surviving. It was possible that Lainey would be no more of a genetic match for him than for Janna, but Clay knew there was also a fair degree of probability that they would share half or more of the same histocompatibility antigens. The implications of that knowledge were something he spent a lot of time contemplating as the day wore on.

Janna and Lainey returned as sunset was painting

the sky. They were both hot, tired and sunburned, though Lainey less than her mother since she wore the wide-brimmed straw hat that he'd seen Janna use once while doing a watercolor en plein air. Janna sent Lainey to take a cool shower while she stood at the kitchen sink drinking glass after glass of cool tap water. The grim look of defeat that settled on her face as she stared out the kitchen window caused a knot of unwilling sympathy in the pit of Clay's stomach.

"No luck?" he asked as he lounged in the hallway opening.

"It's hard to find something that isn't there," she said over her shoulder.

"It's there. You just have to know where to look."

"I showed Arty an old illustration. He says he's never seen it."

"But you asked him to help you anyway?"

It was a long moment before she answered. "I didn't, actually."

"Why not? I'd have thought a guide was just what you needed." Not to mention, he thought, the protection of a man in her boat.

Instead of replying, she turned to put her back to the cabinet, leaning against it, as she asked, "You've known Arty a long time, haven't you?"

"Quite a while. Why?"

"He taught you about the swamp, I think he said."

"Right." Clay waited for her to get to the point.

"You know about his criminal record?"

Clay shook his head. "All that was forty years ago or more."

"He killed someone, according to the gas man."

"He did, and he paid for it. Now he's just an old man getting by the best way he can."

"Staying back in the swamp, avoiding other people. Except for you."

"And a few others such as Roan, Kane, Luke, my older brothers when they're home. And you." He added the last as a none-too-subtle reminder that she'd made a friend of Arty before she found out about his past.

"You have any idea how he makes his living?"

She was brushing her thumb up and down her water glass, a sure sign of how disturbed she was inside. Clay kept his voice as even and reassuring as possible as he answered, "Hunting, fishing, trapping, acting as a guide. He also has a small government check, I think."

"It isn't much."

"Arty doesn't need much." Clay paused, then went on. "He's just a lonely old codger. He'd never think of hurting you. Or Lainey."

"Can you guarantee that?"

He couldn't, so he remained grimly silent.

She gave a short laugh. "Now you know why I didn't ask for his help as a guide. Other than the fact that he said he didn't know dye plants."

"So now you're giving up?"

She gave him a straight look, though still holding her glass in front of her like a shield. "I never give up."

She meant it. Clay liked that, in spite of everything.

By nightfall, he'd had all that he could take of being confined while events went on around him. He waited until Lainey was put to bed with all her attendant procedures and tubes for dialysis and Janna had taken her shower. When he was sure his jailer was tucked in her bed asleep after her long afternoon of hot sun and fresh air out on the lake, he slid out of his waist restraint once more. Moving silently, carrying his shoes, he let himself out of the house.

The old aluminum boat was handy at the camp's dock since Janna had used it earlier in the day. It took only seconds and a few quiet pulls with its beat-up paddle to head the lightweight craft away from the camp and out into the lake. A short time later, Clay was climbing aboard his airboat where she sat screened by a couple of old weeping willows in a back cove near Arty's shanty. Jenny cranked with a quiet rumble at the first turn of the key. Seconds later, he sent her flying ahead of a peacock's tail of blown spume as he headed for Turn-Coupe.

Roan was still up, for the light was burning in the upstairs bedroom at his house known as Dog Trot. Clay tied up the airboat, then walked up to the slope to the kitchen door. His knock was answered almost immediately. Roan stood with one hand on the doorknob and the other on his hipbone as he said, "It's about time, cuz. What took you so long?"

"Expecting me, were you?"

"From the minute I realized you had to be somewhere around Denise's old camp."

Roan stepped back to let him in as he spoke. Clay

gave a resigned nod as he moved on into the kitchen. Old Beau, Roan's pet bloodhound, rose to meet him. As Clay rubbed the dog's big head and pulled his ears, he said, "The film canisters, right?"

"You're the only person I know who tosses the things like other people get rid of used paper towels. So what's the idea? You hiding out from somebody?"

"Promise not to laugh and I'll tell you," Clay said as he swung a chair out from the kitchen table and spun it around before straddling it.

The sheriff of Tunica Parish watched him a second without answering. As if giving himself time to think, he asked, "Cold drink? Beer? Water?"

Clay declined. Roan took out a beer and twisted off the cap before ambling over to the table and dropping into the chair facing Clay. Finally he said, "It wouldn't have something to do with that blond Amazon I talked to out there, I suppose."

"Could be."

"But it's not crooked?"

Clay propped his chin on the high back of his chair as he considered that. Finally, he said, "Depends on how you look at it."

"How do you look at it?"

Roan did have an abrupt way about him. It was intimidating to some, but Clay was used to it. "An error in judgment?"

"Doesn't sound like a laughing matter."

"I had a feeling you might say that," Clay allowed in his driest tones. It was the most he was going to get from Roan, he knew. With deliberation, he told his cousin the whole story.

Roan sat watching him for long seconds when he'd finished. Then a glint appeared in his eyes. He pressed his lips together until they turned white, but there was no way to stop the upward turn of his mouth. He covered the lower part of his face, but his eyes still danced. On a crack of laughter, he said, "Wait till Tory hears this!"

"Your bride wouldn't be crass enough to poke fun at my predicament," Clay said in stern accusation.

"You misjudge her. She'd do it in a nanosecond. And probably will when I tell her how you've been tied down for days at the mercy of a love-starved..."

"It isn't like that!"

Roan's humor faded. "No? Then tell me how it is that this woman has drugged you, kept you under lock and key and made you like it."

"I didn't say I liked it."

"It took you long enough to get free."

"I'm not free." Clay informed him. "Well, for all intents and purposes. I'm going back."

Roan's brows snapped together above his nose. "You're what?"

"Tonight. As soon as I see Doc."

"What do you want with Doc? She didn't hurt you, did she?"

"No, she didn't hurt me," Clay answered in exasperation. "All I want is to check out some facts with him and have him look at some medical records that I found while poking around Janna's desk."

"The little girl's records," Roan said in clarification, adding as Clay noted, "to see…what, exactly?"

"If she could actually be Matt's daughter, for one thing."

"And?"

"And if she's as sick as Janna claims."

"Can't you tell?"

Clay gave him a moody frown. "Doesn't hurt to be sure."

"Then what?"

"It would help if I could get some information on this doctor she's seeing." It was an evasion, but he hoped Roan wouldn't realize it.

Roan reached behind him to a drawer in the kitchen cabinet where he pulled out a pen and notepad. "You have a name?"

"Lainey called him Dr. Bauer or Gower, I'm not sure which. I'm guessing he may have practiced, or still practices, as a nephrologist, probably in New Orleans or Baton Rouge."

"That should do it," Roan said as he thumped his pencil point at the end of the note he'd just written. "What else?"

"I'd like to borrow your phone to call Doc Watkins, see if he's still up, by any chance."

"You're going over there tonight?"

"Have to," Clay told him, his smile whimsical. "I have to be back before bed check in the morning."

"Don't rush off. I'd like to hear a bit more about this female warden of yours."

It was one thing for him to refer to his situation in

prison terms, Clay discovered, but he wasn't wild about anyone else doing it. "Later. I need to do a little work in the darkroom at Grand Point before I take off again."

"You're thinking about photos at a time like this?"

"These are special."

"You're nuts," Roan said without heat. "What about my wedding? You do intend to show up for that?"

Clay held up his hand. "Word of honor."

"I'll hold you to it," his cousin said in grim promise. "But suppose this Amazon of yours checks your bed while you're gone?"

Clay drew a deep breath, then let it out with a slow shake of his head. "Can't be helped. But I'd sure hate to miss it."

Roan threw down his pen and leaned back in his chair. "Right. Now let me see if I can cast my mind back. Just who was it, again, who was telling me not too long ago that I was a goner when it came to a certain woman?"

"Don't go jumping to conclusions. You don't know why I'm going back."

"I suppose it's for Matt, because you need to know, once and for all, if he left something of himself behind when he died."

"Maybe."

"Or because you're a sucker for kids."

Clay gave him a look of disgust.

"Turnabout is fair play or something along that

line? You want to get this Janna Kerr into your bed instead of the other way around?''

''Could be. Or I could also have a feeling that she needs help, needs it in the worst kind of way.''

''Which is it?'' Roan asked, his voice sharp with impatience. ''Make up your mind.''

''I think I have.'' Clay let the words stand without embellishment.

''So what do you need? Besides psychiatric help, of course.''

''Answers,'' Clay said, his voice sober. ''More than anything else, I need answers.''

9

Janna took the old boat out again early the next morning, while Lainey was still asleep. She didn't intend to go far, not with her daughter alone in the house except for Clay. There was just this one small creek-fed cove that had intrigued her the afternoon before. Lainey had been too tired for her to check it out then, but she could do it now in less than an hour.

Quite a few boats were on the lake; more than usual, she thought. They buzzed up and down the nearby main channel, and the waves they made kept her light craft constantly rocking. It was a few minutes before she remembered the weekend fishing tournament Dr. Gower had mentioned. Today was Saturday, she thought, though she'd almost lost track in the confusion of the past few days. She avoided the activity, paddling quietly along close to various small islands and spits of land, keeping her eyes open.

Rounding a bend, she came upon a fancy bass rig with a bright red fiberglass hull, elevated captain's chairs, gauges of all kinds and a motor large enough to run the *QE II*. The two fishermen who occupied the boat gave Janna a pleasant greeting. She would have passed them by without another word, but the one in front hailed her across the water.

"Say," he called, "you wouldn't be from around here, would you?"

"Sorry," she answered, resting her paddle a moment so bright droplets from it caught the sun and she drifted with decreasing momentum.

"We were just wondering what was going on."

She gazed at them across the waves. Their faces were red and shiny from the heat, and their floppy, narrow-brimmed hats were something a Southern good old boy wouldn't be caught dead wearing on his head. Accents from above the Mason-Dixon line were just the final proof that they were from out of state. It was unlikely, then, that they posed any threat. "What do you mean?" she asked.

"We couldn't put our boat in at the landing where the tournament brochure said. Had a small army of cops around it." The man in the rear put down his rod and bent to rummage around in a built-in ice chest until he pulled out a beer. "Ambulance was there, too, rescue squad, fire truck, you name it. We thought maybe there'd been a drowning."

"I don't know anything about it," she said, though she could feel her stomach muscles tighten as if in anticipation of a blow.

The first man said, "I'm sure I saw the medics put a young guy on the gurney. I have to say he looked like a goner, but I suppose they have to carry him in anyway, so the coroner can do his job."

"A teenager?" Janna's voice cracked a little with strain as she spoke.

"Maybe sixteen or seventeen, about that size, anyway. We were too far away to be sure."

It could really be a drowning accident, Janna told herself. This boy didn't have to be a victim of organ theft like the first.

"Funny thing is," the fisherman in the rear seat went on, "I've never seen it take that many cops to check out a boating accident." He popped the top on his beer. "You'd think they were looking for something."

"I heard mention of an airboat and the guy who owns it," the first man added. "Took me a minute to get the picture because they were calling the thing a Jenny or some such name."

Janna had to get back to the camp, and fast. "Yes, well, I guess we'll read about it in the paper," she said as she dug her paddle into the water again. "Good luck with your fishing."

They answered, she thought, but she didn't hear. She was too busy swinging back around in the direction she'd come.

Arty was at the camp when she got back, for his ancient wooden boat was tied up at the dock. She let herself into the house with quiet care, since she didn't want to wake Lainey just yet. She would want to be taken off dialysis the instant she opened her eyes, and Janna had other things on her mind.

Lainey was asleep and Arty was nowhere in sight.

Then as Janna passed Clay's room, she heard voices. The door was firmly closed and Arty was speaking in a rasping near-whisper, as if he didn't want to be overheard.

Janna hesitated a second, then she moved closer to the door and bent her head to listen. The first voice she caught was Clay's in a soft query that she didn't understand. It was followed by Arty's answer.

"Yeah. Floating in the channel again, poor kid. Fresh killed this time."

Clay swore. "The same way?"

"Same bits gone, if that's what you mean," Arty agreed. "But this boy was shot first. A pistol, they say, light caliber, probably a Saturday Night Special."

Janna barely heard Clay's reply for the thunder of her heartbeat in her ears. She pressed a hand to her throat and closed her eyes. Another body, another teenager robbed of his organs, if not killed for them. It was unbelievable.

"Somethin' else you should know."

The grim warning in Arty's voice grabbed Janna's attention again, overriding her horror. She held her breath to listen. Everything was quiet inside the room for long seconds, then Clay demanded, "Well? Out with it."

"You ain't gonna like it."

"So what else is new?"

"The lake's been crawling with law since dawn, as you'd imagine. Officer even stopped by my place asking questions. Thought for a minute or two that I was in trouble, you know. Then he wanted to know if I'd seen you, had any idea why you hadn't been to home lately.''

"Must not have been one of Roan's men.''

"State Police, this guy. I guess Roan had to call them in, being these kids were likely killed somewhere else and dumped here.''

"What did you tell him?''

"Not a dad-blasted thing,'' Arty said, his voice shaded with contempt. "I don't see nothing, don't hear nothing, don't know nothing.''

"He give you a hard time about it?''

The old man gave a humorless laugh. "Tried, being as how I'm fair game.''

Janna heard the bitterness in the old man's voice, and the disgust. He was obviously upset, but it was impossible to tell whether it was from the latest death or this visit from the law.

"You think they've put me on the short list of suspects.'' Clay's tone was thoughtful.

"Looks that way. This deputy mentioned you being a vet and all, said something about that medical training you took years back and how well you know the swamp.''

"Right,'' Clay drawled. "I suppose it never occurred to this guy that the last place I'd dispose of a body would be the main channel? That dumping one there is like trying to hide it in the middle of an interstate highway?''

"Could be they think you did it to make it look like an outside job," Arty suggested.

Clay made a sound of agreement.

"Sometimes folks are so busy trying to be smart that they forget to be logical," Arty commented in disgust. "On the other hand, the best plans can get a kink in 'em." The two men were quiet, probably in recognition of Arty's bad luck all those years ago, when he tried unsuccessfully to dispose of his wife's lover. After a second, the old man went on. "That officer allowed one more thing."

"Yeah?"

"Somebody saw you out in Jenny last night."

Janna drew a quick, soundless breath as she waited for Clay's reply. It wasn't possible. Was it?"

"Did they now?" Clay asked, his voice grim.

"Said they'd recognize you anywhere, that they'd seen you heading down the lake in the middle of the night a hundred times. Jenny's right noisy, when all's said and done. I heard you myself. Woke me up when you got back near dawn this morning, too."

Silence took over inside the closed room. Janna felt sick. Clay was free to come and go. If he'd ever truly been a prisoner, he was no longer. He had been, was now, loose in her house, this man who had so much to hold against her.

Finally Clay asked, "You saying you think I'm involved in this thing?"

"Hell, boy. What's it matter what I think?"

"Roan will never believe it."

''You Benedicts stick together, I'll give ye that.''

That answer could mean anything. Was it possible that he was guilty? It seemed unlikely. But then why on earth was he still here, shut up in such cramped discomfort, if not as an alibi? The only answer that made any sense was that he knew. He knew all about her and Lainey.

''Mama?''

Janna jerked around at the sound. Lainey was awake. It was terrible timing, but there was nothing Janna could do. She moved quickly and soundlessly down the hall to the kitchen where she called out that she was coming as if she hadn't long returned to the house. Then she went to care for her daughter.

It was a good thing that she'd performed the sterile disconnection of the dialysis tubing a thousand times, for her mind wasn't on the job. Too much was happening too fast, and she was caught in the middle with dwindling options.

Clay wasn't a prisoner; somehow she could not get that fact through her mind. She'd like to march into his room and throw his playacting in his face, but she didn't quite dare. He would leave, and she didn't want that. She needed him around a little longer.

Time was running out. She had only one more day to get the extra money Dr. Gower demanded. The Aphrodite's Cup had been a will-o'-the-wisp, the search for it a waste of time. She must scrap the tentative plan to use it as an arguing point for an increase in her already huge loan balance. The trouble was, she had nothing to take its place.

"Hurry, Mama, I want to see Arty."

"You heard him talking, did you?" Janna asked as she valiantly switched mental gears. "He's with Clay right now, but maybe he'll stay for breakfast."

Lainey, holding very still while her stomach incision was cleaned, gave her a confident smile. "Clay won't care if I go to his room with them."

"Maybe not, but I doubt it's a good idea. They could be talking about things they don't want little girls to hear."

"It all right, really. Clay likes me."

"I'm sure he does, sweetheart." Janna searched her daughter's face, noting automatically that she had more puffiness than she should have this morning and her eyes were lackluster as well, an indication that her numbers needed checking. She might also need additional dialysis tonight.

"He told me so," Lainey insisted. "He said I was one of his most favorite people in the whole wide world. Can't I go in with him and Arty? Please?"

"We'll see," Janna said, falling back on the ancient answer of mothers who could think of nothing better. The major question now, she knew, was if Lainey were enough of a favorite that Clay would want to help her. The only thing she could do, now that he was free, was ask.

The ideal solution would be the kidney. Could she risk asking? Suppose she went to him and said, "I'm terrified that I've involved Lainey, your brother's child, in a dangerous situation, one that may mean her death. But I can get her out of it if you'll just cooperate. I don't have the money to pay for an illegal transplant now, but she could have a completely legal procedure if you'll only give her a kidney.''

No, she absolutely couldn't do that. What if he refused? To sacrifice so much for a virtual stranger would be unusual. What if he denied that Lainey was Matt's child? It wouldn't be at all surprising, after the things she'd done to him. And if he did accept Lainey's parentage, it raised the specter of what he might expect in return. Then there was his dislike of needles. He could well bolt at the first mention of surgery, taking all chance of aid with him.

What Janna was laying on the line was nothing so trivial as pride or fear of rejection. It was, as it had been for so long now, her daughter's very existence. For such a huge gamble, she could only trust a sure thing. What she needed then was the money for the illegal procedure.

''Hurry, Mama.''

''Yes, yes, I'm hurrying,'' Janna said as she found clothes and helped Lainey dress, then sat down on the bed beside her and began to brush her hair.

It was possible that she need not gamble at all. There had been the hint, slight but still present, that Dr. Gower might consider an appeal made in the proper manner. A naked appeal, literally. If she could force herself to that, then everything might be all right. All she'd have to do was find a way to live with herself afterward. But how difficult could that be when she might already be trading some young man's life for her daughter's chance to live?

What kind of person was she that she could even think of doing that? She could tell herself that it wasn't proven that Dr. Gower was receiving the illegal kidneys. She could pretend that she hadn't heard this latest news about another body, didn't make the connection. She could look the other way, even lie to herself and say she had no idea what was going on.

Yes, but could she lie to Lainey when she was old enough, curious enough, to ask who had given her a kidney? How could she explain that unwilling sacrifice? Would she even be around to lie then, or would she be in prison for her part in this terrible scheme?

"Mama, you're hurting me!"

She was hugging Lainey much too tightly, smoothing her hair over and over as if that might wipe the stain from her own heart. "Sorry, darling," she said, releasing her with a final brush of a fine blond strand away from her face. "So sorry."

Somehow, she had to persuade either Dr. Gower or Clay to help fund Lainey's surgery. She had to get close enough to one of them so that he would agree; she had no choice. It was wrong, it was crass and manipulative and all the things she despised, but it was also necessary. The only thing left to decide was which man she could trust that far.

The doctor or Clay? Which one could she bear to face with primal seduction on her mind?

It was a fine question. But to it, as in all the rest along this crooked road she'd chosen to travel, there was really just one answer.

10

Arty didn't stay for breakfast. He was nervous about Beulah, he said; she'd filled her nest full of eggs and was likely to take a leg off anybody who came too close to it. Janna thought it was an excuse. He felt responsible enough to check on his friend, and also on Lainey, it seemed, but had little to say to Janna. Of course he knew that Clay could leave at will. It was possible, then, that the two men were conniving at something, though what it might be, Janna was afraid to think.

The day was incredibly hot, a moist, sticky heat that seeped in through the thin walls of the old house and made the two air conditioners work overtime. The sun glared down, laying a sheet of molten-silver on the lake's surface so bright that it hurt to look at it. The heavy air was difficult to breathe. Leaves hung straight and limp on the trees, while the shadows underneath were as deep and dusty as old black velvet.

Clay appeared morose, almost sullen. Janna was so on edge that every sound made her jump. At the same time, depression gripped her so all she really wanted to do was lie on the living-room sofa and escape all her problems in sleep. She couldn't do that, not only for Lainey's sake, but also because of silent dread from knowing she was closed up with a wolf that could slip his chain at will.

Lainey was fretful. She didn't want to help Janna, didn't want to draw, play or have a snack. Lethargic and restless by turns, all she wanted was to lie curled against Clay with Ringo in her arms, listening while he read bits aloud to her from a fishing magazine. When anything else was suggested, she protested so pitifully that Janna didn't have the heart to insist. At least Clay didn't seem to mind sharing his bed with her and the raccoon.

Lunch consisted of cold cuts, boiled eggs and salad, a fast and easy meal that didn't heat the kitchen. Lainey had hers with Clay, though she clearly had no appetite. She'd have done no more than pick at her food if he hadn't teased and cajoled until she finished at least a small amount.

Afterward, Janna cleared away the dishes, then got out her watercolors. The only thing that broke the silence for some time was the swish of her brush in water between colors, Clay's voice as he read a scintillating tale about trout fishing, and an occasional rumble of thunder that indicated a distant summer cloudburst.

Clay came to the end of his article, but didn't continue or turn the magazine page. The silence of creative concentration, broken only by the hum of the air conditioner, settled around Janna. She finished the series of interlocking water hyacinth blooms that she was working on before she finally looked up.

The room had grown so dim with the advance of the afternoon and the gathering clouds that she could barely see across it. She could just make out that Lainey had fallen asleep, lying in the protective curve of Clay's body. He had dropped the magazine he held so it landed on the floor, and rested his head on the bent elbow of his arm. His eyes were closed and his chest rose and fell in a steady rhythm.

Janna laid down her brush and rose quietly to her feet. Walking to the bed's edge, she stood looking down at the pair. How easy it was to trace the resemblance between them while they lay with their faces so close together. The changes caused by Lainey's illness obscured it a bit, perhaps, but it should be plain to anyone with eyes to see.

She reached out a gentle fingertip to smooth Lainey's fine, dark eyebrow then almost, but not quite, touched that same thick arch above Clay's shuttered eye. As she stood with her hand hovering above his face, she was aware of a swelling fullness in her heart. It was stupidly sentimental, of course, but she felt an odd affection toward this man merely because he looked like her daughter.

Even as she recognized it, she was aware of the pull of another enticement altogether. He was a rare male specimen, more attractive than he had any right to be. There was strength in the firm mold of his jaw and the jut of his cheekbones. His long lashes made a shadow along the bridge of his nose. The beard under his skin made a blue-black shadow around the tucked corner of his mouth that tempted her to test it for the rasp of stubble. He was truly fine, so much so that it was probably ridiculous to think anything she could say or do would influence him an iota.

She inhaled, slow and deep, and closed her eyes. Then she opened them again. She could only try.

Ringo roused and lifted his head, his small face with its mask like a bandit appearing sleepily inquisitive. She picked him up and set him on the floor. Then she bent over the bed again and pushed her hands under her sleeping daughter with careful movements. As she nudged the flat surface of Clay's belly, she halted, half-afraid that he'd wake. In that moment of stillness, she became aware of his body heat and the resiliency of his skin under his soft T-shirt. An odd tremor moved over her, like a small earthquake of the senses. Warmth invaded the lower part of her body. She caught her breath, swamped abruptly by such a wave of desire that she felt light-headed with it.

It wasn't fair that he could do that to her without moving a muscle, without even knowing it. She was supposed to be in control here. And yet, she should not have been surprised. She had always, in those long-ago days with Matt, been more responsive at this time of day. Lainey had been conceived, she was almost sure, during a long, sultry, afternoon of napping and making love.

She'd almost forgotten. How could she have let it slip from her mind? It seemed impossible. Regardless, she didn't remember the passion of that afternoon being this powerful, this irresistible.

Clay didn't move. It seemed an insult that he could remain unaffected. She was glad, however, since it gave her a chance to salvage composure. She waited a second longer, collecting her strength, then she lifted Lainey against her chest and straightened to full height. Moving as quietly as possible, she eased out into the hall and along it to the other bedroom. She settled her daughter with the sheet over her legs and her rag doll beside her then tiptoed out of the room and closed the door.

Thunder grumbled almost directly overhead. Janna lifted her head to listen, then glanced down the hall toward the kitchen. Beyond the open blinds at the windows, she could see the leaves on the trees thrashing in a fitful wind. The noise of the air conditioner that pumped cool air down the hall drowned out most of the sound, but it appeared that a summer storm was heading their way. It would be welcome if it would cool things off for a little while.

She moved toward the kitchen. Pulling the glass-topped back door wide, she stood in the opening. The wind swept in, carrying the marshy scent of churning lake water. She squinted against it to see the wind-blown waves of the lake rolling shoreward, reflecting gray under the darkening sky. They washed against the shoreline with the sound of surf, while farther out they wore topknots of dirty white foam. The out-spread branches of the cypress trees swayed, shedding bits of leaves like tattered green lace, while their seed pods struck the water and short stretch of ground between it and the house like miniature cannonballs.

Then she saw across the lake the white curtain of the approaching rain. It swept toward her, dragging a veil of fog behind it where the cool water hit the hot surface. The wind that lifted the tendrils of hair around her face grew cooler and carried the indescribable smell of newly wet earth. Then the first drops splattered the ground and porch steps with fat, liquid splotches. They rattled down, turned to a rapid drumming, became a steady roar.

Janna could feel the tension draining from her to be replaced by reckless exhilaration. She breathed the moist air into her lungs, shook her head with a lift of her chin so the coolness could reach her throat and scalp. For a brief moment, she had the urge to walk into the downpour and stand there until she was wet to the skin.

At a sound from behind her, she turned. Clay leaned with his back to the hallway wall and one foot propped against the baseboard behind him. He was watching her with a dark, almost hungry look in his eyes.

There was no conscious decision, no plan or purpose. She simply started toward him. Her stride was smooth and even, her pace neither fast nor slow. Her muscles glided with the ease of internal heat. Her skin felt fresh and moist with windblown rain. Inside her was instinct and determination. She held his gaze, coming closer, closer until she could almost reach out and touch him.

He blinked, then narrowed his eyes. Suddenly he wasn't there, but was sliding away, stepping aside as if allowing her to enter the bedroom ahead of him. She paused for a startled instant, but there seemed nothing left to do except move past him into the room.

Maybe she didn't turn him on, after all? How ingenuous of her to assume that she could, at will, or that any feeling she had must be mutual simply because he'd made a few suggestive comments days ago. That would teach her to think of herself as a temptress.

Voice brittle, she said, "This should cool things off."

"Or make them more sultry." At her quick glance, he added, "I mean when the sun comes out again and the humidity rises."

"Yes. Yes, I suppose so." She halted, uncertain of how to go on or what direction to take.

"Was there something you wanted to talk to me about?"

She swung to face him. "What makes you think that?"

"Nothing really," he answered, his gaze on a hangnail he'd discovered on his thumb. "I just got the idea that you might want Lainey out of the way for a bit."

He hadn't been asleep after all, then. Or else her attempt to make him more comfortable by moving Lainey had disturbed him. Not that it mattered. He was waiting for her answer. Searching her mind, she grasped at the first thing offered.

"Arty didn't stay long this morning, and he didn't

seem himself. Anything wrong that I should know about?''

Clay gave her a dry look. ''Maybe he's embarrassed because he couldn't impress you by finding a bushel basketful of the Aphrodite's Cup.''

''Oh, please. Arty's old enough to be my grandfather.''

''He's still a male and still kicking, isn't he?''

For some reason, that observation made her feel a little better. ''I'm sorry he couldn't find it.''

''You had your hopes pinned on that plant for some reason.''

She turned away from him, going to her desk where she picked up a drawing then put it down again. Overhead, the rain began to slacken to a slow drumming. Finally she said, ''It was just an idea.''

''But an important one.''

Her lips tightened. ''I could have used the money that it would bring. I thought…it seemed, somewhere in the back of my mind, that if I could just find it, then everything would work out for Lainey. She'd be all right. It didn't happen, so I have to move on.''

''To what?''

What indeed? To escape her own thoughts as much as his question, she asked, ''Are you sure Arty didn't say anything? I mean, you wouldn't think of keeping anything from me just because you felt I shouldn't hear it, would you?''

Clay tilted his head and he dropped into an exaggerated drawl. ''Why, Miss Janna, ma'am, do you really think that, prisoner and all that I am, I'd care two bits about whether you were worrying your pretty little head?''

"I do think so, especially if it was for your own good." Her voice held no amusement.

He stared at her for the space of a heartbeat, his gaze unrelenting. Then a slow grin spread over his face. "I probably would."

She was going to get nothing from him, which was a situation she should be used to by now. Clay could apparently leave at will but was still pretending to be in captivity. Why on earth would he do that when he didn't seem particularly attracted to her? Or was it simply that he was suspicious? Possibly he'd recognized something different about her and was wary of the reason. His next word seemed to confirm it.

"You went back out on the lake again this morning, didn't you? Still no sign of the Aphrodite's Cup?"

She shook her head. "Finding it was a crazy idea, I see that now. Even if I could have synthesized the dye and sent a sample with a set of designs overnight to the company I work with, the legal work for a new commission would never have been done in time. My banker is a good man, but I doubt he'd increase my loan on the basis of some nebulous future benefit."

"Highly unlikely," Clay agreed with irony.

The look she gave him was harassed. "Thank you, I needed to have my stupidity pointed out to me."

"It wasn't stupid," he said, his voice dropping to a softer note. "Just desperate."

She gave a winded laugh. "Exactly. I don't suppose you have several thousand you'd like to lend me?''

He was silent so long that she turned her head to stare at him. His expression was sober and reflective. For an instant she felt something akin to hope. Then he gave a slow shake of his head. "Sorry. Can't do it."

"I assume you have a reason?"

"I don't like this whole idea."

She lifted her chin. "So you're morally offended?"

"I'm afraid Lainey may not survive it."

"That's my worry," she said shortly.

"So it is," he said quietly. "Why aren't you?"

"Because," she said in a voice like the scrape of fingernails on a chalkboard, "it's a worry, not a certainty. No, she may not survive this transplant, but she will definitely die without it."

"There are legal channels."

"Which I've tried. Her blood type is O. The wait for a donor organ is a year or more for her type, compared to only a few months for the others. We've waited almost three years and been turned down twice as candidates because of compatibility factors. We're running out of time."

"So how do you know this Dr. Gower will even check for compatibility beyond a simple cross match?"

"I have to trust him."

"Even though he's accountable to no known

agency? What are you going to do if he slips up? Besides cry, of course.''

The name she called him was not a compliment. Even as she spoke, she was swamped by a wave of despair. He'd put his finger squarely on her most terrifying nightmare.

''She's your daughter,'' he said, the words even. ''It's your privilege to decide what's right for her. In the meantime, here I am. What is it you want with me, Janna, a convenient baby-sitter, a sounding board, maybe an outlet for your frustrations over this deal? Or do you really want a sex slave, after all?''

The temptation to tell him was strong, though she still did not quite dare. Even as she hesitated, she was struck by what he'd said. Why was he there? Why had he stayed, unless it was because he wanted something from her, maybe even the same thing that she had in mind? Given what she'd done to him, however, it could be that he required having her willingness spelled out.

Without quite meeting his gaze, she asked, ''Suppose I said yes?''

''To which part?''

''Any of it. All of it.''

His face lost all expression, though whether from shock or cogent thought she couldn't tell. After a long moment, he gave a short, mirthless laugh. ''I wonder what you'd do if I put it to the test.''

''You could try it and see.''

"I could. But I have to warn you that it would change nothing."

He was wrong. She knew that instinctively. It would alter everything; just perhaps not in the way he had in mind. Her voice low and not quite even, she said, "I understand."

He stepped closer, his gaze never leaving her face. Lifting his hand, he brushed her cheek, pushing aside the silvery curtain of her hair and trailing his fingers through the long strands as if taking pleasure in the silky slide of it through his fingers. His chest filled visibly with the depth of his breath. Gently he cupped her shoulder, smoothing it with his palm while he circled her waist with his other arm and drew her nearer. Her pelvis grazed his with an electric sensation that she felt to the last, tingling nerve end of her body. She saw the pupils of his eyes expand, darkening the rich blue of his gaze to the shade of a midnight sky. Her lips parted. His features tightened then he bent his head abruptly and took her mouth.

It was a tender assault of the senses, an introduction to everything he was, to his unwavering strength and the power of the emotions that coursed through him. She'd thought he was too quiescent before, and she'd been right. It had been a rigorously controlled pose, a cover for the complicated motives that propelled him. She could feel his anger and something more that was impenetrable but almost frightening in its intensity.

His lips were smooth and warm, almost possessive,

the touch of his tongue an assured invasion. She accepted it, gave herself to it and to the rising mixture of languor and excitement inside her. It was right, almost perfect, a promise of sweet surcease and impending joy.

His grasp tightened a fraction, then she felt the easy slide of his hand under the loose batik cloth shirt she wore and onto bare skin. Without haste, as if exploring the texture and heat of her, he glided his fingertips from the indentation of her waist upward over her rib cage until he gently surrounded and captured her breast. Her nipple crinkled immediately into a tight bud. Unerringly he found it with his thumb and brushed it into exquisite sensitivity.

Pleasure, relief and the distant intimation of something more fascinating made her feel light-headed. She melted against him with a soft murmur deep in her throat, wanting to be close and closer still, needing to be submerged in him. Lifting her arms, she wrapped them around his neck and shoulders and gave him total access to her mouth as she accepted right of entry to his. His answering groan was a bass rumble, as he took the kiss deeper while dragging her even harder against him.

It wasn't close enough, wasn't raw enough, hot enough or naked enough. She was losing control, drowning in a hunger greater than she'd ever known. Moist heat spiraled inside her, threatened to embarrass her, particularly when he touched her, lightly, gently, at the very center of her being.

He freed her mouth, drew a ragged breath. With the ghost of a laugh, he said against her cheek, "Your wish is my command, lady. What would you like?"

"I don't know. Please…"

"Please you? I'd like nothing better. Only tell me how."

He was tormenting her, and enjoying it, while she was far past games or reason. "Anyway you like," she whispered. "Use your imagination."

Imagination, that most potent of aphrodisiacs. His was limitless, and more devastating than anything she'd ever dreamed.

She must have helped him, must have moved to the bed and tumbled to the mattress with him, must have released herself long enough to skim away the offending clothing between their bodies before coming close again. She hardly noticed. Or if she did, it didn't impinge on the moment.

She ached for the hot heaviness of his body, needed the certainty of his strength. She longed to be lost in him and never to surface again. His lips, his tongue were the center of her world for this short space of time. The wet hotness of his mouth on her breast sent her reeling deeper and deeper into this splendid oblivion of the senses.

The planes of his chest were firm and lightly coated with crisp yet silky hair under her questing hands. His waist had not even an ounce of excess girth. His belly was taut, the surface flat and hard. And the rest of him was just as smooth and firm, taut and hard as his body. Yes, and hot, so hot.

He didn't rush, but gave her exactly what she needed, when she needed it. Delicate and gentle, fast and rough, he possessed her with teeth and tongue and soft, moist whispers until she could stand no more. Then he eased into her by degrees, giving her only as much as she could take, until she was stretched tight and full, until she could feel the throb of the blood that coursed through him, until her body relaxed every internal resistance and she had him all.

It was repletion, a slow-moving satisfaction so wide and deep that she could feel all tension leaving her, drifting away until she was left in breathless waiting. Then he began to move. The sensation was so exquisite that she gasped and lifted her hands to clutch his wrists. He broke her hold and clasped her hands, fitting them to his, palm to open palm, with fingers meshed. She clung to him while his every rhythmic plunge took her deeper and deeper into perfect beatitude. Never, never had she felt like this, as if she could go on and on in this astounding physical union, as though she had been made expressly for this high-impact rapture. She didn't want to let him go, didn't want him to stop, didn't care if the world ended in the next hour so long as she was in his arms. With tightly closed eyes, she savored the glorious upheaval with every atom of her body.

"Janna," he whispered.

Slowly she lifted her lashes. His blue gaze burned

into hers. She felt its heat deep inside. His weight pinned her to the bed, wedged her thighs open so she was totally accessible, absolutely unprotected from him, and knew it. Slowly he twisted his hips, taking the last possible advantage of her warm, elastic depths.

She imploded in blood-red wonder. Her muscles clenched around him and her body curved toward him. He took her mouth, pressing her back down against the mattress as he rode her internal storm, aiding it, abetting it. But not quite joining it. Not quite.

The cry seemed to come from far away. Fretted with pain and terror, it tore at Janna's nerves. In the same instant, she felt Clay shiver, sensed the hard tightening of his self-control before he was completely still.

She opened her eyes to stare up at him. He met her gaze a long moment, his own dazed, almost anguished. Then he snapped his eyelids closed, spoke on something like a groan.

"Lainey."

"Yes," she whispered.

He released her abruptly, disentangled his long legs and eased from her. Rolling to his side, he lay facing her, breathing hard through flared nostrils. Janna stared up at the ceiling, trying to force her stunned mind to acceptance.

"Go on," he said in low-voiced reassurance. "You have to see about her."

"Yes. I'm...sorry."

He understood without further explanation. "It doesn't matter."

But it did. It mattered to her. It mattered a great deal, for in his forfeiting of his pleasure for her daughter's comfort and well-being she saw something, fully, that she'd known at least halfway all along.

She saw how fatally easy it would be to love Clay Benedict.

11

Clay fell back on the mattress with his arms outflung and his rib cage rising and falling like the gills of a landed fish. He felt like one, too, as if he'd been snatched out of his perfect element into one where it was impossible to survive. The pulsing in the lower part of his body was so strong that he could count his heartbeats where there was normally none worth noticing, and he wasn't sure when he'd be able to fit himself back into his jeans. Not that he'd be forever scarred by the disappointment; he'd get over it, one way or another. Just as soon as he finished wrestling his outraged libido back under control.

He couldn't remember a more wrenching experience, not even in his high school days when routed from the bed of a truck by a cruising patrol unit driven by Roan, then a deputy. He'd been the next thing to gone, maybe even permanently, over Janna Kerr, Clay knew. And he wasn't sure whether to be glad or sorry that he'd been forced to pull up short.

At least he'd carried her over the edge first. That was some consolation, though he wasn't sure if it was male ego or simple fellow-feeling that made him see it that way. Could be it was some of both.

He hadn't used protection.

Clay whispered a curse as the realization struck him. It was stunning, almost unbelievable, after so many years of being careful. Was this what had happened to Matt, the same uncontrollable, all-consuming need, leading to Lainey's conception? If so, Clay took back every hard thought he'd had about his twin's sense of responsibility. He even felt a flash of the old, special closeness to him.

Clay sat up on the edge of the bed with stiff-jointed care, raked his fingers back through his hair, ruffling it vigorously, then clasped the back of his neck. As he massaged it to relieve the tension, he glanced toward the hall. Light streamed from the other bedroom, indicating that it had grown almost completely dark. The rain had stopped, but it seemed a temporary respite from the way lightning still flickered beyond the window and thunder grumbled overhead.

He could hear Lainey crying and the low sound of Janna's voice as she tried to soothe her. Guilt touched him for dwelling on his own trials when the little girl was obviously in greater pain. Listening hard, he tried to get a handle on what the problem might be, but could form no clear idea. It was something more than normal, he thought. The hopeless misery that threaded through Lainey's cries scraped his nerves to the bone and tore ragged strips from his heart.

Pushing to his feet with a hard contraction of stomach and back muscles, Clay jerked on his jeans, then took a step toward the door. The nylon rope attached to his waist brought him up short. It was twisted

around him, a portent reminder that he could go nowhere. Or at least he couldn't without explanation.
Cursing silently, he untangled himself, giving the
rope a hard jerk to straighten it, and then moved from
the room into the hall. He stopped there with his
hands on his hips, staring at nothing while he followed by sound what was happening in the other bedroom. Janna was taking Lainey's temperature, he
thought, though with scant cooperation from the patient.

Short moments later, Janna emerged from her
daughter's room. She flung him a quick glance as she
slid past him to enter the bathroom then looked
quickly away, as if she couldn't stand the sight of
him. Watching her take a clean bath cloth from the
shelf and wet it under the cold water tap, he asked,
"What's wrong with her?"

"I'm not sure," she answered with her back to
him. "I may have to call Dr. Gower."

It was serious then, even potentially dangerous.
"Symptoms?"

"Fever, nausea, night sweats, you name it." She
paused. "Her eyes look glassy to me." She hunched
a shoulder, then moved past him again on her way
back to the bedroom.

To Clay, a crisis was a problem in need of solving.
It felt wrong to be helpless in the face of this one.
The urge to make himself useful, to do something,
anything, besides stand there made him more antsy
than being hog-tied. He hesitated, then called out,
"Anything I can do to help?"

"No. No, thanks," Janna answered, her voice preoccupied. It was also muffled, as if she might have gathered Lainey up in her arms, maybe to change her nightgown or the bedclothes.

Clay swore under his breath. He'd had about all of this passive thumb twiddling that he could take. He'd learned most of what he wanted to know anyway—or would have the information when he'd heard from the tests being run by Doc Watkins. It was possible that he needed a new game plan.

He'd already crossed one foul line, hadn't he? What was one more?

Janna came out of the bedroom again just then, leaving Lainey still crying behind her. Her footsteps were swift and purposeful. He moved aside, and she continued along the hall to the kitchen and dining area. Her cell phone lay on the table, plugged into its charging base. She picked it up and punched in a number, then turned her back to him while she waited for someone to answer on the other end.

She was avoiding him, could barely stand to be in the same room with him. Clay wasn't sure whether it was guilt or newly discovered dislike that moved her, but he didn't care for her attitude. Controlling his irritation with a strong effort, he moved in her direction to the limit of his cable.

She didn't turn around, didn't seem to notice. As she spoke into the phone, she kept her voice low. Clay's hearing was excellent, however, and he had no compunction about using it.

"I need to speak to Dr. Gower," she said with

brisk assurance overlaid by haste, as if she feared whoever was on the other end might hang up. "Could you please give me his home number or have him contact me?" She paused a moment, then said sharply, "Of course it's urgent! Would I bother to call at this time of evening if it wasn't?"

Clay pressed his lips together in a straight line as he heard the panic climb in her voice. Janna didn't frighten easily; he had solid proof of that still attached at his waist. The situation was serious indeed. He listened with care while she ran through Lainey's vital signs and the actions that she'd taken so far, as well as a somewhat longer list of symptoms than she'd given him earlier.

The reply to the spate of information was unsatisfactory, for Janna's back stiffened and anger snapped in her voice. "I am not overreacting, Nurse Fenton. I know my daughter." Janna listened a second. "No, she isn't, but I've been with her day and night for years. I understand things she can't tell me." She paused again, then said firmly, "I really need to talk to the doctor. Yes, I know he needs his rest—so do I! Believe me, this is nothing personal… Look, if you won't let me talk to him, I'll bring Lainey to the clinic… I don't care if it does draw attention!" She stopped, her stance rigid as she pressed the phone to her ear. After a second, she said, "Well, yes, I did say she might need dialysis again this soon, but wouldn't it be better if… But that will take hours!" She drew a deep, hissing breath. "Fine. You do whatever you have to do."

Clay watched with grim admiration as Janna punched the button to end the call. When she turned toward him, he crossed his arms over his chest. "So?"

"The nurse is coming."

"All this way? As late as it is and in this weather?"

Janna tossed her hair over her shoulder. "It's her choice. It isn't storming in Baton Rouge, apparently. And she seems to think that Dr. Gower—"

"What?" he asked when she stopped. Then, as color invaded her face and she remained silent, he added, "That maybe you had a personal reason for wanting to see the good doctor?"

"It's ridiculous," Janna snapped as she looked away, past his shoulder. "I can't imagine where she got the idea."

He'd just bet she couldn't. "Anyway, she's coming instead," he said in clarification. "So the question now is can Lainey wait that long?"

"I don't know," she answered in clipped tones. "Nurse Fenton wants me to put her back on dialysis in the meantime, and I don't see what else I can do."

He straightened. "I know a good doctor in Turn-Coupe. He won't mind being disturbed. Release me, and I can have you there in half an hour, including the time to get to my airboat."

She gave him a tight-lipped stare. "I can take care of my daughter, thank you."

"I know that. It was just a suggestion."

"You're interfering in something that doesn't concern you. Go back to bed and let me handle it."

"Even if I can help?" He tried to keep the incredulous anger from his voice, but wasn't sure he made it.

"I don't need your help. I don't need your advice. I don't need you to ride to my rescue in your airboat. Have you got it yet?"

"I've got it," he said, his voice even. "You don't need me."

She lifted her chin. Her gaze flickered, then she looked away as if unable to hold his gaze. "As I said, I can handle it."

The sound of their raised voices had upset Lainey even more than before. Her crying had turned to screams, something that Clay couldn't stand. He wanted to push the issue, to make Janna listen to him, but not at the risk of doing more damage than good.

As he watched her, tight-lipped and silent, Janna made as if to stalk past him again. He shot out a hand to catch her wrist, bringing her up short. She struggled for an instant, then went still as he tightened his grip. When her gaze met his, only inches from his face, he said softly, "Don't take your nerves out on me, Janna. I don't know what you're afraid of, but I'm not hurting you or Lainey, and nothing I've done was without invitation."

"No, you're innocent, aren't you? If anything happens, it's all my fault, even if…"

"What?" he demanded. "Tell me."

She looked away, biting the inside of her lip. Finally she said in strangled tones, "If Lainey is really sick, the surgery will be delayed. We'll lose the kidney that's been promised, lose it for good."

"I thought you might be afraid she'd die out here," he said with a shake of his head.

"That, too," she said. "And you warned me, didn't you, which would make you right."

The raw edge in her voice acted as a brake on his temper. "I didn't say that."

"It's what you think. Though why you should care, I can't imagine."

"Kids are special. Lainey is special." What he didn't say, but recognized with grim certainty, was that he'd grown attached to the girl. She was sweet and good-natured in spite of her problems. She took them in stride, was so incredibly brave about most of it, that she'd won his heart. That she was a small edition of her mother could be a factor as well.

"Really," Janna said in satirical disbelief. "At what age does that end? When she becomes a teenager maybe? Is that when they cease to be special and become expendable?"

Clay thought of Roan's son Jake, a funny, awkward and wise fifteen, irritating at times with his mannerism and poses, but promising to be a decent citizen and Benedict scion one day. His very being rejected the idea of the boy's death. "God, no," he said. "Kids of any age are hope incarnate, as close to immortality as we'll ever get."

"Touching, or it would be if I believed you." She jerked her arm from his grasp and moved quickly along the hall, vanishing once more into the room where Lainey lay. After a moment, the girl's screams increased in a sure sign that her dialysis tubing was being hooked up.

Janna didn't understand, Clay thought, had no conception of the Benedict creed toward kids. The more the merrier about covered it. Even as he accepted that, another part of his brain processed the salient fact that she had just hinted at knowledge of the dead teens found in the swamp. How was that possible, here in her isolation? It also sounded as if she was aware that he might be a suspect in the deaths. But if that was so, why in heaven's name had she ever let him make love to her?

They had made love, not just had sex. What they shared had been no fast and frantic coupling to scratch an itch, but something special. It had been a dream of sensual exploration, or so he'd thought and felt. Janna had needed him, yes, but she'd also wanted him; he was sure of it.

Yet now that it was done, why was she so set on pushing him away as if she had no more use for him? Two possibilities came to mind. The first was that he was wrong, that it had been about sex after all. The second was that she felt guilty, as if there'd been something behind it.

Either way, it disturbed him.

It disturbed him so much that he was going to get to the bottom of it, one way or another. Now wasn't the time, not while Lainey cried in the next room as if everything had gone wrong in her young life and would never be right again. But it would happen soon, one way or another.

Clay stood the overwrought screams for as long as he could. When he felt the next one would send him around the bend, he swung around and made his way back into his bedroom. At the foot of the bed where the cable was fastened, he bent to catch the frame and give it a hefty pull toward the door. It slid a good three feet. A bit more effort and he had gained the slack in the cable that he needed. With his face set in taut lines, he left the room again, heading down the hall, jerking the plastic coated restraining cable with every hard stride so that it slapped the door facing behind him like a whip.

Janna was sitting on the side of the bed, holding Lainey on her lap while the girl's plastic dialysis tubing snaked down around their legs. She looked up with wide, startled eyes as Clay appeared in the doorway.

"I had to come see for myself," he said in curt explanation for his presence, lifting his voice above Lainey's sobs. "Any change?"

Janna shook her head.

"An alcohol sponge bath might help the fever."

The look she gave him was scathing. "I tried that. It hurts her and she fights it, which just makes her worse."

"Sometimes things have to get worse before they can get better."

"Thank you, Dr. Benedict. I suppose you think you can make her all well."

"I could at least try."

"No, thank you. I told you before—"

"You don't need me, I got that. But what does Lainey need?"

She bent her head, speaking against Lainey's shining hair even as she tightened her arms against the child's wailing struggles. "She's mine. My child, my responsibility." Her voice dropped lower. "My life."

Beyond the windows, the lightning flashed with an almost constant glimmer. The lamp beside the bed, the only illumination in the room, dimmed almost as if the storm was stealing its power. With a glance in that direction, he said, "The generator on the front porch has been around a while, has a lot of hours of use on it. Have you checked to see if it works?"

"I asked Denise about it as backup for the dialysis. I'm not completely irresponsible about my daughter's health."

He clamped his lips shut against the retort he'd like to make. He'd only asked, with no thought of accusing her of neglect. When he could speak again, he asked, "So you haven't cranked it recently?"

"There's been no need."

"But you know how?" he insisted.

"What do you think?"

"Good. You may need it, since electric service isn't too reliable around the lake in bad weather."

She glanced at the machinery that sat humming against the wall at the head of the bed, then to the lamp, and back again to his face. A frown appeared between her eyes. "I see no problem."

"Gasoline engines aren't always cooperative. It might be better to check it out before everything goes dark."

Haunted indecision came and went in her face as she looked down at her daughter. Smoothing the tears from Lainey's pale, contorted cheek with the palm of her hand, Janna said, "I'll cross that bridge when I come to it."

"Unlock this," he said in clipped tones as he indicated his restraint, "and I'll do it for you."

"I don't think so."

"Damn it, Janna, if I'd wanted to hurt you, I've had plenty of opportunity before now."

She didn't even look up. "Go back to bed and leave us alone."

"I can't." The words were the stark truth, though he wasn't sure she was capable of recognizing it.

Voice cool and infinitely remote, she said, "This doesn't concern you."

"Doesn't it?" he asked, then went on before she could answer or make more of the derision in his voice than he'd intended. "Let me have Lainey, then, while you go see about the generator."

He thought she was going to refuse. Her grasp tightened while she lifted her gaze to his face as if searching for hidden motives. Then she gave a tight nod.

He moved forward and sank down onto the mattress, taking the girl in his arms with caution and all the gentleness he could muster. "All right, Lainey," he said in soft yet positive command. "That's enough. Quiet now."

Perhaps because he was calmer or his hold somehow stronger and more authoritative, Lainey turned toward him as she settled into lap, burrowing her wet face into his neck. She sobbed once or twice more, her whole body shaking, then her cries died away to a hiccuping whimper.

Clay felt his heart constrict while savage protectiveness flowed along his veins. At the same time, he was more aware than he wanted to be that Janna had not released her hold, as if she still didn't quite trust him. His bare skin burned where her arm was caught between him and Lainey. For an instant, they supported her between them, their arms overlapping, faces inches apart. Above the medicinal and other inevitable odors of a sickroom, he caught the faint herbal scent of Janna's shampoo combined with a lingering hint of spent passion and female musk. She met his gaze over her daughter's tumbled head, and he saw tears glistening where they pooled in the corners of her eyes.

Need rolled through him like the thunder outside. More than mere lust, it was the urge to hold her close and comfort her, to keep her safe and make sure that nothing ever hurt her again. With that fulsome desire, running just as swift and strong, was a floodtide of compassion for his dead brother who had not lived long enough to marry Janna and bring her home to Turn-Coupe. Matt had never slept with her in the great sleigh bed at the house they called Grand Point, never held her through a cold wet winter into a gentle, sensual spring. He had never seen his daughter, couldn't have since the date of his death had come before her birth. He'd never heard her giggle, never watched the secret intelligence bloom in her eyes, never cuddled her in the circle of his arms.

Whatever last shreds of jealousy Clay might have felt toward his twin melted away. If he had to choose between being a woman's first love or her last, then there could be no doubt which was better. If he could be either Janna's future or her past, then he would settle for the time that was longer. That was, of course, if he was permitted a choice at all.

It was the wrong time and place to speak of it, but he wasn't sure there would ever be a better one. His voice quiet, he said, "You were Matt's mystery woman."

She stared at him as if she couldn't make what he'd just said fit into the interior framework of her thoughts. At last she said, "You knew."

"I knew there was someone just before he died," Clay corrected, "but not who, where, when or anything else about you, including the pregnancy. Matt had his reasons for keeping quiet, I suppose, and he wasn't always the most practical of men, but it isn't—wasn't—like him to turn his back on his own child."

"He didn't," she said shortly as she drew away from him, leaving Lainey to him. "He never found out about her. There wasn't time to tell him."

His sigh of relief stirred the fine curls of Lainey's

hair as he drew her closer against him. It was good to know he hadn't misjudged his brother. "Why didn't you come to his family. We'd have helped you."

"I did that. You didn't."

"What do you mean?" he asked, frowning so his brows snapped together over his nose.

"I saw the news of the offshore explosion on television. That's how I first learned he was missing. When I called Turn-Coupe to find out more, I spoke to your father. He told me that Matt was dead. Just like that. I tried to explain that we were engaged, but he wouldn't listen. He seemed to think I was some con artist after money, or just a girl trying to make a good thing out of a one-night stand when Matt wasn't there to set the record straight. He advised me to send proof of paternity after the baby was born. Then he would consider what price to set on any child of Matt's."

"Jesus," Clay whispered. It sounded like the old man, especially in the weeks following Matt's death. He'd been stiff-rumped and suspicious at the best of times, but grief had made him granite-hard and bitingly destructive. A part of his sorrow was because he'd been hardest on Matt while they were growing up, probably because he was closest in personality to the wife who'd left him. However, Clay had always known Matt held a special place in the old man's heart for the same reason.

"You never contacted him again?" he asked in

stifled tones. "Never tried to talk to the rest of us Benedicts?"

"My baby wasn't for sale." That declaration held infinite layers of contempt before she added more quietly, "Risking having her taken from me wasn't an option."

"But Denise must have known about Lainey?"

"Not at the time, not until recently, in fact, when I asked her about the camp. And I asked because I spent a week here with her the summer after our freshman year at LSU. That's how I first met Matt."

That explained why Denise had suggested he look in on Janna. She'd known Janna hadn't wanted to see the Benedicts, but had also realized that he needed at least an opportunity to learn about Lainey. He owed her, he thought, though it was unlikely that Denise would let him forget it.

"Matt died in November," he said in soft contemplation.

She gave him a look of irony. "We had four months together after he looked me up again in Baton Rouge, that's if you're counting on your fingers."

"I wasn't. Not exactly." He was counting, but not in the way she meant. Janna had met Matt, but not him, because he'd been busy taking medical classes that summer. How different it might have been if he'd seen her first. They'd be comfortable old married folks by now. He'd be a vet, more than likely, since he'd have had little opportunity to follow his artistic bent. The two of them would be the proud parents of three or four kids. If there had been a Lainey, then she'd have been brought up at Grand Point in the more healthy back reaches of the state. She might never have caught the virus that had led to renal failure.

The same train of events could have occurred if his father had been a different kind of man, Clay was sure. Janna could have been accepted as his sister-in-law in all but name, housed at Grand Point where anything might have happened when she got over Matt's death. Lainey could have been a real Benedict by now, a happy normal child romping with all her cousins.

"I'm sorry," he said abruptly. "Sorry the Benedicts failed you and Lainey, sorry we weren't there when you needed us."

"So am I," she said on a deep sigh as she put a hand to her face, rubbing her eyes. "But it isn't your fault."

"I knew there was someone, and I should have looked into it. If I'd made some effort to find you, everything might have changed."

"Why? You didn't know I was carrying Lainey. What would you have said or done that would have made any difference? Matt was gone. That was the end of it."

His smile was brief and without humor, for all that he appreciated her exoneration. Voice even, he repeated the words she'd spoken to Denise, "You didn't need a replica."

"No."

That was certainly plain enough, though he had a

notion that there was something tentative in her face, as if she meant to add to that flat denial. He waited, since he'd been half afraid that she'd come to him earlier because she'd decided she'd settle for one, after all.

Her gaze drifted away, coming to rest on her daughter who was now almost asleep with her cheek resting on the soft mat of his chest hair. After a moment, she said, "I'd better see about that generator."

He didn't answer, which was just as well since she didn't wait to hear it. Seconds later, the screen door slammed behind her.

Clay let out his breath in a slow, almost soundless whistle of surprise for the fact that he'd survived this particular encounter with Janna, first of all, and second, that she had actually followed his suggestion. Still shaking his head, he glanced down at the child he held, then picked up her tubes, checking them, before doing a rough pulse count with his fingertips against her fragile, blue-veined neck. He was still counting the tripping beats when the lamp beside him flickered again, then went out. The air conditioner stopped. The dialysis machine ceased its humming and drained away into silence.

12

She was cursed; Janna was sure of it. At some point in her life, she had taken a bad turn so that everything she touched went wrong. Her parents, staunch in their fundamentalist religious values would say it was when she slept with Matt Benedict without benefit of clergy, and who was she to disagree? That event seemed to mark some midpoint where all before had been okay, if not perfect, and everything that came afterward tainted with disaster.

Except for Lainey, of course. Her daughter was and always had been a blessing.

It was apparently too much to ask that she be able to test the generator before the front porch was plunged into darkness. Clay had been right again. She should have known.

Inside the house, she could hear her daughter crying once more. Lainey hated the dark. Janna was torn between running to ease her fear and working at frantic speed to get the generator up and running. Now, of all times, Lainey needed to complete her dialysis, and without extra pain, or extra hours attached to the machinery. On top of that, a light of some kind was needed to help Nurse Fenton locate the camp in the darkness and the storm. If she missed the gravel driveway, Janna wouldn't put it past the woman to turn around and go back to Baton Rouge without seeing Lainey.

As she hesitated, Janna could hear the deep, soothing tones of Clay's voice. Lainey's cries began to diminish. Her daughter didn't need her mother, after all. Funny, but her reaction was closer to jealousy than relief. It had been the two of them against the world for so long that it was hard to be so easily supplanted, even for a short time.

The rising wind carried a cool mist with it from across the wave-ridden stretch of the lake. In the lightning flashes, she could see the dark and churning surface of the water. It was a violent thunderstorm. It might be minutes before power was restored, or it could be hours or even days. According to Denise, the houses on this side of the lake, most of them empty except for the weekends, came pretty far down on the power company's priority list, so were among the last to receive attention. She had to get the generator going as soon as possible.

Swinging around, Janna banged her way back through the screen door and into the kitchen. Moving by feel, she located the kitchen junk drawer where she'd noticed an emergency flashlight. With it clutched in her hand, she hurried back out to the porch.

Her experience with gasoline engines was nothing to brag about. She'd cranked the family's old push mower while living with her parents, and that was about it. Apartment life didn't include lawns to mow, weeds to cut or trees to trim, and if her car quit, she called a garage. She hadn't lied to Clay; she'd looked at the generator when she first moved into the camp. She'd read the directions for starting it that were printed on the side. But she hadn't actually started the monster, certainly hadn't switched the power for the camp over to it. It was a serious oversight.

After reading hastily through the directions again by flashlight, she flipped the power switch, then pressed and held the starter button. The generator rumbled for a second, then shuddered and died.

Janna took a steadying breath then read the instructions carefully once more. Following them with exaggerated care, she tried again. The only result was an abortive grunt.

"Janna?" Clay called from inside the house. "You may need to clean the plugs."

Turning her head, Janna caught a glimpse of his tall form in the dim recess of the hall. The glow of a lightning glimmer showed him standing empty-handed. Voice strident, she shouted, "Where's Lainey?"

"She's okay, trying hard to be brave for you. I put her back in bed," he answered. "You may have to remove the housing to get to the plugs. Once you have them out, a rub or two with sandpaper should remove any corrosion."

"Denise said they had been recently replaced," she informed him.

"Then try the manual pull cord."

It was a reasonable suggestion. With her jaw set in determination and a foot braced against the crouched housing of the dumb machine, she yanked on the pull cord again and again. The results were the same, a few rumbling grunts followed by silence.

"Don't wear yourself out," Clay advised above the roll of thunder. "Try choking it."

He was the one she'd like to choke. Voice glacial, she asked, "And just how would I do that?"

He told her in detail, adding, "When you're done, give the thing a good, hard pull."

She tried, she really did. She pulled with all her strength, tried until her arm and stomach muscles burned and tears of frustration were whipped from her eyes by the wind. It did no good. Time was passing, slipping away from her, while the stupid generator sat there in sullen noncooperation.

She couldn't do it.

Added to all the other problems and mistakes, it was the final insult, the last abysmal failure. Everything was wrong, so wrong.

The promised kidney was going to someone else. Dr. Gower was going to be convicted for his clandestine transplants, if not as an accessory in the deaths of the teenagers found in the swamp. She was going to prison for purchasing an illegal organ as well as for kidnapping Clay. Above all, Lainey was going to die.

Renal disease was going to claim her daughter as it had so many others, that was if peritonitis, blood chemical imbalance, simple infection or a hundred other ailments harmless to normal children didn't claim her first. And whatever happened, it was going to be Janna's fault. For the rest of her life, in prison or out, she would have to live with the memory of all the difficult decisions and wrong choices that had led to this place, this night, this one last failure. If she could bear to live at all.

Dropping to her knees, Janna put her face in her hands and pressed her fingers to her eyes. She rocked a little with the wind and the anguish inside her, but she didn't cry. Some things were beyond tears.

"Let me try, Janna. Turn me loose and let me give it a shot."

Clay's deep, seductive voice came to her from out of the darkened house. He knew she'd failed, had been waiting for it. Now he was testing her to see if she'd set him free in order to safeguard the person dearest to her heart.

Her daughter or her freedom? It was, perhaps, the last of the difficult choices. Once she'd turned Clay loose, what happened would be out of her hands. Or was that strictly true? According to Arty, Clay had been free to ride the lake in his airboat the night before. If he did have some private agenda that required him to return to his captivity, might it not work in her favor?

She didn't know. All she could do was take the chance. It was possible it was the biggest gamble of her life.

"Janna?"

She made no reply, but pushed upright again. Picking up the flashlight, she followed its beam into the house. Clay blocked the hall with his wide shoulders, a ghostly presence, omnipotent and powerful in the small tunnel of light. She turned aside a second to fish around in the kitchen junk drawer. Finding what she wanted, she stepped to where Clay stood. She shined the flashlight beam full on his face a second. He didn't flinch from its brightness but held her gaze. Turning, she put the light on the stove where it would illuminate what she was doing, then swung back to him.

As she reached around him, searching for the padlock, he put a hand on her shoulder. It was a gesture that could have been a caress but that she took as approval. She ignored it and he removed his hand after a moment. The restraint had tightened with his pull against it earlier; she fumbled with it, taking long seconds to release the lock. As it fell open, she slipped if off, tossed it to the stovetop along with the key so they made sharp, clanging sounds in the quiet. She sent his waist rope after them.

She expected him to step away. Instead he reached for her hand. She searched his shadowed features in the lightning-shattered dimness, afraid of what she might find there. Her fingers were trembling in his warm hold. Would he stay or go now that he was officially free, help her or require some form of revenge for his captivity to this point? Wary, hovering on the edge of panic, she waited to see what he meant to do.

They were so close, there in the narrow hallway.

She could feel his body heat, hear the soft sound of his swift-drawn breath. Her heartbeat stumbled, then increased to a hard throb while a slow tide of memory and need threatened to engulf her. How could that happen, here, now? This wasn't the time, the place, nor the right man. She didn't trust Clay Benedict, and knew he had no reason to trust her. There was no bedrock on which to build anything between them. The attraction they felt was a fluke without permanency or future. She knew it, but was defenseless against its onslaught.

"Please," she whispered, and wasn't totally certain for what she pleaded.

He nodded, then released her and reached for the flashlight. "Right," he said, his voice carrying a trace of huskiness. "The generator."

As he moved past her and through the kitchen to the porch, Janna leaned against the wall and waited for strength to return to her knees. Gratitude was a strange thing to feel at that moment, but she was pathetically grateful for his initiative anyway. A moment later, she pushed upright with a jerk and went to look in on Lainey.

Her daughter had drifted off, though her skin felt even warmer than before. Janna tucked the sheet over her, but there was nothing she could do to help her just now. She made her way back out to the porch.

Clay squatted beside the recalcitrant generator, holding the flashlight under one arm while he polished the end of a spark plug on the rough fabric of his jeans. He looked up as the screen door squeaked

open. Janna held his eyes for an instant, then reached
for the flashlight. When he let it go, she directed its
beam on the spot he indicated.

Scattershot rain hit the porch roof at that moment.
A second later, it became a deluge. Warm, heavy and
incredibly wet, it whipped in on them in a windblown
curtain, sifting like fog through the porch screen. The
wetness snared in the plastic mesh and hung there
like a silver veil, while beyond it was nothing except
a rushing wall of water.

They were both soaked to the skin in seconds.
There was nothing to be done about it, however, except get the job done.

Clay checked and probed and adjusted under the
flashlight's yellow light while rain whipped across his
face and made his hair cling to his head in black
waves. Then he rose with athletic grace and bent to
grasp the starter cord. Janna stepped back out of the
way as he gave it a fast, hard pull.

The generator roared, almost caught. Clay made a
minor adjustment. The rain-wet muscles across his
bare back rippled as he hauled back on the cord again.
The generator exploded into life, then settled to a
steady hum.

"You did it!" Janna cried.

As he straightened, she put out her hand to clutch
his arm. Under her palm, his skin, warm until that
moment, pebbled with chill bumps. He grinned down
at her. "No sweat. Literally."

His face was open, without shadows or guile, in
the flashlight's glow. For an instant, it seemed she

could see inside him to the wide, fearless reaches of his soul, could feel the gentleness beneath the force of his personality, the caring that tempered his strength. He was wet and chilled, but didn't care. He'd been drugged, bound, denied his freedom for days, but had responded to her need, and Lainey's, instead of leaving them stranded.

It was devastating to see him in that light, but there was a problem with it. She had no way to tell whether what she saw was the actuality or only her imagination, if her view of him was true or only as she would like him to be.

His eyes darkened. "Janna."

Fear that she was wrong feathered over her with coldness more painful than the rain that plastered her clothes to her. She retreated a step, then pushed the flashlight at him. "Here," she said in breathless haste. "I have to see about Lainey again."

He made no reply, but stood staring after her as she slammed back into the house. By the time she reached the hallway outside Lainey's bedroom, he had switched the power over to the generator so the light came on overhead to show her the way.

Her daughter was restless, twitching and moaning in her sleep, while her skin was flushed with heat. Janna stood beside the bed, worrying her bottom lip with her teeth. It would be some time yet before Nurse Fenton arrived. Janna hated this waiting. Something inside her shrilled that it was dangerous to delay, that she should be taking action. It was possible she was overwrought, as the nurse had suggested on the phone, but it felt like educated instinct.

She reached to smooth the backs of her fingers over Lainey's tender and puffy little cheek. The skin was hot, so hot. How much of it was fever, how much from the warm night, she couldn't tell. The heat was increasing in the house in spite of the rain. The generator could power the basics, but wasn't designed to run the air conditioners. At least she could open a few windows for air, even if rainwater did splatter inside.

Clay was ahead of her. He'd already shoved up enough window sashes for a decent cross draft by the time she reached the kitchen area, and was opening more. The kettle sat on the gas range as well, and the smell of fresh coffee hanging in the air told her he'd put grounds in the drip pot.

He hadn't changed, she saw. His wet jeans clung to his body like indigo skin. A wet streak trailed down the small of his back to disappear under his waistband, and raindrops spangled the tops of his shoulders. Every step he made left a wet track on the floor in the shape of a bare foot. Regardless, he appeared incredibly competent, healthy and sexy, particularly since she suspected he was naked under his one piece of clothing. If he was conscious of it in any way, he gave no sign.

"Lainey all right?" he asked over his shoulder as he pulled up a blind to keep it out of the way of the sash he'd just raised.

Lightning flared, outlining him at the window in a

silver glow. She turned quickly from the sight, moving to the dish cabinet. As she took down two cups, she answered, "I wish I knew."

"But you really don't think so."

"Maybe I'm wrong. Maybe the whole thing is getting to me."

"Can she wait for the nurse?"

His question carried a knife-edge of doubt. She answered the tone as much as the question. "She'll have to, won't she?"

"Not if you take her out of here."

Janna pressed her lips together without answering. Turning to the table, she set down the cups she held, then pulled out a chair and slid onto it. Behind her, the kettle began to whistle. Clay padded over to fill the coffeepot, then brought it with him as he joined her at the table. For long moments, the only sounds were the trickling coffee, the rain overhead and the thunder that boomed now and then, echoing back from the tree-fringed lake beyond the open back door.

There was tension in the quiet between them, but little real strain; they had moved past that at some time during the last few hours. Janna could feel weariness trying to sneak up on her. She put an elbow on the table and propped her head on the heel of her hand.

"Get some rest," Clay said, his voice abrupt. "I'll keep watch."

"No, no, it's okay." She sat up straight again with an effort.

"Drink this then."

She hadn't seen him pour the coffee, hadn't known that it had finished dripping. Her brain felt as if someone had filled her skull with foam packing peanuts. As she reached for the cup he offered, he wrapped her fingers carefully around it before he took his own away.

The brew was hot and strong, and slid down her throat like the elixir of life. Its jolt was welcome, but not as reviving as she expected.

She risked a quick look at Clay. He lounged back in his chair with his coffee cup resting on his thigh and his legs stretched out and crossed at the ankles. The heat building in the house gave his bronze skin a perspiration sheen to go with the raindrops still glinting like silver beads among his chest hair. His air of relaxation was less than total, however, since he was completely motionless and his gaze was fixed on her chest.

A single downward glance showed Janna that she was attired like a candidate in a wet T-shirt contest. The soft, damp material draped over the curves of her breasts with perfect fidelity, including the tightening of her nipples under the intensity of his gaze.

Deliberately she stared at him until he looked up and his gaze locked with hers. A slow tide of dark color invaded his face and he shifted in his chair in a telltale movement before turning his attention to his coffee.

He wanted her, that much was clear. The question was why. She was bedraggled and exhausted, a hollow-eyed harridan without makeup or even the pretense of civility. The only answer she saw made her feel a little sick inside, especially after her earlier moment of trust.

Revenge.

That was it, she thought, though not revenge of a simple, physical kind. He had no use for crude retaliation, not Clay Benedict. In return for taking his freedom, he meant to have nothing less than her self-respect. He'd joked about being her sex slave, but in reality that was what he was intent on making her.

The pain of that suspicion was so great that she could hardly think, had difficulty drawing air into her lungs. She stood up in a single fast move that sloshed coffee from her cup in a steaming wave. "I think I'll change and lie down with Lainey, after all."

He didn't try to stop her as she moved in the direction of the bedroom. When she paused at the door a second to look back, he was sitting as she'd left him, watching her with the blank look of incomprehension in his eyes. Doubt touched her with cool fingers. She hesitated, said in a tremulous request, "Call me? When the nurse gets here, I mean."

He gave a short nod, but that was all. As irrational as it might be under the circumstances, she missed his smile.

Janna came awake to a touch. Clay stood over her with his hand on her shoulder. The instant she opened her eyes, he released her and stepped back.

"Car coming," he said quietly.

She was so groggy with sleep that it was hard to

focus, still she could see that he'd changed clothes. The rakish, half-naked satyr who had sat in her kitchen was gone. In his place was a neat and somber Southern gentleman in a black T-shirt and jeans, one who looked more alert and purposeful than any man should. Nothing in his face or manner even hinted that he had any designs on her body or her psyche. Why then did she feel as if she had slept unmolested only by grace of his forbearance and self-control?

"Thank you," she said through dry lips.

"No problem." He paused, as if he expected some comment that didn't come, then went on. "The rain has stopped. I'll wait outside for this nurse."

She nodded her understanding. As he left the room, she resisted the impulse to watch him.

By the time Anita Fenton stepped inside the screened porch ahead of Clay, Janna had brushed her hair, splashed cool water on her face and straightened the dress made of hand-dyed fabric in a crazy quilt patchwork design that she'd changed into from her wet clothes. She felt marginally more collected, but was still uncomfortably warm since the power remained out. At least the generator still hummed steadily on the porch.

Anita Fenton, wearing a polyester shirt and slacks set and carrying a molded metal case, glanced at their makeshift power source. An expression of incredulous scorn crossed her face. For a second, Janna was aware of the uncertain grip she held on her temper as she waited at the screen door. Reminding herself to have a care, she said as pleasantly as possible,

"Come inside, please. I'm really sorry to get you out on such a bad night."

"Never mind. I'm here now. Where is Lainey?"

"Sleeping."

"Really." The sarcasm in the woman's tone suggested this was proof she had come on a fool's errand.

Janna, catching Clay's gaze, saw his face tighten with irritation. That helped her feelings for some reason. "This way," she said to the nurse over her shoulder as she led the way toward the bedroom.

At the open doorway, Nurse Fenton pushed past Janna and strode to the bed. Putting out a red-nailed hand, she shook the sleeping child awake with a quick, almost rough, movement.

Lainey raised her lashes. Her face blanched, and she gave a small scream. Eyes wide and fever-bright, she sprang up, then scooted away in the bed until her back was against the headboard. Her retreat disturbed Ringo who had somehow found his way into the bed with her. He leaped in the air from where he had been snuggled between the pillows. Coming down on all fours with his tail straight up, he hissed like an angry cat as he faced the source of danger.

"Shit!" Nurse Fenton jerked back her hand, then swung toward Janna. With an angry flush mottling her face like a rash, she demanded, "What is this?"

"You startled her," Janna said sharply. "And Ringo."

"I have no time for coddling a silly little girl," the nurse snapped. "And I certainly didn't come all this way to be attacked by a wild animal! I'd have thought you'd know better than to allow so unsanitary a creature near your daughter.''

From the corners of her eyes, Janna saw Clay step to the foot of the bed, his face grim and eyes narrowed. To the nurse she said, ''Ringo is perfectly clean, and he helps calm Lainey.''

''Oh, yes? He doesn't seem to be doing such a fine job right now. Are you going to control your child so I can examine her?''

Janna didn't trust herself to answer. Leaning toward Lainey, she held out her hand. ''Come on, honey,'' she said in cajoling tones. ''Nurse Fenton needs to take a look at you.''

''No sticks,'' Lainey said in a high, near-frantic whine, even as she cringed away. ''No sticks.''

''No sticks, I promise,'' Janna murmured in reassurance.

''I may as well do the presurgical blood test, as long as I've come all this way,'' Nurse Fenton said in hard contradiction. Setting her case on the bedside table, she opened it and took out a packaged hypodermic syringe.

The result was entirely predictable. Lainey went into hysterics. Screaming and kicking, she scuttled away to the fullest extent of the tubing attached to her stomach catheter. Janna put a knee on the mattress and stretched a hand out toward her, intending to draw her into her arms to soothe her. A small, flying heel caught her in the mouth, so she fell back, tasting blood. Clay, with a frown between his brows and concern darkening his eyes, stepped quickly around to the far side of the bed.

"For heaven's sake," the nurse said in angry contempt. "Get me a sheet. I'll wrap the little brat up so tight she can't move a toenail." As she spoke, she ripped open the syringe, then pulled out a length of latex ribbon of the kind normally used for constricting the arm to raise the blood vessels.

"I don't think…" Clay began, his voice hard.

"I can handle it," Janna interrupted.

The nurse turned a hard stare on Clay as if just taking note of his presence. "Who is this man, and what's he doing here anyway? Dr. Gower will not be pleased that you aren't following instructions."

"The doctor knows all about Clay," Janna said shortly. She reached for Lainey again and almost had her, but the panicky child made a dive in Clay's direction. She might have tumbled over the side of the bed if he hadn't caught her by her elbow, then sat down quickly on the mattress so she fell into his arms. Ringo, scampering after her, wasn't quite so lucky. He slid over the edge where he clung to a corner of the sheet with his sharp claws for a second, then dropped to the floor.

"Well, finally, someone who can actually hold down the little wretch. Get her arm, will you, while I find a vein." Nurse Fenton, without the raccoon to contend with, pushed Janna to one side and climbed onto the bed. She crept forward on her knees.

Lainey shrieked. Babbling and pleading, she grabbed Clay's neck in a stranglehold, then wrapped herself around him. Her clear plastic dialysis tubing snapped tight across the rumpled sheets.

"I've had enough of this!" Nurse Fenton's eyes flared and her lips clamped in a hard line as she grabbed the stretched plastic tube in a hard fist. "Come here right now, brat, or I'll make you one sorry little girl."

Janna cried out as she saw that the nurse meant to drag Lainey toward her by the tubing attached to the shunt in her stomach incision. The woman was between Janna and her daughter. She was going to be too late to stop her.

Clay shot out his hand like a striking rattlesnake, the movement so fast it was little more than a blur. His hard fist closed over the nurse's wrist in a grasp tight enough to whiten his knuckles. "Drop it," he said in slicing menace. "Do it now, or I'll break your bones like so many toothpicks."

The color drained from Nurse Fenton's face. She crumpled to one side with her mouth open in a gasping cry. Slowly, one by one, she opened her fingers and let go of the tube.

"Back up. Get off the bed." Clay flung the red-haired woman's wrist toward her face.

She followed his orders, even as she threw an accusing look at Lainey. The girl was quiet, though it was impossible to be sure whether her shocked silence was because of Clay's violence or the novelty of having someone protect her from medical personnel. She huddled in his lap as he circled her with a protective arm.

With the space of the mattress between her and Clay, the nurse curled her lips in a malevolent sneer. "You'll regret this," she informed him. "Lainey's kidney will go to someone else. I'll see to it."

"Get out," Clay told her without expression. "And don't come back."

Janna, caught between fierce gladness and horror, drew breath to protest. The look of blazing contempt that he turned on her stopped the words in her throat. He had no more use for one who would condone frightening and hurting a child, she saw, than for the person who would do it.

Voice a little shaky, she said, "But Lainey needs—"

"She doesn't need this."

There was no shadow of compromise in his voice. And he was right; she saw that clearly. It hurt that he'd recognized it before Lainey's mother who should have been the protector of her welfare. "No," she said quietly. "No, she doesn't."

Clay's smile was like a reward. It curved his lips in approval, shone with a brilliant and unearthly blue sheen in his eyes, and beatified the small room. It was a loss when he turned back to Nurse Fenton. In entirely different tones, he said, "You heard the lady."

The woman gave Janna a last narrow-eyed stare. Then she gathered her belongings and stalked from the room. Seconds later, the screen door of the porch banged shut behind her.

Janna let out the breath she'd been holding without

noticing. Then she crawled across the bed and shifted closer to Lainey and Clay. She reached for her daughter, and Lainey put out her arm, leaning near enough to crook her elbow around her mother's neck. She didn't release Clay, however, so that Janna was pulled into a tight, three-person hug. After a second, she felt Clay ease over to reduce the tension on Lainey's tubing, then the warm strength of his arm enclosed her in his hold along with her daughter.

It felt so good, so right, that a hard knot formed in Janna's chest and she swallowed salt tears. Protected, she felt protected, and something else that swelled her heart and filled her with such heat that it radiated from her very pores.

He was quite a guy, Clay Benedict. Whatever he might have done or intended to do, she owed him. In her gratitude to him, she was willing to give him anything he wanted, at least for now. No matter what the form or what it might cost her, she would allow him his recompense. Or even his revenge.

13

A sharp pain in his groin snatched Clay from sleep. Sheer instinct made him try to roll away, but he came up short. He was pinned to the bed. Lainey lay with her back to him and her head and shoulders resting across his outflung arm. She was jerking as if in the grip of some nightmare. It was her sharp little heel that had gouged him as she kicked out in her sleep.

On the other side of the girl, Janna was curled toward him with one foot tangled between his ankles. As he blinked awake, he saw her lashes lift as well. She focused on her daughter who was turned toward her. Fear and comprehension invaded the silver-spangled gray depths of her eyes.

Before he could form a word, she shoved to a sitting position on the mattress and reached for Lainey. She dragged her daughter across her lap. Leaning backward, she plucked a child's hairbrush from the nightstand then thrust the slender, blunt-ended handle into Lainey's mouth. Deftly she extracted her swallowed tongue.

Lainey was having a convulsion.

It wasn't the way Clay had dreamed of waking up when he'd gone to sleep in Janna's bed.

With a wrenching contraction of stiff muscles, he surged to his feet. He stared down at the arched, shuddering body of the little girl whose eyes were rolled back into her head so only the whites were visible. As he watched, she went limp, barely breathing. Janna had been right in her mother's intuition. The situation was bad.

God, he felt helpless. Guilt seized him as well, as if he'd somehow wished this on Janna with his insistence that she face the possible consequences of bringing Lainey so far into the swamp. Certainly there was no satisfaction in being right.

Something had to be done. There was only one possibility that he could see.

He hesitated a second, then asked in soft query, "Janna?"

"Yes," she answered in a voice like tearing silk.

"The hospital. We have to go."

"I'll be back from Arty's with the airboat by the time you get her tubes out and throw what you want to take with you into a bag."

She frowned at him. "My car's outside."

"Twenty minutes to Turn-Coupe by water, three hours to Baton Rouge by car. Your call."

She closed her eyes while she drew a deep breath. Then she opened them again. "Hurry."

"You've got it."

On the way out, he snatched up the cell phone from the kitchen table and punched in a number. Seconds later, he was talking to Roan. In less than half a minute, he had the promise of an ambulance and police escort waiting for them when they docked at Grand Point. Tossing the phone back down, he hit the porch at a dead run.

The rain had stopped, but the lake steamed in the dark like a giant cup of black coffee. Digging a paddle into the murky liquid, he sent the boat flying toward Arty's place.

When Clay returned, Janna was standing on the dock with Lainey, wrapped in a sheet, in her arms. She was pale and her hair straggled around her shoulders in long, shining hanks, but he'd never in his life seen anything that twisted his guts with so much longing, respect and possessive passion. Leaping to the dock, he bundled mother and daughter into the airboat, and then shoved off again. As the gap widened between the rickety dock and Jenny, he sprang back onboard. Dropping into his seat, he turned to Janna. "All set?"

She nodded with a jerky movement of her head. "Just go."

Something in her face as she met his gaze in the dashlight clutched at his heart. He felt the full weight of responsibility for this move press down on his shoulders. Over and above that, he acknowledged a flash of pride that she had enough confidence to follow his lead, plus something more that he didn't dare examine. The dependence and gratitude in her face were unwanted, even as he felt his stomach muscles clench to board-hardness with his determination not to fail her.

Voice deeper than expected, he said, "Hang on."

The airboat roared into life, then Clay sent it flying toward Turn-Coupe. Trees, water, fog, blown spray; these things whipped past and around them. He narrowed his concentration to the stretch of water just ahead of the boat as he negotiated twisting channels and stretches of open lake he knew so well that he could have followed them blindfolded as well as in the dark. The airboat skimmed the water, bouncing on a soft cushion of air and spume, dancing around curves, answering his slightest touch instantly and with consummate grace. Time spun past as well. He glanced at Lainey. In the faint glow of the running lights, the girl appeared comatose, uncaring for the wind of their passage that whipped her hair across her white face. Clay pushed Jenny into a higher speed.

Minutes that seemed like eons later, he swerved from the main channel into the long, fingerlike cove that would lead him home to Grand Point. Ahead of them, he caught the welcome flash of blue and red lights, saw the shapes of an ambulance and Roan's police unit. Over the airboat's roar, he called to Janna, "Almost there."

"Yes. I see," she said with a catch in her voice before she brushed Lainey's hair away from her closed eyes then pressed her lips to the top of her small head. She looked away then, but not before Clay caught the sheen of moisture in her eyes.

A mere fragment of time later, he was slowing, letting the airboat slide up to the Grand Point dock under its own impetus. Hands reached out to pull the boat in and secure it. Med techs in blue-and-white saluted Clay and spoke quietly to Janna as they took Lainey from her. They transferred the child to a waiting gurney with care and dispatch, then loaded it into the ambulance. Janna climbed inside and settled at the head of the gurney. The doors closed, and the emergency vehicle rolled away.

Clay put his hands on his hips as he stared after the ambulance, watching it disappear around the bulk of the main house, headed for Turn-Coupe. His responsibility was over; Lainey's well-being was out of his hands. He should have been relieved, but only felt empty inside.

Roan had left his patrol unit and walked out to stand beside him on sun-warped boards of the dock. "You did it, huh? Got the woman and the kid here where you wanted them?"

Clay met his cousin's stern, assessing gaze in the blue flash of the lights from his patrol unit. "It's not like that."

"Isn't it? Even a little?"

He shook his head. "If Lainey doesn't make it..."

A corner of Roan's mouth took on an odd curl. "Think her mother will blame you?"

"She could."

"With reason?"

"God, no!"

"What I thought."

As his cousin fell silent, Clay said in brooding tones, "Lainey should be at Children's Hospital in New Orleans at the very least, maybe even Oshner's

Medical Center. Someplace with a major kidney unit.''

"Simon Hargrove's a good man," Roan said, speaking of the head physician and surgeon at the Turn-Coupe hospital. "He knows what he's up against and is waiting to get started. He'll make the right decisions for her."

Clay nodded. It would have to be enough. For now.

"Think I'll head on over there, see to it that the kid gets checked in all right," Roan said, tipping his head in the direction of his police car. "You coming?"

"Try leaving without me," Clay answered.

Janna was seated in front of the admissions desk, filling out forms, when Clay hit the hospital emergency room. He lifted a hand, but didn't stop. From somewhere in one of the back examining rooms, he could hear Lainey moaning. Following the sounds, he found her stretched out on an examining table while Dr. Hargrove checked her and the duty nurse, who happened to be Clay's cousin, Johnnie Hopewell, tried to keep her still.

"It's okay, punkin," he said quietly as Janna's daughter turned piteous eyes in his direction. "I'm here."

The nurse, a plump, motherly sort with curling dark hair and a hundred-watt smile, looked up. "Speak of the devil," she said cheerfully. "I was just telling Lainey that you'd show up any minute."

"Darn right," he replied though his gaze was on the little girl on the table.

"Benedict," Dr. Hargrove said in greeting as he reached across the patient for a handshake. "Glad you're here. Our girl is not good. She's had a sudden spike in her blood pressure, maybe from emotional causes, maybe from infection. It probably brought on the seizure her mother described, as well as her unconsciousness when she first arrived. She seems to have a degree of paralysis on her left side, and I'll bet my next year's house note that her hemoglobin is low. We can't rule out other problems without a battery of tests. But the main thing is to get her stabilized and her blood pressure down. Speed counts as much as accuracy right now."

Clay nodded, since the news wasn't too far from what he'd expected. "Think you can handle it here?"

"Yes, if I'm right," Hargrove answered with precision. "It's a matter of finding the right combination of drugs as fast as possible. But she can be airlifted to Baton Rouge or New Orleans, if that's what you want."

"It's her mother's decision." The Flight for Life medical helicopter had been an option in the back of Clay's mind all along. It was common practice for rural hospitals to airlift critical patients to more sophisticated centers, and it would mean access to expert treatment for Lainey.

"My mistake," Hargrove said. "I need to know, though, one way or the other."

Clay gave him a level look. "You can still get things started, can't you?"

"I have the mother's signed permission, if that's what you mean."

Every second counted, Clay knew, and his gut instinct warned that time was running out. The elevated blood pressure could still cause a full-blown stroke with attendant brain damage, complete paralysis or even death. If Lainey were his child, he wouldn't want treatment delayed an instant longer than necessary.

"Do it," Clay said. "I'll clear it with her mother."

Johnnie, who had been following the exchange between him and the physician, said, "This young lady said she'd let me give her a couple of little sticks if I promised to use this stuff I have here to numb the skin and keep it from hurting. Well, and if you'd hold her hand."

Clay could see that the "little sticks" in question were going to stretch to several for tests, medications and to insert a heparin lock for the IV solution and antibiotics that waited nearby. Even knowing Lainey was in good hands, the best available within a hundred miles, Clay still cringed inside to think of it. He could feel sweat pop out between his shoulder blades and across his forehead. The last thing under the sun that he wanted to do was to stay in the same room when so many needles were plunged into anyone, especially Lainey. It was too much like feeling them pierce his own skin.

And yet, how could he refuse? Lainey was willing

to endure it if he stood by her. Her courage touched him as nothing ever had before. He couldn't chicken out while she needed him, was ashamed that he would even think of it. It was such a little thing, after all, and the knowledge that he could help her by doing it seemed to ease the ache in his heart.

Clay picked up the small, cold fingers that lay on the disposable paper sheet tucked under Lainey's frail arms. His quick wink brought a watery smile to her pinched face, but the terrified resignation that lay behind the effort almost killed him. In that moment, he'd have given anything to be able to take the pain for her. Anything.

"Yeah, she's a brave kid, and my sweetheart to boot," he said, his voice husky and his eyes never leaving hers. "Hold on tight, punkin. It'll be over in a few seconds."

Lainey gave him a solemn nod, then her thin fingers curled firmly around his palm. He held her tense gaze a brief moment longer, until her small nod signaled that she was ready. Then he looked across her at Johnnie and Simon Hargrove, and his hard stare said plainly that they'd better make damn sure that they didn't hurt her an iota more than necessary and that the seconds he'd promised were all that it took to get the job done.

By the time Janna arrived five minutes later, Lainey lay quiet and still with her eyes closed so her long lashes rested on her small, puffy cheeks. Clay glanced up as the door opened. He saw Janna put her hand to her mouth while the color receded from her face until it was bloodless.

"Sedated," he said in sharp explanation. "Just a mild tranquilizer and Benadryl to prevent a reaction to the packed blood cells they've started. It made her sleepy. That's all."

Janna stared at him a long moment, then looked toward the different IV racks around the head of the bed. Finally she met the gaze of Clay's cousin who had been detailed to remain with the patient and check her blood pressure at ten-minute intervals. As Johnnie added her nod of reassurance, Janna looked around for a chair. Locating one against the wall, she dropped into it then closed her eyes and leaned her head back against the wallpaper behind it.

"There was so much paperwork because I don't have insurance," she said, her voice uneven. "I don't know what I'd have done if Roan hadn't stepped in and told them to let it go. This is a strange hospital for Lainey, with doctors and nurses that she doesn't know. I was afraid she'd be terrified. They kept saying you were with her, but I couldn't be sure."

Clay wanted to ask why she would think he was unreliable, but it wasn't the time or place. Voice even, he asked, "You saw Hargrove?"

"He told me the next twenty-four hours will be crucial." Her lips curved in a hard, tight smile. "Of course they always are."

"Then you know about the possible airlift."

She opened her eyes. "He mentioned it. Apparently you didn't think it was necessary."

"Not so. Say the word and it's done."

She studied him as she absorbed the message behind his simple statement, that he was perfectly willing to defer to her wishes. Finally she said, "I've heard mothers of other renal patients talk about helicopter airlift. It costs thousands."

And she'd said there was no insurance, Clay remembered. He tilted his head. "You'd be for it if cost wasn't a problem?"

"But it is."

"I got that part. Not to worry, there are ways." Clay tried for a casual, offhand note, but wasn't sure how well he succeeded. The look his cousin Johnnie gave him said she suspected that what Clay had in mind involved his own pocketbook, still he knew she wouldn't interfere.

"Charity." The corners of Janna's mouth turned down and she looked away toward the window where the light from outside security lamps made an artificial dawn. After a second, she asked, "Do you think she's in good hands?"

"You can't beat Hargrove and his staff. As for the hospital, it may not have every space-age gadget in the book but it has everything that's important."

Her chest rose and fell with a deep breath. "They seem to care about what happens to her instead of seeing her as just another problem. I've had enough of big hospitals, anyway. I think…I'd just as soon she stayed here."

For a single second, Clay felt a surge of sheer masculine satisfaction that she'd accepted his judgment.

Then reality set in. If anything happened to Lainey, it would be his fault. Again. Still, he could take that possibility so long as he was allowed to stick close enough to fix anything that might go wrong.

"I'll tell Hargrove to move her into a private room," he said, and turned toward the door.

Janna frowned and opened her mouth to speak, but Lainey made a small, moaning noise at that moment. Janna came to her feet in a rush and stepped to the bed. Reaching out an unsteady hand, she brushed her daughter's arm as if to draw comfort from the touch as much as to give it.

Clay watched her for a second, though he was almost sure she'd forgotten he was there. She was pale and her hair was tangled from the rough night and rougher airboat ride. Her clothes looked as if she'd slept in them, which she had. But no other woman had ever made him feel such drawing pain around his heart. He wanted to take her in his arms, to shelter and protect her and make everything right in her world. He wanted her to turn to him, to accept what he had to give, including the deep mingling of his body with hers in that most ancient of comforts against pain and grief. There was raw need in his impulse but that wasn't all of it. It felt timeless, elemental, the ultimate answer to the fear of hovering death.

It wouldn't work. She had no use for him or his protection, especially if it involved physical contact. The sooner he accepted that, the better off he'd be.

Clay turned on his heel and went quietly from the examining room.

Roan was standing near the glass doors of the emergency room entrance, talking to a med tech, when Clay strode into the vestibule. As his cousin turned toward him, the fluorescent lighting from overhead gleamed on the star of his office. With a last word for the uniformed medical attendant, he walked to meet Clay.

"So what's the decision? The girl staying or is Hargrove shipping her out?"

"Staying," Clay answered in clipped tones.

Roan gave him a long look. "You don't sound too happy about it."

"I never knew making decisions about the best thing for a kid was so hard."

"Welcome to the real world. But I guess this means I can tell Luke to stand down?"

"Luke?"

"I've got him on alert, out at the airport."

Clay stared at his cousin a long moment. Luke's small plane and his crop-dusting experience had come in handy before, but he didn't fly for just anybody. In any case, the Flight for Life helicopter would have been point-to-point service and have carried medical personnel to care for Lainey. "Why?"

"I figured Oshner's in New Orleans would be the most likely transfer. The girl would go on the helicopter, of course, but that would leave her mother stranded four hours away, just when she was needed most."

Surprise threaded Clay's voice as he said, "Good thinking."

"It's a family emergency," his cousin told him, his gaze clear. "One of our own is in trouble."

"Me? How's that?"

"Don't play dumb."

Clay stared at Roan a moment before understanding moved over him in a shock wave. "The blood and tissue tests?"

"Positive, according to Doc Watkins. He said you and young Lainey Kerr are so much alike that you should have the same fingerprints. The only way she could not be Matt's daughter is if she was really yours."

Fierce gladness welled inside Clay. Then the suggestion in the tail end of Roan's words drew his brows together so tightly that he could feel them mesh above his eyes. "That's a shitty thing to say. If you think—"

"I don't, no. But some might, the way you're hanging around her."

"To hell with them."

A ghost of a smile came and went across the stern lines of Roan's mouth. "Thought you might feel that way. So how are you going to explain it when the clan arrives?"

"Meaning?"

"Kane and Regina, Luke and April, maybe even Tory, though you know—"

"The wedding's next month and she's busy. Yeah, I know."

"Just a friendly reminder. You don't show up, she might take out after you with a pistol."

"As if you'd let her."

"Can't always stop her. You know Tory."

He did. His soon-to-be cousin-by-marriage was as unpredictable as she was gorgeous. Clay liked her a lot, but that didn't mean he was going to plan his life around what she wanted. He said, "I'll be there. Unless something more important comes along, like taking Lainey to New Orleans, after all."

"Fine." The sheriff paused. "It's a shame we didn't know about Lainey sooner. Looks like Janna could have used some help."

"Yeah. But there's always after this is over." The comment was a dipstick of sorts, a small test of the family waters.

"Lainey will have more cousins than she knows what to do with, that's if she makes it."

"She'll make it," Clay said. "At least, she will if her uncle has anything to do with it."

Roan set the Stetson he'd been holding back on his head then tugged the brim down until he was watching from under its shadow. "So that's the way it is?"

"That's the way it's going to be."

"She's a Benedict and a Benedict she'll always stay."

"One way or another." Clay's tone carried not a hint of compromise.

Long seconds ticked past while Roan surveyed him and Clay stared back, shoulders straight and gaze unflinching. Then Roan's taut features relaxed a fraction. "What about her mother?"

"I'd prefer it if she was around, but if not, well, so be it." The muscles of Clay's shoulder were so tight with tension that it barely lifted with his shrug.

"I hope you know what you're doing."

"Yeah," he said in grim agreement. "So do I."

14

She must have been a little insane the night before, Janna thought, or else so strung-out and exhausted as to be incapable of rational judgment. There could be no other reason why she'd allowed Clay Benedict to take over and railroad her into bringing Lainey here. In the bright light of morning, it seemed incredibly stupid. She might as well have hired a stunt plane to tow a banner announcing the presence of her daughter with end stage renal disease in the same area where the mutilated teens had been found.

She'd risked her best chance of a transplant for Lainey, not to mention imprisonment, and for what: a set of broad shoulders and a pair of dark blue eyes? The short answer was yes. Yes, and also because the simple truth was that she had not been completely rational since the day she met Clay Benedict.

Janna glanced at him where he sat on the room's single straight chair while she rested on the narrow love seat that made into a single bed. His lean cheeks were shadowed by beard stubble, his hair tousled by wind and rain and the rake of his long fingers, and he still wore the black T-shirt that he'd jerked on with jeans and running shoes with no socks. Still, he appeared ready and able to rearrange the world once more if it was required.

It wasn't fair.

As if he felt her gaze on him, he turned his head. Their eyes met for an interminable moment. Then abruptly, deliberately, she looked away.

She was grateful to Clay for his efforts, of course. It was possible that he'd saved Lainey's life. But what good was it if her daughter was going to die eventually anyway?

But it wouldn't happen today, thank God. At least, it seemed less likely now than it had twelve hours ago. Lainey still looked incredibly small and fragile in the hospital bed, but she was breathing easier and her color was better. The numbers on the digital blood pressure monitor that sat beside her bed were slowly descending toward normal. She had awakened once from her sedated sleep, but had only looked at Janna and Clay then smiled and went to sleep again. That was probably the reason her mother had the capacity to think, now, about the future.

They had dodged the bullet one more time, she and Lainey. But how many more times did they have before their luck ran out?

Abrupt changes in blood pressure, like the one that had triggered this emergency, had always been a problem with Lainey, as with any renal patient. Her BP had to be checked eight times a day, every day that rolled around. Anything could make it rise, from an argument over whether she'd brushed her teeth to a relatively harmless stomach upset. Janna feared the cause for this dangerous incidence had been Lainey's terror over the threats of Dr. Gower's nurse. It would not have happened if Janna hadn't called her in the first place. Or perhaps it would have if the cause was an infection that the tests Nurse Fenton had wanted to do would have shown—in which case it was wrong not to have permitted them. Either way it was her fault.

Such thoughts made bad company. They certainly didn't make the time pass quickly.

Nurses came and went on their changing shifts, always checking, constantly monitoring Lainey's vital signs. The hospital public address system chimed with unknown signals and scratchy calls for a multitude of hospital personnel. An older man moaned a woman's name over and over from a room farther along the hallway. Tray-laden carts rattled along the hard terrazzo flooring outside. The frequent interruptions and constant noise made even dozing impossible. Janna had turned on the television around midmorning in the hope that it would provide white noise to cover the racket outside. Instead it became another irritant. She left it on, however, since it filled the oppressive silence between her and Clay. After a while, she no longer heard it as she stared with burning eyes at the opposite wall.

Toward noon, Roan came and took Clay away. His summons was official, Janna thought. Though the sheriff kept his voice low, she was sure she heard him mention the state police and questions. Clay had little to say when he returned, just that it was routine business, nothing to worry about.

She stared at him with a worried frown. "What do you mean by routine?"

"They wanted to know where I've been the past few days."

"What did you tell them?"

"That I was with you, of course. That you had me sort of tied up." The look he gave her was clear, yet carried both amusement and heat in its depths.

"You didn't?" she asked, her voice faint.

He smiled. "I did, but I don't think they took it literally."

"You didn't go into details then."

"You've got to be kidding. I'd as soon not become the biggest joke in the parish."

"No, I can see that." Her relief was so great that she felt weak with it, although she could see that being with her at the camp gave him an excellent alibi. It did not escape her that it provided one for her as well. "Do they want to question me?"

"Not just now. Roan persuaded them that it can wait."

It could wait, but not forever. At some point, she was going to have to decide what she was going to say. Or if she would be around to say anything at all.

Janna had skipped lunch; she wasn't hungry and certainly didn't feel like facing the hospital cafeteria alone. Clay had eaten with Roan but on discovering that she'd gone without, walked down to the cafeteria and returned with a plate lunch for her. She ate the meat loaf, cabbage and corn bread to be polite, though she hardly tasted it. Afterward, she tried to convince him that he might as well go home, that she and Lainey would be all right. He seemed to agree, but never quite made it out the door. Why he was so intent on staying was a mystery she was too tired to unravel. Then in late afternoon it became blindingly clear.

Janna heard the voices first, low female tones in a pleasant give-and-take that ceased just outside the room. She looked up as the door opened, expecting to see yet another aide or nurse bent on taking vital signs.

The two women who stepped inside could not have looked less like hospital staff. One was willowy and chic in matching blue silk slacks and shirt and with her sun-streaked brown hair coiled in a cool and regal coronet on top of her head. The other had a soft and maternal appearance with her freckle-dusted skin, russet hair pulled back in a rubber band, loose dress of lavender linen skimming her body, and sleeping baby held in the crook of her arm.

Janna sat up straight on the love seat as she looked from one to the other. "I'm sorry," she began, "but I think you must have the wrong room."

"Come in, come in," Clay's voice cut across hers as he rose to his feet with a warm grin firmly in place and his arms open in a wide gesture of welcome. He enveloped the women in quick, affectionate hugs, then bent swiftly to brush his lips over the fine dark fuzz on the baby's head. Only then did he turn toward Janna.

"Meet a couple of my favorite Benedict women, Janna," he said. "The one holding the future prom queen is Regina, married to my cousin Kane, and the other is our local claim to fame, an author-type married to my cousin Luke, though better known as April Halstead. Ladies, this is Janna who's been staying at Denise's old fishing camp. The sweet thing in the bed is her daughter, Lainey."

Benedict women. There had been a time when Janna would have been overjoyed to meet them, a time when she'd even dreamed of joining their ranks. Now her first reaction was suspicion. It was followed by something very close to fear.

"What are you doing here?" she asked, her voice tight.

April divided a quick glance between Clay and Regina, then stepped forward. "Roan called us since he thought you might need reinforcements. I hope you don't mind?" She extended her hand. "It's a pleasure to meet any friend of Denise's. Or Clay's."

The woman had the kind of bedrock confidence that came from a lifetime of being beautiful and more than a few years of being famous. At the same time, she was perfectly natural, with a warm smile that carried an underlying sweetness that was as disarming as it was enthralling. She was everything a Benedict should be, and everything Janna was not. She was also impossible to dislike.

"Thank you," Janna said in cool tones as she accepted the hand April offered. "It's nice of you to bother, but we're fine."

"Does that mean your daughter is better?" Regina asked, moving forward in her turn. "I have a son only a little older than your Lainey. I can't imagine what it would be like for Stephen to be so ill."

"Lainey isn't quite over the hump," Clay answered for Janna, "since it's only been eighteen hours or so. But she's stable and she's a fighter."

"We hope, that is, I'm sure everything will be fine." It was Janna's standard answer to all such queries, and had been for years, the main reason being that she didn't care to go into the gruesome and sometimes depressing details. She was also wary, just now, of a growing tendency to include Clay in her thinking, as if they had a common bond. They certainly didn't, regardless of his actions during the night or even their brief closeness the afternoon before.

"I'm so glad," Regina said simply. "But you really should get some rest, you know. Stress does strange things to people. April and I thought you might like a chance to take a shower and sleep a few hours, if the crisis is almost past. Clay could drive you out to our place, The Haven."

"Or you can crash at Chemin-a-Haut," April put in at once.

"I thought we might just go back to Grand Point," Clay said.

April gave him a quick sparkling look. "Did you, now?"

"Really," Janna said at the same time and with a total lack of enthusiasm.

"No ulterior motives, ladies, I promise," he said, raising his hands, palm out, in a gesture of surrender. "I just figured it would be easier for the hospital to know where to contact us."

"Since they know you're concerned, I see." Regina's voice was deadpan and her face completely innocent. Possibly too innocent?

"Now look," Clay began.

"I appreciate the offer, all of you," Janna said, raising her voice. "But Dr. Hargrove said it will be twenty-four hours before we can breathe easy. I'm not going anywhere until that time is up, and maybe not even then."

"Mama?"

That plaintive call, muffled by the nasal oxygen tube, came from the bed behind her. Janna spun around as if on oiled wheels and moved to her daughter's side. She was aware of the others gathering closer as well, but ignored them in her concentration on Lainey. Touching her hand, she said, "Here, honey."

"Thirsty."

It was such a common complaint, since her fluid intake had to be rigorously controlled, and yet that one word, the first she had spoken in hours, affected Janna with such joy that tears rose in her eyes. "I'll see if you can have an ice chip or two."

Lainey nodded, then allowed her gaze to roam around the room. A small smile curved her lips as she saw Clay, but faded when she noticed the women beside him. She stared from one to the other with puzzlement in her face. "Who are they?"

"These ladies are some of Clay's family come to visit with him," Janna said, forestalling any other explanation. Lainey didn't need to be upset by anything more.

"Hello," Regina said. Even as she spoke, her gaze moved from the child's small features to Clay's face, then back again. "You're a beautiful girl, just like—"

"Like your mother," April said hastily as she flashed a glance toward Janna.

"Do you think so?" Janna inquired without inflection. It almost seemed they were making mental comparisons between Lainey and Clay, but that would mean they knew her daughter was a Benedict. They could only know that if Clay had told them, perhaps during a call while he was gone to lunch or on that secret trip away from the camp that Arty had mentioned.

Who else knew of it? The answer to that question was crucial. The more people who knew, the less likely it was that she could ever contact Dr. Gower again. Particularly if one of the many who shared the secret was the sheriff of Tunica Parish, Roan Benedict.

Lainey had been lying quietly with her gaze on Regina, apparently caught by the ornate amethyst pendant that lay just below the hollow of her throat. Now she spoke up again. "That's a pretty necklace."

Regina put a hand on the stone. "It belonged to Kane's Grandmother Crompton. Kane's grandfather gave it to me when Courtney Morgan was born." Her smile turned droll. "I think it was a bribe, to be sure I'd keep producing kids until he has a great grandson."

"A family heirloom," Janna said, her voice expressionless.

"I suppose so. It will belong to Courtney one day."

"In the meantime, no one is better qualified to look after it," Clay said easily. "Regina is an expert and dealer in antique jewelry, though she mostly buys and sells on the Internet these days."

"I'd never sell a single stone of anything from Kane's family, of course, since I don't want to be drummed out of the clan," the red-haired woman said with a low chuckle.

Janna could imagine how she felt. Once she had thought that being accepted by the Benedicts would be the grandest thing imaginable. She'd longed to be a part of that huge extended family as some longed for paradise, still yearned for it like a child with her nose pressed against the window of a candy store.

She might well be close to gaining her wish, or so it appeared. But all she could see, all she could think about, was the threat that came with it.

"Thirsty, Mama," Lainey said, returning to her complaint as her attention waned.

"I'll find Hargrove," Clay said. "Maybe see if we can get his okay on those ice chips."

Janna didn't object, but the look she gave him as he left the room accused him of cowardice for choosing that moment to escape.

Clay returned a few minutes later with the doctor in tow. Janna remained with Lainey while she was being checked, but Clay stepped outside with his cousins' wives. Their voices made a low background murmur. It was impossible to tell what was being said however, even if Janna's main concentration hadn't been on what Dr. Hargrove had to tell her about her daughter.

"Her heartbeat is clearer and stronger," he said as he took the earpieces of his stethoscope from his ears and folded the flexible tubing in his hands. "But it still has the distinctive sound that indicates mild pericarditis, or fluid around her heart. You know, I expect, that it's enlarged as well?"

Janna inclined her head in assent. She could have recited Lainey's many symptoms in her sleep. "She didn't complete her dialysis last night. She has excess fluid from the fill stage."

"It's possible that's a part of her pericarditis, all right, but we can't be sure. We're watching her fluid build up and will start dialysis as needed. Unless you'd prefer to see to it yourself?"

"Yes," Janna said quickly. "Yes, I would." No one else would be as gentle or as careful during the long drawn-out process as she would be. No one else could understand Lainey's pain so well.

"Whatever you like. We'll make the equipment available." The doctor paused, then went on. "Just remember that you aren't superwoman. From what I hear, you've had Lainey's care on your shoulders without relief for too long. It won't help her if you collapse.''

''That's not going to happen.''

He snorted, a soft sound of disagreement. ''You're dead on your feet this second but too keyed up to know it. Fatigue is funny. It can catch up slow or it can hit you like a fast freight train, but it will get to you one way or another.''

She met his gaze across the bed. ''I don't suppose Clay Benedict suggested you talk to me, did he?''

''Would it make any difference if he had?''

''None whatever.''

''Then no, Clay didn't say a word. It's just that I'm a poor, overworked country physician who'd as soon not be called out to see about you and Lainey two nights in a row.''

''I'll do my best to remember that,'' Janna said, and discovered that her lips could still curve enough to return a friendly smile.

''My other prescription,'' Hargrove said, ''is to let someone help you. You don't have to do this alone.''

He reached to touch her hand, a light, impersonal brush of his fingertips that offered human warmth and understanding. At the same time, she thought she saw distinctly masculine appreciation in his eyes. She liked him, she discovered, and what was more important, she trusted him. With that last realization, came the knowledge that she didn't quite trust Dr. Gower, hadn't for some time. It was an idea with unpleasant ramifications. She had no time to consider them, for Dr. Hargrove was speaking again, giving care instructions on his way out of the room.

"Any questions?" he asked as he stopped with his hand on the door's edge.

"One," she said, her glance satirical. "You wouldn't be a Benedict cousin, would you?"

"On my mother's side. How did you know?"

"It figured." She gave a wry shake of her head, then added, "Thank you. For everything."

"Just doing my job."

The door closed behind him. It opened again almost immediately, however, admitting Regina and April. Clay was only a second or two behind them and carried a cup of crushed ice in his hand.

"You look a bit happier," April said. "Everything is okay then, for now?"

"For now." Everything would never really be okay until Lainey had a new kidney, but there was no point in saying so.

Taking the cup from Clay with a quick word of thanks, Janna fished an ice chip from it and fed it to Lainey. The small face of her daughter lit up with pleasure while she crooned in the kind of ecstasy most kids reserved for chocolate ice cream.

A small silence fell. In it, the noise of the television seemed loud. Behind Lainey, one of the women caught her breath with a strangled sound. Turning her head slightly, Janna saw tears standing in Regina's eyes before she gathered the baby she held closer to her and pressed her face to her small cheek.

Her gaze was not focused on Lainey, however, Janna realized. It was on the wall-mounted television screen.

The news was on, showing a coiffed and suited anchorwoman in front of a neat but featureless ranch-style home as she announced the identification of the body of the teenager recently found in the swamp near Turn-Coupe. Her expression suitably somber, she turned to the woman who stood beside her in faded, baggy shorts and with disheveled hair, angling the microphone in her direction. "Tell us what your feelings were, Mrs. Bianca, when you learned that your son had been murdered for his body organs?"

"He was just a boy!" the woman cried, staring into the camera with swollen, red-rimmed eyes that leaked tears. "He finished his last year of Little League Ball just last week. He wasn't wild, didn't do no drugs. He made good grades in school, played in the marching band, wanted to be a marine biologist when he grew up. He was a good kid! What kind...kind of monster could do...do this to him?"

Hard on her last cry, a grainy picture appeared on the screen. Obviously a school photo, it showed a boy with a lopsided grin, a cowlick in his dark hair and the gleam of mischievous intelligence in his dark brown eyes. In a voice-over, the anchorwoman spoke of the continuing police investigation into the recent deaths of two teenagers. Then she returned the program to the studio anchorman who began to talk about the mayor and plans for a new football stadium.

Janna felt as if a hard fist gripped her heart and

was squeezing it. Her chest hurt, her jaws ached as she clenched them, and her brain felt on fire. It was one thing to know about a teenager's death, but something else to see his face, to understand that he had really and truly lived but did so no longer. Dear God, she couldn't stand it. And it didn't help to hear Clay's whispered curse in the subdued quiet.

"I'd like to kill whoever did it with my bare hands," April said in tones of soft loathing.

"Think about that poor woman." Anguish threaded Regina's voice, and her arms tightened around the baby in her arms. "What a horrible thing to have to live with, knowing that your child died in fear and pain."

The baby she held, disturbed, perhaps, by the movement, gave a small wail. The adults turned toward the sound, partly in concern, but also, Janna thought, in relief from the mental pain of what they'd just seen.

The sound attracted Lainey's attention as well. "A baby," she said in a small voice that was thin and scratchy from disuse. "Can I see?"

Regina looked at Janna. "Is it all right?"

Coolness descended over her as if she were being splashed with ice water. "She isn't infectious, if that's what you mean."

"No, no!" Regina's fine, redhead's skin almost glowed with her fiery flush. "I just didn't want to get in the way or tire her or...or maybe hurt her without knowing it."

"I'm sorry," Janna said in abrupt embarrassment. "Yes, it's fine."

Regina's smile was still a shade anxious and she glanced at Clay as if for corroboration. At his nod, she stepped forward, holding out the baby. Lainey opened her small arms as naturally as breathing, and Regina, carefully avoiding her tubes, settled the infant against the girl with its tiny head resting on Lainey's small shoulder.

The little one, disturbed by the move, opened her dark eyes. Baby and child regarded each other in solemn and silent communication. Then a slow smile bloomed across Lainey's face, rising to shine in her eyes. "Oh," she breathed in quiet wonder. "She's beautiful. And just perfect."

"You, too, honey," Regina said softly. "You, too."

Warmth toward Regina filtered through Janna. But at the same time, she allowed herself to accept something that she'd kept carefully cordoned off in her mind until that moment. Other mothers also had their perfect, beloved children, and for them, as for her, the idea of death for those children was unendurable.

It might have been that incident, though it could have been Dr. Hargrove's half-comical warning or even simple exhaustion, but the idea of allowing Regina or April to sit with Lainey for a short time began to seem like a possibility.

There was no dramatic turnaround in Lainey's condition over the next hours, but she did improve by slow degrees. Her blood pressure eased downward until it was as close to normal as it ever came; her excess fluid drained the way it should once dialysis was begun, and the sound of her heartbeat faded to its usual sandpapery whisper. Her low-grade fever remained and she was still a sick little girl, but the danger of losing her was no longer immediate.

April and Regina Benedict had not stayed long that afternoon. Clay saw them out and didn't come back for several minutes. Janna assumed a family conclave of some kind was held in the hallway, but Clay didn't mention what was said when he returned, and she didn't ask. Afterward, however, there was a constant stream of visitors, most of them cousins of one degree or another. The first was Betsy, who was plump and outspoken, with frosted blond hair and an almost overpowering friendliness. Kane Benedict, the stern yet engaging attorney who was married to Regina, showed up around sundown, apparently on his way home. Luke joined him shortly afterward, a Benedict whose dark hair, warm smile and effortless charm gave him a strong resemblance to Clay. They left only after Roan returned, as if they felt some obligation to wait for the changing of the guard, or so it seemed to Janna.

It was almost a relief when Roan left again at last, since it seemed that the small hospital room had become a male enclave with a surfeit of tall, overwhelmingly masculine men stuffed into it. Of course, even one Benedict male added to Clay's constant presence seemed one too many. She was glad he was there doing the visits, regardless, since she had no idea what to say to his cousins and her brain seemed too sluggish to produce anything more than mere commonplaces.

Johnnie, the nurse who had been on duty when Lainey was admitted, stuck her head in the door just before the shift changed, around ten-thirty. Seeing Janna and Clay, both sitting upright but silent and half asleep, she raised her brows. "You two still here? Jeez, the stamina of youth. Never fear, reinforcements are on the way. I saw April pulling into the parking lot just now."

"April has arrived," the author said from behind her. Easing past Johnnie's broad form, she stepped into the room with a laptop computer under one arm and a woven bag over her shoulder from which protruded the unmistakable roll of a piece of unfinished needlepoint. "I've come to stay, too, and I don't want to hear any arguments. You're dead on your feet, both of you. Dedication to a child is a lovely thing, but there's no use being a martyr about it."

Janna, staring at April through eyes that were heavy with fatigue, was torn between annoyance and a strong urge to fall on her neck in gratitude. Lainey would be safe enough with her, she knew. And yet it was so hard to overcome years of being her daughter's sole guardian and protector, years of being all she had to depend on.

"No martyrs here," Clay said, climbing stiffly to his feet and stretching with his hands at the small of his back. "You can take over until daylight, anyway. Right, Janna?"

"You go," she said. "I can sleep on the love seat."

"No way." He moved to stand over her, taking hold of her hand. "The twenty-four hours are up now, and everything is under control. You need a real bed and a few hours of nice, cool darkness without racket or people coming and going every ten minutes. On your feet, Kerr. You're going if I have to carry you."

Any other time she'd have blasted him. Now she stared into the rich blue of his eyes, seeing the hard determination that covered his concern, and she couldn't quite manage it. She sighed, then let him pull her to her feet.

It was still necessary, however, to warn April exactly what to watch for and when, to show her a couple of small details about the continuing dialysis, and tell her all the things that Lainey liked and disliked. She kissed her sleeping daughter and brushed a hand over her cheek, then turned away. After two steps, she swung around again for yet more instructions. She was still talking when Clay took her by the shoulders and steered her from the room into the hall.

The night air that greeted her beyond the hospital doors was soft and pleasantly warm after the air-conditioned frigidness she'd left behind. A gentle breeze lifted her hair and brought the scent of the crape myrtle that stood in the islands of landscaping around the hospital building, with spent blossoms littering the ground around their feet like fallen confetti. Breathing that tantalizing scent, Janna became uncomfortably aware that her clothing, her hair, even her skin carried the sour, chemical odor of the hospital.

The parking lot was nearly empty as she and Clay walked toward it. The security lamps placed at regular intervals made yellow pools of light in the metallic paint of the few cars that were left and picked out the black streaks of skid marks in the concrete. It was quiet, almost too quiet, or so it seemed to Janna. She was used to big metropolitan medical complexes where people were always coming and going and the sound of traffic was omnipresent. There were no streets at all on this side of the hospital, however; it faced only a wooded area thick with pine trees and an undergrowth of briars and the vines crowding along its edges. The security lamps didn't reach far into the thicket.

Clay touched her arm, guiding her in the direction of a dark green SUV parked about halfway between the woods and the building. Glancing at it, she asked, "Are you borrowing someone's transportation?"

"It's mine," he said with a shake of his head. "Luke and Roan went out to the house and drove it back for me."

"You being so sure that I'd leave when you thought I should?" she asked, her voice even.

"Being so sure I didn't want to walk." He took out a key and unlocked the SUV's passenger side door, then pulled it open for her.

She flung a quick glance at his set face. Aware that she had said the wrong thing, she tried to find a way to rectify it as she climbed into the high vehicle. Clay gave her no help, but held the door with grim patience as he waited to close it behind her.

Abruptly the night exploded. Fire spurted with red light from the margin of the woods. Dull thuds sounded against the side of the SUV.

"Get down!" Clay yelled, even as he gave her a hard shove that sent her sprawling across the center console. The door slammed behind her.

Shots. Someone was shooting at them!

Even as her brain made sense of the noise and motion, another burst of gunfire rang out. Clay's footsteps pounded around the vehicle. He needed to get inside, and fast.

Stretching out her arm, Janna found the driver-side door lock and released it just as he snatched open the door. He flung himself inside, inserted the key and turned it. The engine roared. Clay reversed out of the parking slot, then almost immediately stood on the brake so they skidded to a halt. He slammed the SUV into Drive and gunned the accelerator. They left the parking lot with a scream of tires and the stench of burning rubber.

15

Janna pushed upright as the SUV swerved out of the hospital driveway and they took off down the dimly lighted road that led away from town. She twisted in the seat to look back, but saw no sign of a gunman. The only thing moving was a couple of med techs who ran out the front door of the hospital. No more shots sounded in the night.

She settled back, holding her seat with clenched fingers. As she glanced at Clay, she saw that he was watching the hospital and the road behind them in the rearview mirror, dividing his glances between it and the blacktop unreeling ahead of them.

"What was that all about?" she demanded in strained tones.

"You tell me."

"Why would I know anything?"

The look he gave her was sharp and not at all concerned with her comfort. "Just a guess."

"Maybe we should go back? What if it's some psycho who plans to shoot up the hospital? Lainey is in there."

"He was firing at you. I'd just as soon not let him too close to his target again."

Something in his voice suggested that he would have returned if he were alone, or most likely never left in the first place. She might have been grateful if she could believe the bullets were meant for her. "What makes you say that? I was already in my seat when the shooting began."

"Whose side of the vehicle is full of holes?" he asked with inescapable logic. "How many of those holes were made after I ducked around to my side?"

"He might have been after anybody. It could be one of those stupid, random things where some crazy person goes over the edge and starts shooting at anything that moves." She continued to argue because she couldn't bring herself to admit that he was right. If the man in the woods had really targeted her, then there could be only one reason. And it wasn't one she wanted to discuss with Clay, much less with the police who were sure to show up.

"The shots weren't wild and the shooter was sane enough to keep hidden. Besides, the odds against dying while playing it smart are a lot lower than they are for being killed while acting dumb."

She crossed her arms over her chest as a shiver rippled over her. "I still can't believe it."

"Doesn't matter. It happened." He reached for the cell phone that hung in a support attached to the dash and began to punch in numbers with his thumb.

"Wait! What are you doing?"

"What does it look like?" His eyes were narrow as he waited for her answer, but at least he didn't press the final button to send the call.

"If you're reporting our part of this to Roan, I wish you wouldn't."

"Why is that?"

"Suppose whoever was out there was shooting at you? Suppose they think you're interfering and decided to scare you off?"

"Your doctor friend, you mean."

His voice was flat. It wasn't surprising. She'd just suggested that any danger to him was unimportant. It hadn't been her intention, but the result was the same. "I know you don't think much of my—my arrangement with Dr. Gower, but I can't just forget it after going this far."

"You don't have to go any farther."

"But I've paid out so much."

"And he still wants more. It's crazy, Janna! It's criminal."

"It's Lainey's life! Don't you care about that? Haven't you seen how anything—a cold, a cut finger, too much fluid or not enough, a fright or upset—can become a life-and-death emergency?"

"There are other ways."

"They don't work for her! She's your brother's child, Clay. You're her uncle. Doesn't that matter?"

The look he gave her was murderous. "Of course it matters. Why the hell else do you think I let you keep me tied up for so long? It hurts in my gut every time I look at her. I'd do anything to help her. She's like having a part of Matt back, or finding a part of myself "

He dropped the phone between his thighs then

reached into his T-shirt pocket. Taking a piece of paper from it, he spun it toward Janna. She reached to catch it, but missed. As it fluttered to the floor-board, she leaned to pick it up, staring at it in the greenish lights of the instrument panel.

Matt. Lainey's father, in the photo that was her most prized possession. "Where did you get this?"

"Lainey."

She had given the photo to Clay. Her voice a thread of sound, Janna said, "She thought this was you."

"She wondered."

Lainey had wondered, but she hadn't asked her mother, hadn't mentioned it at all. What else had her daughter told Clay Benedict in all those long hours they had spent together? What games of pretend had she played with the man who looked so much like her father? If she had made a substitute of him in her mind, what would happen when she lost him?

But there was more to this equation. If Clay had stayed because he knew about Lainey, what did that mean? He could have wanted more information, but it would have been simpler to just reveal that he knew the truth and ask for details. However, the Benedicts were big on family. They looked after their own. Matt's father had wanted to separate Janna from Lainey by buying her child. Suppose what Clay wanted was simply to take her?

"If it matters so much to you," she said finally, "I'd think you'd want her to have every chance to live."

"That it matters so much is the reason I don't want your precious Dr. Gower anywhere near her with a scalpel. His shady way of doing things will kill her as surely as her kidney disease."

Doubt assaulted Janna, familiar yet almost crippling now, after seeing the boy on television that afternoon. "You don't know that! There's no way to know. But don't you see that I have to try? If I do nothing and she dies then it's all my fault." Her voice broke on the words and she turned her head to stare out the windshield to hide the tears crowding into her eyes.

He was silent so long that she thought he wasn't going to speak, then he said, "You think it's your fault, her kidney disease? Janna, it can't be. That's impossible."

"She had a virus. I thought it would go away, that it wasn't serious. I didn't have time to take her to the doctor. I had a commission to fulfill, a living to make, and would have lost a whole day sitting in some doctor's waiting room. She'd always been so healthy, and I thought—" She stopped, swallowing against the hard, constrictive knot in her throat.

"All children have viruses. That Lainey's turned into renal failure was a million-to-one chance, something you could never have guessed and even her pediatrician might have missed."

"I'm her mother. I should have seen it sooner, and might have if I hadn't been so wrapped up in other problems. Now there's a chance that I can fix it. Don't you see?"

''Yeah, I see.'' He gave her a long, hard look and
opened his mouth as if he meant to annihilate her.
Then he closed his lips so tightly that they made a
thin line. Reaching for the phone, he jammed it back
into its dashboard holder then settled deeper into his
seat. Controlling the SUV with one fist on the wheel,
he sent it flying down the dark country road.

Janna didn't know where they were going. She had
been neatly separated from her daughter, had been
shot at and was now headed out of Turn-Coupe at
high speed with a man she barely knew. Suspicion
invaded her mind. It occurred to her that the firing
might have been meant to frighten her, to make her
easier to control in a neat reversal of her kidnapping
scenario. Clay could be abducting her right now without her realizing it. At any moment, he could turn to
her and tell her that it was payback time.

Paranoid, the word should be her middle name.
Clay wouldn't do that. He couldn't after everything
they had been through in the past few days.

Could he?

She flicked a glance at him from the corners of her
eyes. His face was set in stern lines and the dashlights
reflected with a hard turquoise sheen in the blue of
his eyes. He seemed remote, unapproachable, as if he
might be turning over a problem in his mind with
which he wanted no interference. It could be anything, she thought, from which of his cousin's houses
it might be best to dump her at, to where he could
bury the body when he was done with her. Or it could
be the recognition that he might make an excellent

candidate for a relative kidney donation for Lainey, and had come very close to being tapped for it with or without his permission. If he got that far, he should also work out that her wariness of him stemmed in large part from worry over whether he suspected that she might have been in discussion with Dr. Gower over that possibility, and what he would do about it.

From deep inside her rose the strong urge to abandon all her plans for Lainey and simply ask Clay to be tested as a legal kidney donor. It wasn't the first time she'd wrestled with it; the impulse had been with her for hours, even days. What held her back was a multitude of reasons, beginning with the memory of his dismissal of it when her daughter had asked, and ending with the way he'd taken charge since they had left the camp. Behind them all was fear.

Family was everything to the Benedicts. They looked after their own. Clay disapproved of everything she'd tried to do for Lainey. He had given orders for her medical treatment as if it was his right. He'd called in his family for support, introducing Lainey to them with all the quiet ceremony of an initiation into the clan. With iron will cloaked in charm and concern, he'd separated her from her daughter this evening. And just now his voice had held the same implacable contempt that had sounded in his father's nine years ago.

Suppose that, by some miracle, he agreed to be tested and was found to be a compatible donor? The sacrifice of a kidney would surely require a reward. What if he asked that Janna give up her daughter to

him? It was what his father had intended if she had
been able to prove she was carrying Matt's child.
Clay's own mother had been forced to leave her sons
behind when she divorced his father, or so Denise
had told her. It seemed like a pattern.

Lainey was all Janna had. Was it better for her to
risk the clandestine surgery while remaining with her
mother who knew exactly how to care for her, or to
have the advantage of a legal transplant under Benedict protection? Janna didn't know. She just didn't
know.

They sped past dilapidated gas stations, trailer
homes with shiny trucks parked out front, rows of
long chicken houses perched under security lights and
farms with old white houses nestled under ancient
oaks. The blacktop curved and turned through long
wooded stretches where giant trees on either side
made a tunnel of their branches, and passed one or
two big old plantation houses set well back, almost
hidden from view. They crossed several small bridges
over nameless creeks and bayous, whipped past briar
and plum thickets and made ditches full of ghostly
black-eyed Susans wave in the wind of their passage.

Finally Clay turned the SUV onto a driveway of
white gravel and oyster shell that crunched under the
tires. They wound through grounds where huge live
oaks and magnolias stood like dark, glassy-leafed
sentinels on a spreading lawn, the lake beyond made
a mirror for the rising moon, and the air smelled of
unseen roses and a hint of basil. They rounded a

curve and his home that she'd glimpsed earlier, though without really seeing it, appeared before them.

It was a sprawling architectural mongrel that predated the Civil War by several decades. Its two-storied center section appeared oldest and hinted at late 1700s French West Indies influence. A wing in the neoclassical style of the 1850s flanked it on one side, and a long, barracklike addition of turn-of-the-century vintage stood at a right angle on the other. The gallery, or porch, on the bottom floor of the center section continued along the newer addition, and these two sections formed a protective corner for a combination garden and entrance court. Centered by a wrought-iron fountain that played a soft water tune as it fell into its basin, it was floored with tiles in the Moorish style and filled with a sprawl of roses, day-lilies and verbena set off by the tropical foliage of canna and taro.

"Welcome to Grand Point," Clay said as he pulled up on the driveway that curved in front of the house.

The casual tone of his voice was not quite enough to cover his pride and affection in the place. Janna didn't blame him. His home, for all its amalgamation of styles and features, had an indefinable grace and an aura of sheltering comfort. Added to over many generations of growing families, it wasn't small. Janna counted at least ten chimneys sprouting from its various sections, and guessed that there must be something like three dozen or more expansive rooms under the different rooflines.

Though she'd heard much about Grand Point over

the years, from Denise as well as Matt, she'd never expected to set foot in it. That she was here under the present circumstances left her as melancholy as she was awed. To cover her reaction, she asked, "Do all the Benedicts name their houses?"

"Seems a bit pretentious, doesn't it? People seldom do that anymore, but it was common at one time." He opened the driver side door and stepped out, moving around to the passenger side. She'd already lifted the handle and pushed it open, but he gave her his hand to help her make the long step down to the ground.

Keeping her voice as light as possible, she said, "I hope we aren't disturbing anyone."

"No one here to disturb."

That was what she'd wanted to know, of course, but she wished he'd chosen another way to put it. "You live alone? I mean, it's obviously an old family home, and you have brothers, I think."

"A couple of them. We all share a legal interest in the place under Louisiana's inheritance laws, but that's about it. Adam, the oldest of us, says he's had enough experience living in an old house to last a lifetime and much prefers modern glass and steel with all the latest conveniences. Wade likes the place well enough, but he's a petroleum engineer working overseas so he comes and goes, mostly goes. I'm the only one who wants to live at Grand Point. At least for now."

They moved across the courtyard as they talked, skirting the fountain and climbing the tiled steps to pass under the dark shadow cast by the high porch ceiling. A double front door loomed in front of them. Clay unlocked the heavy right side and pushed it open, then reached inside to flip on a light switch. As he stepped back, Janna moved ahead of him into the house.

There was no foyer, no entrance hall as such, but only a large open room that spanned the width of the house. It had an ornate marble fireplace centered between French doors that were draped in crisp red and white toile de Jouy. This was the focal point for the mixture of antique rosewood furniture and modern overstuffed oxblood leather sofas gathered around the Turkey carpets that defined the sitting areas. The keynote once more was grace combined with comfort.

As Janna paused to look around her, Clay shut the front door with a solid thud, closing them inside. Slowly she turned to face him. If he meant to take advantage of their isolation, or make his move toward retaliation, it would surely be now.

"Would you like a snack?" he asked, moving past her toward double doors that opened to one side. "It's been a while since we had dinner, and you didn't eat much anyway."

"I don't think so," she answered. Food was the last thing on her mind.

"Something simple? Toast and milk? Fruit? Ice cream?" He turned on a light in the connecting dining room, then moved on out of sight, presumably in the direction of the kitchen.

Surely no man so intent on extending hospitality

could have revenge on his mind or even aggressive seduction? She'd worried for nothing. With an involuntary shudder, Janna called after his retreating back. "No thanks. The thing that holds the most appeal right now, the one thing I'd really, really love, is a hot bath."

He stopped in a doorway on the far side of the dining room. Turning back toward her, he propped one hand on the facing and brushed his chin against his shoulder with a bearded rasp. His expression wry, he said, "A shower and a shave wouldn't hurt me, either. We can eat afterward."

"Don't let me stop you if you're hungry now," she protested. "Just point the way to a bathroom."

"Through here. This is the bedroom wing that I use, on the far side of the kitchen." He tipped his head toward the dark hallway behind him.

She moved to join him. His gaze tracked her, turning opaque as she drew nearer and paused where he stood so it was impossible to tell what he was thinking. Her heart tripped into a stronger beat while her lips parted of their own accord.

His lashes flickered down to conceal his expression. He lowered his arm and stepped back, indicating with a brief gesture that she should move ahead of him into the connecting hall. Turning on lights as he went, he guided her past two closed doors then stopped at a third. He pushed inside, and walked quickly to a closet where he pulled out an oversize sleep shirt in white with hot-pink lettering, then handed it to her.

As she took the shirt, it fell open to reveal a picture of a bored woman with her arms crossed over her chest and a dialogue bubble above her head that read, Trust Me…I've Had Sex, And It Isn't Like That. As she held it up, she gave him a laconic look. "Yours?"

"My mother's," he answered, his smile a little crooked. "She uses this room when she comes to visit. Feel free to take whatever you need from the closet. Or from the bathroom, either, for that matter."

She thanked him, and he nodded. He didn't linger, didn't even act as if he might, but simply walked out and closed the door behind him.

He had been, for all intents and purposes, the perfect gentleman. Amazing.

She was grateful, of course. She was tired to the bone, had been wearing what she had on for more than twenty-four hours, and was worried, still, about Lainey. She'd been shot at this evening and had more problems about that incident and everything surrounding it than she could comfortably handle. Fending off sexual overtures was the last thing she needed, even if she and Clay Benedict had been in bed together a small eon ago, before Lainey's latest medical nightmare began. Yes, she was truly appreciative.

Why, then, did she feel so deflated?

The bath was hot and revitalizing. She shampooed her hair as well, removing the last of the hospital smell and replacing it with a clean hint of roses and herbs. Combing out the long strands, she towel-dried them then pushed them behind her back.

It didn't seem like a good idea to go to bed while her hair was still wet. Though she was tired beyond words, she was too keyed up for immediate sleep. Added to that was a feeling of unreality overlaid by restlessness. It had been so long since she'd been relieved from the minute-to-minute responsibility for Lainey that she didn't feel right without it hovering over her. It seemed that she should be somewhere else, doing something else, that she had no right to be idle with only herself to look after.

She also felt a little hungry, after all. And she couldn't expect to go to sleep on an empty stomach.

The sleep shirt was perfectly decent, covering her from neck to knees. There was nothing sexy about it since it skimmed over her breasts without emphasis and hardly touched her anywhere else. Even turning back and forth in front of the closet door mirror, she couldn't see so much as an outline of her body through it. Not that she had any reason to worry too much about turning Clay on, she thought. He didn't seem all that interested. Besides, he'd probably already eaten and gone to bed.

Wrong.

Clay was perched on a tall stool in the big, rambling kitchen with its white cabinets and tall, leaded glass windows that featured Art Deco stained-glass designs in their centers. He wore only a pair of gym shorts, and moisture from his shower slicked back his hair and clung to tops of his shoulders in droplets. Janna's mouth went dry the instant she saw him.

She must have made some small sound, for he half

turned, his body rigid and gaze alert. As he caught
sight of her, he relaxed again, giving her a smile.

"Change your mind? There's plenty here."

"If you don't mind."

The feast spread out on the slate gray-cabinet top
included wafer thin deli-sliced ham, a wedge of ched-
dar, buttery crackers, apple slices and brownies en-
riched with nuts and chunks of caramel. Clay was
using a paper towel for a plate, and he reached to pull
off another one for her from a heavy brass holder.
Leaving his stool then, he stepped around to the cabinet to take down an extra glass. Carrying it to the
refrigerator, he asked over his shoulder, "Milk, iced
tea, juice or something fizzy?"

"What, champagne?"

"Cola was what I had in mind, but there's Bor-
deaux, if you want something stronger." He reached
for a bottle that sat far back on the top shelf.

"No, no, bad joke. Milk is fine," she answered as
she slid onto a stool. It was what he was drinking
and sounded good with the brownies. With any luck,
it might also help her to sleep.

He filled the tall glass and brought it to her, then
returned to his stool where he faced her with one long
leg outstretched as a brace. When he nudged the ham
and cheese in her direction, she picked up a slice of
each and a cracker to go with them, then watched as
he selected a brownie. They sat eating for several
minutes while silence grew thick between them.

Janna reached for her milk and took a long, cold
swallow. It felt good going down, soothing to the

nervousness in the pit of her stomach. As she set the glass back on the cabinet top, she brushed her fingers along the side where condensation had formed. Finally she looked up at Clay. "I should thank you for not calling Roan earlier," she said slowly. "It means a lot to me."

The look he gave her was impenetrable, without warmth. He wasn't happy with his decision, she thought. It was even possible he'd made no permanent decision at all.

"I know you don't approve of what I'm doing," she went on. "You think it's wrong and even dangerous. Maybe you're right, I don't know."

"Maybe?"

"All right, probably," she said in tight agreement. "But I can't just forget it."

"Who are you trying to convince, Janna? Me or yourself?"

She looked away from his level gaze. "You don't understand."

"I think I do," he answered in quiet contradiction. "But what about me and what I think? I'm her uncle. Doesn't that matter?"

"You don't know her."

"I've known her for days. I've held her, talked to her, watched her smile. She's family, blood of my blood. That's sacred for a Benedict. It means everything. But you can't buy a life with a life, Janna. It's a devil's bargain that smears everything it touches and kills the soul. It will destroy you, and Lainey."

"I can't help that," she said, her voice aching in her throat.

"What are you going to tell Lainey one day when she asks who the person was who gave her back her life? What are you going to tell yourself if you keep this bargain and she dies anyway? How are you going to live with it, any of it?"

Agony took her appetite and her breath. He was so merciless in his hard anger and honorable stance, and so very right.

She pushed her milk away from her, then slid from the stool. Turning blindly away from him, she said, "I don't know how. I don't know what's best or worst, what's noble and good or even what's cruel and selfish. All I know is that doing nothing is also a choice, one that's more than I can bear."

"Other people also have choices, Janna," he said after a moment. "Sometimes you do what you must."

She didn't answer, wasn't sure whether he was talking about her or himself. Did he call out to her again or slide from his stool as if he meant to follow her? She thought he might have done both, but couldn't be sure. She saw nothing, heard nothing. Head high and back straight, she walked away from him, and didn't stop until the door of the room she'd been given closed behind her.

The room was dark, but she didn't turn on a light. Finding the bed in the dark, she sank to its cushioned surface and sat with her head forward and her hands braced on either side of her. She ached as if she'd been beaten. Her mind was empty, yet something dark and unendurable hovered at the edges.

It was quiet, too quiet. The old house that was the ancestral home of Lainey's father seemed to press in upon her. It weighed her down with its traditions and moral clarity and high expectations. It caused her to feel unsure of herself. It made all her defenses based on moral ambiguity and shades of gray seem foolish if not disingenuous. It forced her to stare her responsibility in the face.

If she continued on her present course, she would be exchanging her daughter's life for that of another child. She would be condemning a young innocent to death and his mother to eternal grief.

She couldn't do it.

She might once have been able to, might have convinced herself that the suspicious deaths had nothing to do with her, that she was not to blame for what others might do, or that her need outweighed all else. No more. She was forced to accept the fact that she could not make Lainey's life right with that kind of wrong. She couldn't snatch this bitter, bitter cup from her daughter's lips and pass it to someone else.

Nor could she allow Clay to be implicated in what she was doing or be endangered because of it. Regardless of his intentions, he didn't deserve that. The last thing she wanted was a repeat of the shooting incident this evening. Next time, they might not be so lucky.

She must put whatever trust she could find in Clay and cancel the surgery. She would see Dr. Gower and take care of the latter tomorrow. She would tell him she couldn't get the extra money, tell him that the discovery of the bodies in the swamp made it too dangerous, that Lainey was too sick or too closely watched by the Benedicts, something, anything to make him see that it was impossible to continue. That was, of course, if he meant to proceed after the hue and cry over the bodies in the lake and Anita Fenton's threat to withhold the kidney.

Time seemed elastic, endless. She could feel her heart beating, almost hear the soft rush of blood through her veins. She was aware of where she sat, how she sat, the steady, corrosive paths of her thoughts and where they were taking her, but she was outside it all. Pain and fear were there, but their edges were muffled. She felt so strange, unreal, like an automaton that had come unwound. She needed something, had to have it, but couldn't quite identify it.

As if from a great distance, she watched herself rise from the bed and leave the room. She walked along the dark hall, feeling her way along the wall until she came to the bedroom where she'd heard the sound of a shower earlier. The door was open a crack. She pushed it wider and stepped inside.

"Janna?"

Clay's voice came from the big sleigh bed. She moved in that direction like a bat honing in on vibrating sound waves. Placing a knee on the high mattress, she lowered herself beside him, reaching for him.

His arms closed around her, warm and comforting

and so very, very real. And abruptly the pain and the fear were just as genuine, so she was lost in a world of hurt and fear and unending, unbearable grief over the decision she had made.

"Hold me," she whispered as she turned her face into his neck and huddled close. "Please, please hold me."

16

Clay didn't mind.

He accepted the warm, shivering, pliant woman into his arms, his bed, his mind and his heart. This was his purpose for living. He had been created for this and nothing else, to keep this one woman safe and whole and to banish her demons of the night.

He meant to do no more than that; he really didn't.

Yet she felt so right, fit so perfectly against him, into him. He'd thought she might never want to touch him nor be touched by him again after the things he'd said. That she would come to him tonight had seemed a distant fantasy. He still thought it might be some form of a waking dream. Until he felt the soft press of her lips against the strong column of his neck.

He was just a man. He might have the best of intentions, but he had no immunity against the feel of soft skin, the woman scent that went to his head like fine brandy, or the powerful surge of the blood in his veins at the smallest hint of cooperation with his potent imaginings.

He could have rolled over her, into her, in a single fast act of penetration. The urge to do just that was strong, so strong. The lingering residue of his despairing anger at her refusal to be influenced by him drummed the need against the inside of his skull. Still he retained enough self-awareness there in the quiet darkness to know it would be inadequate. A fast, hard rut was a fine thing on occasion, but it would be over too soon. Janna required more, and so did he. He needed a deeper and longer connection. Tomorrow would come too soon, and he might never hold her, never see her after she found out what he meant to do at first light.

So he brushed her forehead with his lips in his first tentative move of the ancient *pas de deux* of love and waited for a response. It came, the delicate brush of her fingertips through the crisp yet sensitized hair that covered his breastbone, as if she could absorb some knowledge of him through touch alone.

He lifted his hand to her hair, threading his fingers through the damp strands, easing the long length from under her. The cool silken glide of it along his palm stoked the fire that burned low in his belly. Ignoring that building heat, he traced the curve of her ear, memorizing the small whorl and the petal softness of the lobe, before trailing along the gentle turn of her jaw to the point of her stubborn chin. The slightest pressure there tilted her face toward him. Then with a deep drawn breath, he set his lips to hers.

The kiss was sweet and powerful, and as long and deep as he intended to love her. He plumbed the heady recesses of her mouth, taking pleasure in the satin surfaces, the tiny, jell-like beads of her tongue, the slow and sinuous play of one slick surface against the other. His mind expanded as he took the taste and feel of her deep inside him and carefully stored away their myriad variations as vital sense memories.

When did he shift his hand to her hip? He didn't remember. The discovery that she was naked under her borrowed sleep shirt burst into his consciousness like a silent explosion. That she had sat in his kitchen like that only a short time ago, virtually unprotected even as they quarreled, brought a wave of hot need that tightened his grasp so he turned toward her, pulling her close against him.

She came willingly, fitting herself into his body until she felt locked to him. Compulsively he explored the slim line of her thigh, the curve of her hip, then skimmed along her backbone. The movement slid the folds of cotton knit higher until he was forced to ease away while he disentangled her from the sleep shirt. Flinging it into the darkness behind him, he got rid of the loose sleep shorts he wore, then pulled her against him once more. He spread his fingers over the tender fullness of her hip, pulling her into him until the warm, diamond-shaped valley between her thighs cradled his hard, pulsating length.

Perfect, the fit was so perfect, so exact that it was as if she was made for him alone. The sensation of his strutted flesh against her soft, cushioned heat was such exquisite torture that a low groan vibrated in his throat. Janna's breath caught, so her breasts pushed more firmly against his chest.

A shiver rippled over the woman he held, leaving goose bumps in its wake. Feeling it, all his deliberate, gentlemanly intentions vanished, displaced by naked, raging desire.

God, but he wanted her, wanted to taste every inch of her, delve into every fold and recess, to touch and hold until he knew her smallest secrets and felt her shudder again, out of control, in his arms. He had to have her completely and know that for this moment there was no shadow of anyone or anything between them.

And he did. Half-crazed with longing, totally absorbed, he pressed his face between the warm silk rises of her breasts. Climbing the peaks in slow, dizzying spirals with his tongue, he captured the tight peaks with cautious pressure of his teeth, then drew them into his mouth to abrade the raspberry nipples with the rough edge of his tongue. He smoothed his lips over her quivering abdomen and the resilient and flat surface between her hipbones, enjoying the fluttering reaction of her muscles. He tested the softness of the curls that protected the joining of her thighs, laved the fine-grained skin on the insides of her thighs with his tongue, then swooped down to delve into her soft, magnolia-petaled, citrus flavored folds. Gently he plumbed them until she writhed and gasped in his hold, and was so liquidly, scaldingly inviting in her openness that his willpower and rigorous self-containment shredded like a banana tree in a hurricane.

He would have taken her then in pounding oblivion if she hadn't raised up, shifted away, then bent to take him with her mouth in such hot yet delicate encasement that he couldn't move, couldn't think, couldn't make a sound without the risk of exploding.

Nothing, nothing had ever been so endlessly right in all the vital march of his days. He endured it, exalted in it while holding, barely, to sanity and restraint. Until heart and stamina could take no more.

Shivering, forgetting every compulsion or intention he'd ever had, abandoning all hope and pretense of delicacy, every convention except the mutual and primal joining, he gathered her close and buried himself in her depths.

It was the most perfect thing of all. It was the glorious dance of flesh against pulsating flesh, two people striving together with panting breaths, slick skin and mindless transmission of ineffable joy. It was stupendous, transfiguring, a storm of wonder that burst over them, shook them, carried them, then left them spent and gasping. It abandoned them, in the end, leaving them on their opposite shores, with their opposite values and intentions.

Afterward, Clay held her until her muscles relaxed, her breathing slowed, deepened, and she slept. For him, however, all hope of rest was gone. He lay staring into the darkness, soothing his hand down her back over and over, as he accepted, finally, all that he had never known, would never know, and all that he was going to lose.

''What have you been doing with yourself? You look as if you haven't slept in a week.''

It was Roan who spoke, looking up from his pa-

perwork, as Clay stepped into his office. Clay gave
him a sour glance before throwing himself into the
chair across from the sheriff's desk. "That's because
I haven't."

"But I thought you and Janna went home last night
to— Never mind."

Clay refused to rise to the provocation that lurked
in his cousin's gray eyes. He appreciated the fact that
Roan could make a semisalacious joke, however. Until he'd met Tory and learned to relax a little, he'd
been much too uptight for that kind of banter. "Janna
slept," he said now. "I didn't. Getting shot at can do
that to a guy."

"So you were involved in the hospital fireworks,
after all?" Roan leaned back in his chair. "I thought
it was too much of a coincidence that you'd just left."

"Somebody told you, I suppose?" Clay asked in
disgust. People always told Roan everything.

"Johnnie."

"At least nobody shot up the hospital the way they
did when Tory was laid up there."

Roan inclined his head. "But it's still getting to be
entirely too popular a place for ambushes. So did you
see who did it?"

"Not really. Did you?"

"Long gone by the time we got there, though he
might not have been if you'd given me a buzz. Why
was it, again, that I got the news from someone
else?"

"We weren't hit," Clay said with a twitch of one

shoulder. "Getting Janna the hell out of there seemed a tad more important."

"More important than seeing to it that it didn't happen again?"

Clay propped one ankle on his knee and studied the laces of his running shoe. "Janna thought it might be a warning. She didn't want you brought into it because..."

"Because she was afraid I'd put this Dr. Gower out of business."

"Something like that."

"Hell, Clay."

"I know. I tried to talk her into reporting it, and into forgetting about this under-the-table transplant, but she's determined."

"In spite of all you can do?"

Clay gave his cousin a level stare. "I did try, believe me."

"I thought you were more persuasive. I mean, look how you charmed Tory."

"That was different." The words were defensive.

"How? She's a woman, Janna's a woman."

"If I have to tell you how, then you're worse off than I am," Clay said with precision.

"Meaning you had nothing to lose where Tory was concerned?"

"Something like that," he agreed, then realized with irritation just how much he'd given away. "Damn it all, Roan..."

"Unfair, I know. So sue me."

"I'll let you make up for it instead, by telling me

what you found out about the shooting. Or anything you may have dug up about this doctor.''

''Found out he was a medic in 'Nam, went to med school after he returned stateside. Could be he saw more than his share of wasted human organs while out there.''

''Or how easily young men can die?'' Clay suggested.

''You saw him, even if you didn't talk to him. What do you think?''

Clay frowned as he tried to get a firm hold on his impressions. Finally he shrugged. ''That nurse of his wasn't exactly what I'd call well-balanced, but I didn't see enough of the doctor to tell.''

''Everybody says he's a hard worker, donates a lot of time to the project close to his clinic. On the other hand, several teenagers, mostly gang members and punks, have turned up missing over the past couple of years. Nobody took much notice except their mothers and maybe their aunts and grandmothers. I mean, it's a rough area, crack houses on every corner, all-night Ecstasy bashes, drive-by shootings as common as sneezing, and it's a slow Saturday night when at least a half dozen don't hit local hospital ERs for knife wounds. Who misses a few punks, one way or another?''

''They should be missed,'' Clay said, his voice tight.

''I'm not saying it's right, just stating facts.''

''You think somebody is taking advantage of the death toll?''

Roan stared at him a long minute. "You want my best guess? I'd say someone took advantage of it for a while. Then maybe a patient about to have his organs harvested came back to life, or could be there was no convenient corpse when one was needed. This person went from taking from the newly dead to stealing from the living. Since it was twice as profitable to take both kidneys and not much more dangerous, they started making a clean sweep, so to speak."

"Such a way with words," Clay drawled with a wry glance at his cousin. Then he frowned. "Most of these kids we're talking about are from ethnic groups other than white, aren't they?"

"Not all, but people desperate for a new kidney don't care," Roan pointed out.

"Of course not, but our culprits have to be aware that there's less chance of rejection with cadaver transplants when the donor is from the same ethnic group. No such thing as discrimination politics in organ donation. It just doesn't work. So if Gower is doing transplants on patients like Lainey with organs of unknown origin, then he's endangering them."

"You been doing Internet research or something?"

"Or something," Clay agreed.

"Could be he doesn't care. Besides, dead patients don't complain, or their families who've been involved in illegal activity."

"Which scares the hell out of me when I think of how close he came to using a scalpel on Lainey," Clay said.

Roan made a grim noise of agreement. "At least that won't happen."

"Meaning the investigation is on track?"

"And moving right along. The Baton Rouge police are set to raid the clinic before noon today."

"Without you?" Clay asked in mock surprise.

"Not exactly. It's out of my jurisdiction, but I've been invited to come along for the bust since the evidence for it came from this office. A helicopter is standing by. I'll be heading out of here any second."

Clay felt no surprise whatever. There wasn't a Benedict alive who didn't think he could do a better job than anyone else at practically anything in which he had an interest—or who didn't hate to be left out of anything exciting.

He said, "Don't let me hold you up."

"I won't. Oh, and you can tell Janna about it after lunch. It should be all over by then."

"Are you suggesting that she'd try to warn Gower if she heard sooner?"

"Who knows? But it's best not to take chances."

Clay picked a dried sand burr off his shoestring. "Maybe I'll wait then. You'll let me know how it goes?"

"Sure. I'm anxious to see this clinic shut down myself, regardless of whether the good doctor is involved in organ harvesting."

"I don't know what Janna will say about it. Nothing good, I imagine, especially when she finds out that I helped set up this raid. She thinks Lainey's going to die, you know."

"Is she?"

Clay set his lips in a firm line. "Not if I can help it."

"But can you?"

That was, of course, the question. "I'm working on it."

From Roan's office in the courthouse, Clay went by the combination flower and gift shop that lay on the other side of the town square. Immediately afterward, he headed for the hospital. He needed to relieve April, for one thing, but he was also anxious to see Lainey. It seemed he'd been away from her for days instead of mere hours.

As he stepped into the hospital room, she appeared different, more beautiful, more open, even a little older. It was, he thought, the effect of returning health. She held out her arms to him and he went straight to the bed, barely glancing at April who sat reading a book, before he swept his niece into a one-arm hug.

"What have you got?" she asked, her voice muffled by his shoulder.

"Nothing," he said, keeping his gift shop purchases, a super-soft stuffed raccoon to replace Ringo who was in Arty's care and bouquet of pink sweetheart roses, behind his back. "Why would I have anything?"

Lainey twisted and turned as she attempted to see around him. "For me," she said. "Is it a present?"

"You're a very pretty young lady, but I don't know why you'd think I might bring you a present."

"Because you like me!" she cried.

"Nope," he said, bringing the gifts around and depositing them on her lap. "Because I love you madly, deeply and forever."

She blushed, she really did, and barely even glanced at the things on the sheet that covered her. "I love you, too," she said with a smile that was going to annihilate the boys in a few years.

"Now if only your mom felt the same," he quipped, trying to keep it light to cover the squeezing sensation around his heart.

Lainey's blue eyes took on a twinkle. "Maybe if you brought her a present?"

"*Excellent* idea," he said, falling back with his hand on his heart, pretending to be stunned by the suggestion. Then he twisted his face as if in difficult thought. "What do you suggest?"

"Chocolate candy?"

It was, Clay knew, Lainey's favorite thing, and one definitely not on her diet list. "We'll see, punkin," he said, ruffling her hair an instant before turning to April.

She wasn't alone. Luke had slipped into the room behind him while he was talking to Lainey. Clay turned in time to see him pull April from her chair and into his arms, then bend his head to give her a long and hungry kiss.

"Well, heck fire, Luke," Clay drawled. "It's only been one night."

"One long and lonely night," Luke told him over his shoulder, "with me rattling around in the big house at Chemin-a-Haut like a referee's whistle with nobody to blo—"

"Watch yourself, Benedict," April said hastily. "We have a small pitcher in the room."

"I'm not a pitcher and I don't have big ears," Lainey declared from her thronelike bed.

April, her face a little flushed, recovered with aplomb. "Of course not, sweetheart. Would you like some grape juice before I leave?"

"Sorry," Luke said with a grimace, as he reached to shake hands with Clay. "Got a little carried away there. Not that it's unusual."

Clay understood perfectly. And wished that he didn't since it seemed unlikely that anything as simple as a quick apology was going to fix things with Janna. "If you're not in a big hurry, could you and April stick around a few minutes longer while I talk to Dr. Hargrove? I won't be long, promise."

"We'll be glad to," April answered for her husband.

Luke's dark eyes gleamed through his lashes as he flicked a glance at his wife then winked at Lainey. "Not to worry," he said easily. "Spending time with gorgeous females is one of my favorite things, especially when they're held down in bed with all kinds of tubes and cords so they can't get away from— Ouch!" Luke massaged his shoulder while an injured look sat on his strong sun-bronzed features. "Now what was that for?"

"Punch him again," Clay advised April as he

rolled his eyes. Then he swung around and left the room in search of Simon Hargrove.

"Young Lainey is doing great, seems to be one of those kids who go from fine to death's door in seconds, but bounce back just as fast. Her signs are good, and so were her numbers when they ran a blood test a few minutes ago. She's almost clear of fever. If there's somebody who will be conscientious about giving her antibiotic for the next couple of days, I don't see why she can't go home this afternoon."

"You're sure?" Clay tilted his head as he waited for the answer. They stood outside the door of an examining room in Hargrove's office, which was a couple of blocks from the hospital.

"I'll write the orders and leave them at the nurses' station."

"Just what I wanted to hear, Simon, thanks." Clay hesitated, then added, "There's just one more thing. I don't suppose any of Lainey's blood drawn this morning is still in the lab?"

The physician narrowed his eyes a fraction. "Might be."

"I'd hate like hell to have you stick her again, but I'd like another blood test done." He went on to outline exactly what he had in mind.

"We can do that," Hargrove said with a slow nod, "though we may have to send it to an outside lab for verification, to Baton Rouge or New Orleans."

"Whatever it takes."

Hargrove fished a cell phone from his pocket and punched in a number. It was apparent when he began to speak that he'd contacted the lab. Seconds later, he ended the call and pocketed the phone again. With a quick smile, he said, "No sticks for Lainey. Report to the lab and they'll stick you. After that, it's a matter of waiting for the results."

Clay winced, shuddered and then squared his shoulders. "Right. Thanks again."

The handshake Hargrove offered Clay was firm and lasted just a little longer than necessary. The look in his eyes carried warm approval. "This kid, she's special, yeah?"

"Yeah."

"So is her uncle."

Clay didn't know how to answer that, so he said nothing.

It took longer at the lab than Clay expected, since he had to wait on the paperwork and that put him at the end of a long line. The process left him a little light-headed, so the lab technician made him drink a glass of juice and stay flat on his back for a half hour, then recommended an early lunch. All in all, it was after twelve o'clock before he headed back to the hospital.

As he turned the corner, he saw Luke waiting in the hallway outside Lainey's door with his features set in grim lines. Clay almost broke into a run. Voice sharp, he called, "Something wrong?"

"Not with Lainey. Where's Janna?"

"Grand Point. Why?"

"I don't think so. I could have sworn I saw your

airboat heading out past the house this morning. If you weren't in it, then..."

"Shit," Clay said with feeling. "Why the hell didn't you say something earlier?"

"It never occurred to me that someone else would take your Jenny. Then it took me a while to remember and make the connection, since a stunning female distracted me. But April was telling me while you were gone about the shots fired last night. She also said Janna seemed at the end of her rope. I put that together with the airboat, and the fact that you were here but Janna hasn't shown up yet, and decided you ought to know."

"Yeah." Clay looked down at the pattern in the terrazzo floor. From what Luke said, Janna must have left Grand Point the minute he was gone. Since she'd taken the airboat, her destination had to be the camp. It sounded as if she was up to something that she didn't want him to know about.

She had an old piece of a car parked at the camp, which meant that she could go anywhere once she was there. But what could she have to do that was so urgent? The only thing he could think of was the extra money for the transplant. It was possible that she'd taken this opportunity, while Lainey was safe at the hospital, to see the banker she'd mentioned.

Yes, and maybe she'd gone to see Gower. The very idea made Clay feel as if someone had used a noose to take a half hitch around his heart.

"Roan called while you were gone," Luke said, interrupting his thoughts.

"Roan?"

"He said to tell you the raid went off as planned except for one small problem."

Clay definitely did not like the sound of that. "What problem?"

"The doctor and his nurse lit out some back way that the police didn't know about or expect. They were spotted, though, and a couple of patrol units are giving chase."

"And Roan with them, I suppose?"

"You know it."

"He say what direction they took?"

"No, and I didn't think to ask. But if they're smart, they won't stop until they reach Mexico or South America." Luke hesitated a second, then he added, "If Janna was going to see this doctor, she was probably too late. Anyway, Roan would have mentioned it if she'd been there."

"Right." Somehow, Luke's comforting words didn't do a lot of good.

"Not much you can do about it now except see if she comes back."

He could follow her, look for her, Clay thought. But which direction would he go? And what would he say when he found her—"You can't do this kind of thing without my permission"? But she could and she had, and there was no way he could change that.

So he would watch out for Lainey and he would wait.

But when Janna Kerr got back the two of them were going to have an understanding. One way or another.

17

The camp looked exactly as they had left it, Janna thought. Nothing had changed. It seemed strange since so much else was different.

She eased the airboat up near the dock then cut the engine, letting the unwieldy craft glide forward under its own momentum until she was close enough to step out onto the catwalk. It was a relief to have arrived with the thing in one piece. Though she had watched Clay easily crank and maneuver the airboat, there had been a few dicey moments before she got the hang of it. She'd taken more than one wrong turn on the way back here, too; the twisting, branching lake channels through the lanes of cypress tress were deceiving, especially when she'd seen them last in the dark. Several times, she'd almost turned back.

The difficulties of the boat ride weren't her only concern. It had felt wrong to borrow Clay's boat without his permission, wrong to leave without telling him what she meant to do, wrong to leave him at all. Why, she wasn't sure. He'd left her, after all.

Desolation, pure and simple, had been her first re-action to waking up alone in Clay's bed. It had been even more disturbing to discover that he was not even in the house, that she'd been stranded without a car or any other transport except the airboat. It was vaguely possible that he'd left without saying good-bye because he was reluctant to disturb her, but it felt like desertion.

Clay owed her nothing, of course. She'd had more from him than she had any right to expect considering what she'd done to him. He'd helped her, taken care of Lainey, given her shelter and even a degree of surcease. No promises had been made, no permanence implied.

It didn't matter. The desolation remained.

"Well, there you are."

Janna jerked upright from where she had just secured the stern line of the airboat. "Arty," she exclaimed as she whipped around. "You scared me half to death."

"Didn't mean to," he said as he moved from among the trees where his faded shirt and shapeless pants allowed him to blend into the landscape. "Me and Ringo have been keeping an eye on the place is all, like Clay said."

"You've talked to Clay?" She shaded her eyes from the bright, molten sunlight that poured onto the dock as she studied Arty's lined features above his beard.

"Not exactly. He sent Luke out yesterday to let me know what happened with the little gal and ask me to take care of Lainey's pet 'coon. Luke passed the message."

"Oh." It hadn't crossed her mind that Arty would

be concerned, and it should have since she knew how attached he'd become to Lainey. Nor had she given more than a passing thought to poor Ringo. "That was considerate."

"Clay's like that."

"Yes." She turned away, reaching into the airboat and retrieving her shoulder bag of woven brown straw in order to hide her disturbance. "Well, Lainey is much better this morning. She was chattering away when I spoke to her on the phone."

Arty frowned. "You didn't stay with her last night?"

"April looked after her. She's still with her, since I had something I needed to do."

"That's okay then," the old man said with a semi-satisfied nod. "You'll find everything's good here. Quiet as a tomb."

His description sent a small shiver along her spine that she tried to ignore. "No visitors?"

"You expecting any?"

The deadline for supplying the extra money Dr. Gower wanted had come and gone. Nurse Fenton's threat to cancel the surgery notwithstanding, she would not have been surprised to hear that either she or the doctor had come to collect it. Keeping her voice light, as if it didn't matter, she answered, "You never can tell."

"No sign, far as I can see." He paused. "You come back for something then? Something I can help you with?"

He wasn't prying, she told herself as she moved

toward the house and he fell into step beside her, but only trying to be of service. "I just had an errand."

"One somewhere else besides Turn-Coupe, that would be." He glanced toward her old clunker of a car, the rear of which could just be seen beyond the far corner of the camp house.

"Right."

"But you'll be coming back here?"

"Today, you mean? I suppose, since I'll have to return Clay's boat."

"And after? When young Lainey is out of the hospital?"

How could she tell? It depended on so many things beyond her control. "I don't really know."

"Oh, aye," the old swamp man said with a sage nod. "That'll be for Clay to say, I reckon."

"Clay?" The look she gave him was something more than inquiring.

The weathered mahogany of his skin turned almost purple with embarrassment. Casting a harried look toward the lake shallows where his old boat was beached, he answered, "Nothing, nothing. Guess me and Ringo better be headin' home now so's you can get on with your rat killing. You tell young Lainey that old Arty said hello. You hear?"

Janna heard and she agreed. She waved him off, then turned back toward the house.

What Arty had said remained with her, however, as she stepped into the hot, airless confinement of the house with its smells of old, discarded furniture and the grease of a thousand pans of fried fish. Clay had been the soul of helpfulness, but had no right to say where she and her daughter went or what happened to them, none at all.

Janna changed out of the shorts and shirt she'd borrowed from the things left behind by Clay's mother, slipping into a loose-fitting linen dress in cool aqua-green linen instead. She secured the long length of her hair in a soft knot on top of her head with silver pins and applied a modicum of makeup by feel as much as by her reflection in the poorly lighted bathroom mirror. Armored by the transformation into something near comfortable elegance, she locked the camp house behind her and set out for Baton Rouge.

The drive seemed to take forever. Her overstimulated emotions churned uncomfortably inside her. She worried that April might have other obligations so that Lainey would be left alone. What Clay might be doing, thinking or planning was a constant threat. It was a distinct relief when the Mississippi River Bridge loomed ahead of her, and she could swing north on the other side past the state capitol building surrounded by its green areas.

A short time later, she was in the section where Dr. Gower's medical center was located, an area of barbecue joints, pawn shops, hot-sheet motels, liquor stores, defunct car washes and half-deserted strip malls. The center was actually located at one end of such a mall. The term was an exalted one for the run-down collection of examining rooms and small surgical unit where he worked. It had once housed an optical store, Janna thought, and was still connected on one end to a department store building with going-out-of-business signs splashed across the brown paper that masked its empty windows.

As she stepped from her car in the parking lot out front, the humid heat struck her, along with the smells of coffee and fumes from the chemical plants along the river. She was still a little early, since Dr. Gower was seldom in his office before ten o'clock. She hadn't stopped for breakfast, and really wasn't hungry now, but refused to consider that the emptiness and weakness inside her had causes other than a skipped meal. A quick cup of coffee and order of beignets from the coffee shop next door to the defunct department store might help.

In fact, the sugar and caffeine rush made her feel worse. She was painfully aware that the whole point had been delay, putting off the uncomfortable and inevitable, and that she could afford no more of it.

It seemed quieter than normal as she walked down the covered sidewalk in front of the strip mall. Traffic was light on the street running past it, and cars gave a wide berth to the white patrol unit that eased along before turning at the corner. The parking lot was deserted except for the vehicles that probably belonged to the people who worked in its few stores. She saw no sign of the BMW that Dr. Gower normally drove, but that meant nothing; he often parked in the back so he could come and go through a rear door.

The medical center had a brown brick facade in a style popular during the seventies when the area had been more prosperous. Entry was through a glass door filmed with the grime of years. The inside walls were stained and covered with curling posters, the vinyl floor had a buildup of old wax in the corners so deep it was yellow-brown, and the exposed fluorescent light fixtures overhead gave the whole thing a lavender-gray, cadaverous aspect.

The receptionist, a new girl Janna had not seen before, sat at a brown metal desk in the center of the room with only a phone and a cheap intercom centered on the expanse. She looked up from filing her plastic nails into a handful of purple-black weapons. No, Dr. Gower was not in, she said, but Nurse Fenton might be able to help her. As she started to direct Janna back to the assistant's office, Janna waved off the instructions. If there was one thing she knew, it was her way around the center. Behind her, she heard the receptionist buzz through to the doctor's assistant anyway.

"So," Anita Fenton said, her mouth set in an unpleasant line as she turned from where she had been working on a computer terminal at right angles to her main desk. "I suppose you want me to reschedule your daughter's surgery?"

"Actually, I don't," Janna answered, glad that she'd been given such an opportune opening for what she wanted to say. "I've come to tell Dr. Gower that I'm removing Lainey's name from the list of transplant prospects." She took the chair in front of the cheap desk with her shoulder bag in her lap and her hand clasped on top of it.

"You're what?" The woman seemed to swell with her anger.

"I thought you'd be pleased after your visit to the lake."

"Nonsense. I was a little annoyed, I'll admit, but that's only natural given the circumstances. Surely you didn't take what I said seriously?"

"I'm afraid I did, but it doesn't matter now. I just feel that it's best if we stop right here."

"But you are committed, you've paid the initial fee and everything is in place. You *must* continue."

"The fee is the main reason I'm here," Janna said firmly. "I'll need it returned, since I'll have to pay for a legal transplant procedure, eventually, as well as Lainey's care between now and the time a kidney becomes available."

Nurse Fenton's lips tightened like a prune. "You can hardly expect a refund."

"But you are the one who said the procedure was canceled. I'm only following up on your ultimatum. I really do need the money."

"I explained about that misunderstanding. You do realize that this is a serious matter, Ms. Kerr? Your daughter could very well die."

"I realize that." She did not appreciate this obvious attempt to play on her fear.

"Dr. Gower will not be pleased. You have been fully briefed about the way these things are handled, you're privy to information that could be dangerous to him personally and to the experimental work he's engaged in here."

"Experimental?" Janna felt the hair crawl on her scalp.

"Research into ways to preserve organs and with various drug combinations to neutralize rejection of cadaver transplants. The work cannot be hindered."

"I was never told that Lainey would be a test subject," Janna objected.

"It was implicit in the process. Surely you realized that?"

"No," Janna said with force. "No, I didn't, and it makes me even more determined to withdraw my daughter from the program."

The face of the woman across the desk from her seemed to congeal. "I think you'll find it difficult to extract yourself, Ms. Kerr. You are, or have been until this moment, a willing accessory to a criminal procedure. In the event of prosecution, you will be as guilty as any in the eyes of the law."

"I realize that," Janna said, her voice clear, "and I'm willing to take the consequences."

"Very high flown. But what will become of your Lainey if you go to prison?"

"Are you suggesting that you'll have a hand in any charges that may be filed against me?"

"I'm suggesting that it would be unwise to think of going to the authorities since you would only implicate yourself."

Janna stared at the woman for a long moment. Then she said, "You're afraid I'll go to the police. I suppose I should. However, I suggest Dr. Gower close this center voluntarily. I don't doubt that he had good intentions at one time, or that he's saved a few patients that might not have lived otherwise, but something has gone wrong. Teenagers are dying minus vital organs, and I think there's a connection. It has to stop.''

"Are you threatening us?" Incredulity and rage burned in Nurse Fenton's eyes as she came to her feet and rounded the desk to pause at its corner.

"I suppose I am." Janna hadn't intended it when she stepped into the office, but it seemed required. Since she'd come this far, what was going a little further?

"You're making a huge mistake."

"I sincerely doubt it. It's only a matter of time before the authorities make the connection."

The phone in the reception area rang, demanding and shrill, a sound plainly heard through the thin walls. The murmur of the receptionist's voice came in answer, followed shortly by an intercom message that sounded in the office just down the hallway. Seconds later, a man could be heard speaking. Anita Fenton glanced toward the phone, then at the inside door that connected her office to that adjoining one, but made no comment.

"I need to be going," Janna said as she got to her feet and settled the strap of her straw bag on her shoulder. She wasn't cut out for this kind of confrontation. Her knees were wobbly, her hands sweating and her stomach felt as if it had no bottom. And yet, for now at least she had no regrets.

"I'll have to consult with Dr. Gower," the nurse

said. "He'll want to talk to you, I'm sure, since I believe he is here now. Take a seat in the waiting room, please."

"I don't have time to wait. Lainey is in the hospital and I need to get back to her."

"She's fine." The woman's voice hardened. "It's you who has a problem."

The nurse knew about Lainey. Maybe she'd tried to contact the camp, discovered they were gone, checked nearby hospitals until she found her. The memories of the shots fired the night before echoed in Janna's mind, triggered by the grim look on Anita Fenton's face. Had they been meant as a warning? Or as something more lethal?

"I don't think I do," Janna said quietly. "Tell Dr. Gower that I appreciate everything he's done for me and I'm sorry, but I can't go through with it. That's all."

The woman's lips twisted. "You appreciate it?"

"The hope he gave me. It was good to have that, at least for a while." She'd come here driven by guilt and the remnants of a sense of obligation for the vanished promise of a miracle, but that was over.

Janna turned toward the door, then stepped into the hall that led to the reception area. As she glanced in that direction, she saw a police car pull up outside with lights flashing.

Abruptly the connecting door swung open inside the office she'd just left. Dr. Gower charged into the room, his eyes wide and his face so pale that the blotches on it stood out like oil spots on a white sand beach. "It's a raid, Anita! My contact from down-town called. The damned sheriff of Turn-Coupe, up near Horseshoe Lake, can provide evidence and a wit-ness against us. Destroy the files. Then we have to get out of here right—"

He came to a halt, staring at Janna through the office's open door. Surprise and concern chased themselves across his face. Before he could speak, however, the sound of shouts and sirens came from outside.

The front door of the reception area down the hall-way swung open to hit the wall with the sound of breaking glass. The receptionist screamed.

Close on the sound, a harsh voice bellowed, "Po-lice! On your feet! Hands in plain sight!"

Comprehension invaded Dr. Gower's eyes, turning them dark as he stared at Janna. "Oh, my dear," he said in pained tones. "What have you done? What have you done to me?"

18

"We have no time for that," Anita Fenton said with icy disdain in her eyes. "We have to get out of here. Now!" Diving toward the computer terminal, she tapped the keys briefly, then popped out a disk, leaving the drive grinding and whirring in erase mode.

"As you say," the doctor agreed, his gaze brooding. "I think we will all use the escape route."

Hard on the words, the doctor swooped down on Janna and caught her wrist, pulling her back into the office. He clamped an arm around her waist, then propelled her toward the open door that led into the second office beyond.

"Wait!" Janna struggled, trying to set her feet.

"You must come with us," Dr. Gower said urgently.

"And keep quiet!" the nurse said in a harsh whisper as she slid past them, then ran to another door that was set into the back wall, this one of rusting steel and with an Exit sign above it. Cursing under her breath, she put her shoulder to the heavy panel while shoving on the handle. As it swung open with ponderous slowness, she held it while reaching out with clawlike hands to drag Janna and Dr. Gower into what appeared to be a storeroom. When they were inside, she slammed and locked the steel barrier behind them.

"What are you doing?" Janna demanded as she pulled free for a second. "You can't hide in here!"

"Shut up, I told you," Anita snapped. "Unless you feel like answering a lot of very unpleasant questions."

On the other side of the door, they could hear the voice of the receptionist raised in protest. Janna had seconds to make a decision. If she screamed and gave them away, there was no telling when she might see Lainey again. But how could she go with these two when they might have been responsible for the deaths of at least two teenagers?

"Of course she'll be quiet," Dr. Gower said. "She isn't stupid."

"She'd better not be." From her purse, the red-haired woman pulled a handgun and pointed it at Janna's midsection. "Let's get the hell out of here before I'm tempted to make little Lainey an orphan."

The doctor's face tightened in the gloom, but he made no protest. Turning, he led the way at a fast trot from the storeroom and through what was undoubtedly the back area of the old department store. They hurried past dust-covered clothes racks, naked and staring mannequins, piles of broken hangers and scattered drifts of rat-eaten cardboard. Janna went with them; she had no choice, though her mind worked at super speed to find an alternative.

As they passed into the open sales section of the empty building, they could see the collection of police units and uniformed muscle beyond the display windows with their torn masking paper. Keeping well back, they skimmed through that semiexposed area as quickly as possible, though it was likely that the mirrorlike glaze on the windows prevented them from being seen. Entering another suite of offices, they plunged through them to the rear where they reached another steel exit door. This one opened into the steam and bustle of a kitchen. They were in the coffee shop, Janna realized, even before she'd inhaled the distinctive smells of chicory coffee and frying yeast dough that she'd noticed earlier.

A man with a dingy white cap on his head and an apron tied around his middle, turned from the deep fryer he was tending to stare at them. "What the hell?" he began. Then he saw the pistol and closed his mouth with an audible pop.

Dr. Gower spared him only a single glance before turning toward the kitchen's rear. Yet another exit door was set into the dirty brick wall, next to a collection of trash cans, brooms and mop pails. From the one time that she'd approached the medical center via the back way, Janna was sure that it led into a fenced-in cul-de-sac for deliveries and garbage pickup. She felt rather than saw the movement when Nurse Fenton started toward it.

Instantly Janna spun in the opposite direction. She didn't hesitate, but ran for the swinging door that separated the kitchen from the front of the coffee shop.

"No!" the doctor shouted. Janna glanced back to see him thrust Anita Fenton's arm upward so her pistol pointed toward the ceiling. She expected to hear the crack of a shot at any second, but it didn't come. Instead there was only the hard thud as she hit the door, then the *squeak-squeak* as it flapped back and forth behind her.

No one came after her. Nurse Fenton, or more likely the doctor, must have decided against drawing that much attention. It seemed like a wise plan. Janna slowed her pace as the few customers craning their necks to see the police action at the front windows turned back to stare at her. She gave them a strained smile. Then moving with as casual an air as she could manage, she walked deliberately out of the shop.

The number of police cars and uniformed men had grown, forming an effective barricade outside the entrance to the medical center. She ignored them studiously, like any ordinary citizen who didn't want to be involved. Her car seemed miles away, but she began to walk toward it.

Seconds passed. Her footsteps sounded unnaturally loud on the pavement. Then the car was in front of her and she was reaching for the door handle. As she unlocked it, she heard a commotion of shouts, car engines and sirens in the rear of the strip mall that sounded as if Dr. Gower and Anita had been spotted leaving and the police were giving chase. With only the mildest of curious glances in that direction for the benefit of anyone watching, she slid into the furnace heat of the vehicle. The seat burned through her dress but she hardly felt it. Fumbling with her keys, she slid them into the ignition and started the engine. Then, carefully, slowly, she drove away.

No one tried to stop her. No one followed her that she could tell. She had appeared as she had intended, like a coffee shop customer with better things to do than gawk at such a common spectacle as police action in that part of town. Reaction hit her. She began to shake. The hard tremors ran over her entire body, making her muscles jerk so uncontrollably that she could hardly hold the car on the road. Afraid she might cause an accident, she pulled in at the first service station she came to and parked with the engine running. Bracing her arms on the steering wheel, she rested her forehead on her stacked hands and closed her eyes.

She was safe. She had gotten away.

She should have stayed; she knew that. She should have approached the police and told them everything she knew. Because she hadn't, the doctor and his murderous assistant might well go free. Free to start over, free to experiment again on the desperately ill, free to go after those who had betrayed them.

Nurse Fenton was behind the deaths of the teenagers; there seemed little doubt of that. It was she who normally made Dr. Gower's financial arrangements, after all. Though she functioned as a nurse, she had considerably more medical training and expertise in her capacity as a physician's assistant. Did she do it for the money, because she had some kind of stake in the center, or was it for love? As hard as it was to realize, women did sometimes invest in the obsessions of the men they cared about, even to the point of committing heinous crimes.

Regardless of her reasons, Anita Fenton had to be stopped; Janna was clear on that. If she went back now, would it make a difference? Would it really, when the police seemed in control of the situation already?

She didn't know. And she didn't see how she could afford to reveal her part in the sordid business when it might mean prison. She couldn't leave Lainey to be cared for by people who didn't know and understand her condition, had no instinct for when she was in serious trouble. No, she couldn't do it. And yet the guilt over running away was a fierce, rending pain inside her.

Why couldn't the raid have happened just a few minutes later, when she was far from the medical center? Why did she have to be caught in the middle of it? Why couldn't she have had the simple peace of being without blame for this, at least? Was that too much to ask?

It was, of course. The damn sheriff of Turn-Coupe, as Dr. Gower had called him, was Roan Benedict. Sheriff Benedict was Clay's cousin. If there was evidence against Gower, then Clay had supplied it. Clay was the witness whose testimony had doubtless proven the critical element in the decision of the Baton Rouge police to raid the center. He knew what was happening in the swamp because she'd kidnapped him. If she were going to be implicated in this mess then it would come about because of that. In all likelihood, she would have to tell her story to someone eventually.

Clay had worked with Roan to shut down the transplant operation, had been working with him, perhaps, since the first night he left the camp. Even while he was making love to her, he had been busily seeing to it that she had no life.

It shouldn't matter what he'd done. Janna had come finally to the recognition that she couldn't endure saving her daughter at the expense of another young life. However, Clay didn't know that. He thought she still meant to go through with the illegal transplant. And since he did, his actions were in deliberate opposition to what Janna had proposed for her daughter's health and welfare.

He didn't care what she wanted. He didn't care about Lainey. He only cared about his damned Benedict notions of right and wrong, justice and honor. He felt his way of handling the situation, his reading of it, was superior. He had been so horrendously sure of it that he'd left her no choice except to do things his way.

Well and good. He'd been right and she'd been wrong. The illegal transplant had been a desperate idea, one that should never have been attempted. She didn't blame him for that, or for doing everything in his power to stop Dr. Gower. What she did blame him for was not discussing it with her.

He had taken the decision into his own hands, this man who had never had a child, never been a parent.

He had discounted Lainey's life. He'd thrown it away for the sake of some abstract sense of justice. He might say he had discounted it for the greater good, but that didn't matter when the person who must pay had a child's laughter and a child's tears.

He'd sacrificed Lainey. He'd given up Janna's daughter for a principle, and for that Janna could never forgive him. And she could certainly never allow him to lay any claim to her, no matter how powerful the reason.

Janna lifted her head, staring through the windshield with unseeing eyes. So what was she to do now? The first thing was to see her daughter, hold her in her arms and feel her small heart beating, smell the sweet child's fragrance of her. Then the two of them would pack their things and leave the camp and Turn-Coupe behind, maybe go back to New Orleans, find a cheap apartment close to The Children's Hospital. They would put as much distance as possible between them and Turn-Coupe and the Benedicts. Especially Clay Benedict.

After a few minutes, Janna's trembling eased. She took a deep breath, then shook herself. Moving like an automaton, she put the car in gear again and pulled back out into the traffic, headed for Turn-Coupe.

The hospital bed was empty.

Janna stood staring at the expanse of white sheet where her daughter should be while anguish curled itself around her heart. An empty bed equaled death; she'd seen it far too often during Lainey's long sojourns in the pediatric renal units of various hospitals. It was almost certain when the room had been stripped of personal effects and cleaned, and no family or nurse-sitter was present.

The bed was freshly made and with the sheets turned back on one corner. The wastebasket had a new liner. The closet was bare, as was the bedside table. April was nowhere in sight. What else could it mean? The only other possibility she could imagine was almost as paralyzing as the first.

"Hi there! I guess you're looking for your little girl, huh?"

Janna spun around to face the nurse who stood in the open doorway. In a voice that sounded as if she'd been running for miles, she asked, "Where is she?"

"Jeez, honey, take it easy. She's okay, really. Clay just took her home."

The face of the plump, dark-haired nurse was creased with sympathetic distress. It made little impression on Janna, since she remembered very well that this particular nurse, Johnnie Hopewell, was a part of the Benedict clan. "You mean Dr. Hargrove released her?"

"Yeah, about an hour ago. She was basically over the problem, and he thought she could recuperate at home just as well, considering she was in such good hands. Boy, was that kid ready to get out of here."

"And Clay took her...where, exactly?"

"Home with him, like I told you. To Grand Point."

So much for putting trust of any kind in him. With

her voice gathering strength, Janna said, "He can't do that. Lainey is my daughter, mine. I gave no permission for her to be moved."

"But you came in with Clay." Johnnie frowned in perplexity, as if she couldn't see the problem.

"That doesn't mean anything!"

"Means he's got a strong interest in the welfare of your little girl. There's no cause to be upset, hon, really there isn't. Clay dotes on that kid, as anybody with half an eye can see. He wouldn't hurt her for the world."

"You're saying he can walk into this hospital and take any child he wants just because he likes them?" she demanded. "That's outrageous! What about release forms, a legal signature? Payment, for God's sake! Who the hell does he think he is?"

"All arranged, every bit of it." Johnnie's smile curled one corner of her mouth. "He's a Benedict, sweetheart. That's the way they are."

She should have known. Tunica Parish was Benedict country. Here, they were kings. They could do anything they wanted and get away with it. Or thought they could.

It was her greatest fear made real. Clay had taken Lainey. He had taken her away from her mother. Still, it was so hard to believe. She didn't want, couldn't bear, to believe it.

"Are you sure Clay wasn't going back to the camp?" Janna insisted.

"Didn't hear him say, really. I suppose he could have been, or might even have taken her to April and

Luke's house, since they were here. But I sure got the idea they were headed for Grand Point.''

''Bastard,'' she whispered.

Clay had taken Lainey home with him, he really had. But if he expected to get away with it, Janna thought in grim resolve, he would soon discover his mistake.

''Now wait a minute, hon,'' Johnnie exclaimed as Janna brushed past her and stalked into the hall. ''Don't you go doing anything foolish.''

Janna didn't answer. She didn't even look back.

19

Grand Point sat like an oasis at the end of a long journey. Its white walls reflected the broiling late-afternoon sunlight in places, but the great oaks that arched above it provided deep, motionless shade around its base and its tropical landscaping looked lush and fecund rather than prostate with the heat. Janna drove to the rear to park her car, then got out and mounted the tall back steps of the center section. The shadow of the deep and wide gallery that enveloped her at the top was a cooler prelude to the refrigerated atmosphere inside the door.

She paused a second in the central parlor. The house was so still. No childish giggling or chatter disturbed it, no deep male voice. The only sounds were the slow ticktock of a pendulum clock on the mantel and the soft whir of a ceiling fan in some bedroom down the connecting hall. Yet Clay was here somewhere, or so she thought. His SUV sat on the driveway and the back door of the house had been left unlocked. Turn-Coupe residents might not be as careful about security as people in larger towns, according to Denise, but they weren't foolhardy. Though they often left their houses open during daylight hours, they locked them at night or while they were away.

In her simmering anger and concern for Lainey, Janna had walked in without knocking. Now she hesitated, unwilling to retreat but knowing full well that she had no right to go any further. Engrained manners could be a disadvantage at times. Though it felt ridiculous under the circumstances, she opened her lips to call out a greeting.

A scratching noise accompanied by soft, gruntlike panting snared her attention. She shut her mouth and tipped her head to listen. It was growing louder, she thought, and seemed to be coming from the bedroom wing, yet the size of the rooms in the big old house made it impossible to be sure.

She turned in that direction, frowning as she listened. What she was hearing sounded almost familiar. She couldn't quite place it, however, not even after she'd moved into the kitchen and through it to the hall that led into the bedroom section. An odd dread slid down her spine. She stopped an instant at the entrance to the hall, then raised her chin and stepped inside.

Keeping close to the right hand wall, she moved with stealthy footsteps toward the bedroom Clay had designated for her the night before. She hadn't used it for long, of course, but it was at least not quite so off limits as the remainder of the house. In any case, the scratching seemed to be coming from the other side of that door.

It stopped as she drew closer. She put out her hand,

then brought it back and stood listening. Nothing. She caught the knob again, turning it with slow care, then pushed the door inward to open it.

Ringo.

The raccoon scuttled out of the way, then sat back on his haunches and looked up at her with bright, inquisitive eyes. Janna let out her pent-up breath in a short, hard rush of relief. As if taking that as a signal, the furry little beast dropped to all fours again and waddled past her in a break for freedom. Beyond the door, he turned in the direction of the kitchen. Janna watched him go, wondering where he had come from since Arty had had him when she'd talked to the old trapper earlier. Then she dismissed Ringo from her mind as she turned toward the bed.

Lainey lay in the middle of it, turned on her side with her hair spread over the pillow. One hand was tucked under her cheek as she slept, while the other clutched her rag doll. She nestled into the curve of Clay's body, as she had slept so often at the camp, looking small and fragile against his long length. He was asleep as well, with his chin resting on Lainey's silky blond hair and one strong, brown arm thrown protectively over her.

At least Janna thought he was asleep. That was until he opened his eyes and stared straight into hers. And seeing the accusation that burned there, she felt her dying anger return with double the force.

Face grim, she lifted a brow and tipped her head toward the doorway in an invitation to speak outside the room. Without waiting to see if he meant to comply, she turned and stalked out. She didn't stop again until she was back in the central living room. The instant Clay stepped through the door from the kitchen, she attacked.

"What do you mean by taking my daughter from the hospital?"

"Lainey wanted to leave," he began.

"Of course she did! She hates hospitals. But does that mean you can do anything you like with her? Dear God, the unbelievable Benedict arrogance of it! Who do you think you are to make decisions about my child?"

His eyes darkened. Slowly he put his hands on his hipbones. "Where were you that you couldn't take her home? You left for Lord knows where, maybe someplace to beg or borrow the money to pay a quack not fit to trim Lainey's toenails, much less anything more critical. I did what I thought was best."

"What *you* thought? You barely know her, or me, and you're making life-and-death decisions for us? Why should you think anything? What right do you have to touch Lainey, much less take her away from me?"

"I wasn't taking her way from you."

"What do you call it then? She's here instead of at the camp where she—"

"Maybe this is where she belongs."

"The hell you say! She belongs with her mother. I'm the only person who can take care of her, who understands what she needs when she cries, who can do all the things that make her happy and comfortable.''

''You need help.''

''And you're going to help me right out of custody, aren't you?''

''I wouldn't. I'm not.''

''Where the hell were you when I really needed help?'' she asked without bothering to listen to what he had to say. ''Where were the Benedicts when Lainey nearly died three separate times, when I couldn't pay the rent for the medical bills, when I was so tired that dying myself sounded like the only way I'd ever be able to rest?''

''I didn't know, none of us knew.'' He stepped closer, put out his hand to touch her arm,

Janna backed away from him. ''You didn't want to know, damn you! But that's all right, because I got by just fine without you. I had Lainey by myself and I took care of her by myself. I raised her and I loved her without anyone, especially anyone by the name of Benedict, and I can go on doing it.''

''For Pete's sake, Janna,'' he said in tight impatience. ''You aren't thinking straight.''

''And you are? You scheme and plot with your cousin behind my back to see to it that the transplant Lainey needs is no longer available, and you actually think that's better?''

His head came up. ''How did you find that out?''

''Never mind how! You did it, and that's enough for me.''

"The surgery was too dangerous. There was no way she could go through it."

"I *know* that," she cried, flinging up her hands. "Why do you think I went there today except to tell Dr. Gower that it was off?"

"You did what?"

"You heard me. Yes, and what did I find? You and Sheriff Benedict had seen to it that the center was shut down. You'd made the transplant impossible."

"Let me get this straight," he said, his gaze as black and hard as volcanic glass. "You meant to cancel the transplant, yet you're steamed because I stopped it? I don't see the difference."

"The difference is that you decided in your stupid Benedict male conceit that you were right and I was wrong. Taking kidneys was legally and morally depraved, and that was what mattered. You put my daughter at risk for a principle, not because you cared whether she lived or died."

"I did it to protect her!"

"You did it because—because you had to be right!" she shouted, her voice shaking with the rage that choked her and made hot tears spring into her eyes.

"Now wait a damned minute," he said with rough anger in his voice. "Lainey is my niece. I may not have known her as long as you but I still love her. Do you really think it was an easy decision, closing down Gower's center? I had to weigh her chances with every bit as much care as you did. I may have made a mistake. If I did, if she dies, I don't know how I'll live with it. But what I did was not because I didn't feel anything for her or want like hell to see her live a reasonably normal and healthy life.''

Janna stared at him with aching eyes. Could she have misjudged the situation? The possibility opened up vistas that she didn't dare consider. She was still trying to dredge up the courage to ask what he meant when a quiet shuffle came from near the door into the kitchen. She turned her head in that direction, half expecting to see Ringo.

''What a shame to interrupt such a cathartic shouting match,'' Dr. Gower said as he stepped into room. ''Especially when it made such a timely distraction. But I'm afraid I'm in something of a hurry.''

Janna's heart congealed in her chest. She opened her mouth, but no sound came out. Eyes wide, she could only stare as the doctor half-pushed, half-led Lainey into the room, using the child like a shield as he held her with one arm crooked around her neck. But her gaze was riveted to the scalpel that he held to her daughter's small white throat.

''Mama,'' Lainey whispered. Then she looked at Clay. ''Daddy?''

Janna didn't dare move, barely breathed. She lifted her gaze to Gower's as she asked, ''How did you get in here?''

''This house has dozens of doors and windows, not all of them latched,'' he replied in finicky precision. ''So convenient—especially those on the far end of the house. Then you and Benedict were too engrossed

in your quarrel to realize that I was around.'' He
smiled with a tight movement of his thin lips. ''As
for the rest, I followed you from the center, my dear.
It was pitifully easy. You were so upset that you
never looked back. Why you even waited for me to
catch up— Don't!''

The last was for Clay who had eased forward as if
he meant to jump Gower. Clay wrenched to such an
abrupt halt that a tendon made a popping sound in
his leg.

''I didn't wait for you,'' Janna declared in an instinctive effort to distract Gower again. ''I was
just...''

''Upset by the turn of events, I do understand. I
was a little spooked myself, to tell you the truth. As
for Anita, well, she actually tried to give herself up
when she saw the police were waiting for us.''

''Tried?'' That question came from Clay.

''I couldn't allow it, could I? I mean, she would
have made far too dangerous a witness against me
since she knew everything. Besides, she had the disk
with all the records and refused to give it to me. Her
jealousy had become tedious as well.''

''She'd become a liability,'' Clay suggested.

''Just like dear Janna, here. Well, and you, too,
since she brought you into our little arrangement.''

Janna stared at him in dread as she asked, ''You're
saying that you killed her?''

''No time to take her kidneys, of course, though
I'm sure she had a fine, healthy pair. Pity.''

Nurse Fenton was dead. It seemed impossible

when she had been so full of life when Janna saw her last. She gave a slow shake of her head.

"Don't look so horrified," the doctor said. "She barely felt a thing." He smiled as he shifted the position of his scalpel to the hollow beneath Lainey's left ear, the starting point for a classic slash from behind the victim. "A scalpel is a beautiful and merciful weapon for someone who knows how to use it."

Lainey's eyes were huge in her small, puffy face. She hadn't made another sound, though unshed tears rimmed her lashes. She understood what was going on, understood it too well, Janna thought. Torn by fear and frustration, she sent a burning look from her daughter to the man who held her as she exclaimed, "You're insane!"

"Really? It's insane to try to prevent people from testifying about my humanitarian efforts in the field of kidney disease? I'd say that was exceptionally sane. It would only be crazy if I didn't care."

Clay was poised and ready for any break that came, Janna thought; she could sense the tension in his stillness. All she could think to do was stall until something gave him a chance. "You have nowhere to hide after what you've done. I'd have thought you'd be better off far away from here."

"I considered it. Then I thought of your lover here, and how much I'd dislike leaving without settling with him. I'm aware that I have him to thank for today's raid."

"Don't mention it," Clay said in hard irony. "My pleasure, believe me."

The doctor turned on him with mottled color riding his sharp cheekbones. "You destroyed my practice, a life's work in transplant research and experimentation, and you're proud of it?"

"I closed a human chop shop that used desperate people as guinea pigs and disadvantaged kids as a convenient source for body parts. Yeah, I'm proud."

"What ignorance. You made the lives of the young men whose organs were harvested worthless, not I. My research gave them a reason for having been born in that dreary project where few people cared about their existence and three-quarters of them would die from drink and drugs and stupidly vicious gang wars. I tried to help them. I spent years curing them of head lice and worms and sexually transmitted diseases and a thousand other illnesses, and what happened? They went to prison or died anyway. Why should their lives not benefit someone since they were so determined to throw them away? Why should they not serve my noble purpose instead of costing taxpayers the price of a cell or a funeral?"

"You don't know what the two you killed might have done with their lives," Clay replied with cold contempt in his face. "They were alive until you came along, and in life there's hope."

"I thought that way, once. For a long time I only took the organs of those who died on my operating table. But there were so many, and their constant dying was such a waste. Such a waste." Dr. Gower looked away, and for a second his face was a mask of grief. Then it hardened again. "Lay people always get so emotional over these things. They don't understand that life is cheap, that thousands upon thousands of people die every day, or that literally hundreds of millions have lived and expired over the millennia with no more trace left behind than—than will be left when that ridiculous creature goes." He nodded toward Ringo who had waddled into the room and was sniffing at Clay's ankles.

"So cheap that you tossed them into the lake like empty beer bottles," Clay said

"As good a place as any to dispose of them, I thought, especially from a fishing boat. Bass fishermen are boring to watch…people give so little attention to what they do."

"The lives of these young men were worthless, so you say," Janna observed in flat disparagement, "but I'm sure you feel differently about your own."

"My life has value because of the knowledge that I'll leave behind and the patients whose lives my methods and expertise have saved. For every project rat who didn't care whether he lived or died there was a patient who was so desperate to live that they would take any risk, do anything."

"Pay any amount?" Janna suggested.

"You're thinking of the extra sum I asked from you. What of it? Financing is necessary for any great endeavor."

"Without that money you'd have let Lainey die, regardless of how much she was loved or how desperately she wanted to live."

"The choice of who is saved has to be made by someone."

Lainey, turning to look up at the doctor behind her, said distinctly, "Only God is supposed to do that. You're a bad man."

"A monster, in fact," Janna agreed in low tones, then went on because it seemed she had so little to lose. "You're a vulture, feeding on other people's pain and misery. You're the one who doesn't understand the value of life. You think it's cheap because it comes and goes so fast. But every single second we spend on this mean and dusty little planet is a glorious joy. Taking it from anyone is a crime, but stealing it from the young who have not yet learned its worth is an atrocity beyond bearing."

"I'm disappointed in you, Janna," Gower said with a sigh. "Of all those I've tried to help, I thought you came closest to understanding my vision."

"Bull," Clay said, in heavy disgust. "She tickled your ego because she's beautiful and was so grateful for the hope you offered. You loved it that she was totally dependent on you."

Dr. Gower gave a dry laugh. "You may be right. There was always the possibility that she'd require consoling if the transplant for dear little Lainey failed."

"Never," Janna declared in fierce rejection.

"No?" The doctor's voice turned hard. "But I think you considered being very kind to me in lieu of the extra money for your daughter's surgery?"

He was right. She might well have succumbed if

Clay had not been there, if the bodies of the doctor's victims had not been found, or if Lainey had not gotten sick. What would she not have done for her daughter's sake?

The need to destroy the man who might have manipulated her that way, and who was doing it now by holding her daughter, rose in Janna like a hunger. It wasn't just his suggestion, though it was sickening enough; it was the casual way he referred to Lainey, his easy dismissal of the fact that she might have died. She'd understood the mothers of the dead teenagers before, but now she grasped their pain and need to retaliate with a visceral and primitive force that rose to her brain in blood-red heat and threatened to crowd her heart from her chest. Beside her, Clay cursed in a soft undertone as he eased forward again.

"Enough of this," Dr. Gower declared. "I don't have the time." Shifting Lainey quickly to the crook of his right arm, holding the scalpel edge to her neck with one hand, he plunged the other into his pocket and took out a length of nylon cord of the kind used to secure fishing boats. "You will oblige me, Janna, by using this to tie up your lover. You should be good at it, after all."

She glanced at Clay. His attention was focused on the kitchen and the bedroom hall that lay behind the doctor and Lainey. Then as if he felt her watching him, he turned his gaze, dark blue and unfathomable, to meet hers.

Time became elastic, stretching endlessly while they stood in communication that had no words. Finally he said quietly, "Do as he says. It doesn't matter."

"Why? You're stronger, so a greater threat. Tying you up will make it easier for him to cut all our throats."

"Why?" the physician demanded. "I'll tell you why. Because you value your daughter's life."

Janna's eyes were clear as she turned back to him. "I don't see that you can let her live once she's watched you kill Clay, or me. We might as well let you try to figure out another way."

"You can do that if you'd like to observe firsthand exactly where an incision for a kidney transplant is made."

"No!" Janna shuddered at the mental vision created by the threat. She said again, "No."

"Do what he says, Janna," Clay commanded in a voice devoid of emotion.

What other choice was there? She stepped forward and held out her hand for the nylon cord.

As she moved, a shadow materialized in the room behind the doctor. Alligator Arty crept forward and then eased around the door frame. A flash of silver-blue in his hand marked the razor-edged gleam of his skinning knife. He was near, so near. Still he needed to be much closer before he could jump the doctor without endangering Lainey.

Then Gower heard the quiet rustle of his clothing, or perhaps caught a shadow of movement. He whipped his head around.

What happened next was like a kaleidoscope of

images, shifting, sliding, changing in a blur of color
and motion. No thought or plan moved them but only
desperate chance and heart-jarring effort.

Janna whipped the cord she held across Gower's
face. He released Lainey as he staggered back, grunt-
ing, lifting his hand to his eyes. Clay hit him with a
hard shoulder in that instant. Even as he struck, he
snatched up Lainey, tucking her against his chest. The
doctor cursed and struck out with a slicing blow. A
red streak appeared across Clay's back and his swift-
drawn breath hissed through his teeth. He hurled himself and Lainey out of reach. They crashed into Janna
so the three of them struck the floor in a tangle.

Then Arty was there, jerking the doctor backward
in a chokehold with the point of his skinning knife
denting the flesh of Gower's neck. "Hold, you mangy
bastard," he growled. "Move a muscle and I'll gut
and skin ye like a muskrat."

Lainey was crying with great, gulping sobs. Janna
reached for her, scanning her body with anxious eyes,
but could see no damage. She had only a second to
look before her daughter lunged to wrap her arms
around her neck. Janna held her, rocking her back
and forth. Even so, she was aware of Clay struggling
to his feet next to her with the back of his shirt rap-
idly turning wet and sticking to his skin.

He turned toward Arty and his prisoner. The old
man's face was as expressionless as a bronze death
mask, his arm corded with stringy muscle as he held
on to Gower. The doctor was making strangled,
wheezing noises while the slick soles of his Italian

leather shoes scrabbled for purchase on the polished floor.

"Let him breathe," Clay said, the words calm, reasonable.

"Don't think so," Arty said after judicious consideration. He dug the point of his knife deeper so blood welled around it. "He was about to kill our sweet little gal."

Gower, his eyes so wild they were mainly whites, gasped as he cried out, "For God's sake, man!"

Clay stopped. "Roan won't like it if you kill him— and I think I just heard his patrol unit drive up."

"You did?"

Janna was almost as skeptical about that as Arty appeared to be. That was, until she heard a car door slam outside.

"Besides, he'll get the death penalty anyway," Clay went on. "I'll see to it personally. And I think he'll dread death by lethal injection more."

Arty squinted at Clay. "You sure? Wouldn't take but a second. I could drag him out the back way, drop him out there in the swamp, only hid a lot better than he left them kids."

"Not in front of Lainey."

The old trapper looked to where the girl was huddled against Janna. Regret crossed his wrinkled features behind the partial screen of his beard. Then he heaved a sigh and loosened his grip. "Reckon not, damn it all. I mean, dang it."

"Yeah," Clay said in laconic agreement.

Janna knew exactly how they felt.

20

The sun was setting by the time the last question was answered for Roan, who had indeed arrived on the track of the doctor. The ordeal was not as bad as Janna had feared it would be. She was treated as a victim of Dr. Gower's unconscionable scheme and a future witness against him. No hint of her being accused as an accessory was ever raised. For this, she thought, she had Roan to thank, that and her good luck in having the doctor's last act of madness take place within his jurisdiction. The mantel of Benedict protection had been quietly and efficiently flung around her, though mainly for Lainey's sake, she was sure.

Finally the sheriff and his deputies shoved Dr. Gower into the back of a police car and took him away to a cell at the courthouse in Turn-Coupe. The elderly physician who Roan had called, and who was referred to by everyone as Doc Watkins, followed them soon after. He had taken ten stitches in the deepest portion of the slash in Clay's shoulder. That had been a trial, since Clay had demanded that Lainey be checked first, even though he was bleeding like a stuck pig, then had tried to refuse the injection that would numb the cut before stitching. But when Lainey offered to hold his hand while he was stuck, Clay took the needle without flinching.

The last set of taillights disappeared down the driveway. Clay went to his bedroom to clean up and put on another shirt. Rest had been the only prescription Doc Watkins had for Lainey, and Janna gave her a light dinner and took her off to get ready for bed. Since dialysis had been done at the hospital, the process this evening wasn't a long one.

Lainey was keyed up from the excitement. She wanted Janna to lie down with her while she went to sleep, as well as having her rag doll and Ringo in bed with her. She also had a tendency to cling. Still, the results of the confrontation could have been worse, Janna thought, much worse.

"I was scared when that bad doctor came and got me," she said, her voice muffled against the front of Janna's dress as she huddled close against her mother's side.

"You were very brave. I was proud of you."

"I didn't cry because I knew Clay wouldn't let that bad doctor hurt me. Or you."

"No." It was strange, but Janna had felt something close to that same confidence.

"And I knew there was no way that you'd ever let him take me away to his hospital, either."

"No, not ever," Janna whispered, smoothing her daughter's hair away from her face, pretending that there had never been the least doubt.

"Clay wouldn't, either, because he said so. Just like he wouldn't let that nurse do anything to me."

"He's brave, too." Janna could barely force the words through her tight throat as she remembered how he had let himself be slashed with the scalpel to save her daughter.

Lainey nodded wisely. "He told me just a little bit ago that he wouldn't mind needles and their sticks anymore, not if I'd always hold his hand."

"Did he?" Janna felt like crying though she wasn't sure why.

"I called him my daddy."

Janna closed her eyes, pressing them tight. "I heard."

"I know that he's not, but sometimes I like to pretend."

"That—that's all right, sweetheart. I'm sure he won't mind."

"No, he said he wouldn't."

Janna could think of nothing to say to that. Several minutes passed. She thought Lainey had finally drifted off when she spoke again.

"Mama?"

"What, love?"

"It hurts being sick, but I don't want to die."

"No, love," Janna whispered against her hair, valiantly swallowing tears while she rocked her daughter slowly in her arms. "None of us do. None of us do."

When Lainey fell asleep at last, Janna covered her with a sheet against the coolness of the air conditioning, then eased out of the bed and tiptoed from the room. Nothing moved in that bedroom wing of the rambling house. She wasn't sure what Clay was doing now, whether he felt like eating or if his shoulder was paining him so much that he'd decided to lie down. She debated going to bed herself; she was certainly tired enough. But she was as wound up as Lainey, much too restless for an early night. In the hope that a short walk in the evening air would calm her, she made her way to the central parlor, then slipped out the back door.

She stood for a moment on the back porch, searching for some sign of Clay. Nothing moved in the dimness. After a moment, she moved down the steps toward where the lake glimmered among the trees and the large boathouse and dock lay off to one side.

From the dock's catwalk, she stared out over the water that reflected the last rose-purple of the dying evening. It should have been peaceful, but there was no peace inside her. She clasped her arms around her rib cage, holding tight because it seemed that otherwise she might fall to pieces.

Tomorrow or the next day, when Lainey was well enough for the upheaval, she would go away from this place, from Grand Point and Turn-Coupe and the lake with its stately cypresses, its egrets and alligators. She would leave dear old Arty and Ringo, too. And she would leave Clay. She would take her daughter and drive back to the camp where they would pack their few belongings then return to some apartment in Baton Rouge or New Orleans, as she'd planned before. There the two of them would get on with whatever time they had left together.

She had to go because staying was too painful and no one had suggested that they were to be permanent guests, anyway. If leaving was even more of an agony, it was something she intended to ignore until, perhaps when she was a very old lady alone in some nursing home, she no longer felt the ache.

She had made no real plan beyond the illegal transplant, as if she'd thought that would solve all her problems. She'd need to work hard, she supposed, to keep up with the continuing medical expenses. If she submerged herself in color and design, perhaps she could forget, and also find the strength to face whatever happened next. She'd discard the swamp fabrics with their soft, grayed lavenders and browns, however. They had too many memories attached, too many hopes and dreams. In any case, the series was incomplete without the elusive blue-green color that she'd envisioned; it needed that spark of difference to lift it above the ordinary. She'd start over, find a new vision. At least she could try.

Behind her, the back door of the big house closed with a solid thud that echoed from the tree rimmed lake in a dull boom. Janna glanced over her shoulder in time to watch Clay descend the steps, moving with easy grace and one hand tucked into the top of the watch pocket of his jeans. The white shirt he'd changed into was loose fitting and had half the buttons undone over the bandaging for his injury. He paused as if looking for something, or someone. Then he continued down to the ground and started toward her.

"How is your shoulder?" she asked with determined brightness as he came closer.

"Fine." He shifted it experimentally. "Probably be sore tomorrow, but no serious damage."

She knew very well that the cut had gone deep, slicing into muscle, but refrained from prying into the details since he made light of it. "I'm sorry it had to happen. I feel so stupid for leading Dr. Gower back here."

"Forget it. You didn't know what he was really like."

"That's just it, I should have." She shook her head. "Who would have thought he'd go that far. It's still incredible to me that he really killed those kids."

"It takes a certain mindset to accept that kind of thing in people you know," he said, his features grim. "Be glad you don't have it."

He meant a cynical mind that lacked trust and always looked for the worst in people, she suspected. "I must have been willfully blind. When I think of what he meant to do to Lainey..."

"Don't," he said shortly. "No point in dwelling on things that didn't happen."

"No." She paused, then said after a moment, "I suppose I should get back to the house and check on her. She might be upset if she wakes up and finds herself alone in a strange place."

"No hurry. Arty's in the house. He'll look after her."

A quick smile came and went across her face. "He's so good with her."

"He's her slave, pure and simple. I'd hate to have been in the doctor's shoes if he'd left even a scratch on her."

"You really think Arty would have used his knife?"

"In a heartbeat. The doctor's hide would have been on Arty's wall, and his carcass in Beulah's belly."

She grimaced and shook her head.

"Sorry. That may have been a bit graphic, but it's true."

In an abrupt change of tone, she said, "I was never so glad to see someone in my life when he showed up. Or so shocked."

"He brought Ringo for Lainey, because he thought she might be pining after her pet. At least that's what he said. Sometimes people like Arty, those who live close to nature, have an instinct about these things."

"Danger, you mean?"

"Especially when it threatens somebody they've come to care about. He's just as attached to you, you know. You took him in, let him be your friend when most women would have run screaming from him. It means a lot to him. He didn't like the way you went off, either, without telling anybody where you were going. So he came to see what I meant to do about it."

"You?"

Clay squinted at the fading light on the water. "He has old-fashioned standards. He thought whatever feeling there was between us gave me an obligation to look after you.''

She looked away. ''I see.''

''The only trouble was, he couldn't tell me where you'd gone.''

Was he suggesting that he'd have made an effort to find and protect her if he'd known? She'd like to think so, but didn't quite dare. She said, ''Arty is a grand old guy. I'll never forget him after this afternoon.''

Clay looked at her through narrowed eyes, but if he found her choice of words prophetic, he made no comment. After a second, he asked, ''Why didn't you tell me what you meant to do? Why keep it a secret?''

''You'd have tried to stop me.''

''Hell, yes. It was a suicide mission.''

''I know that now. At the time so much had gone wrong that I wasn't thinking too clearly.''

''You knew too much. You were in danger from the instant his nurse understood that you were seeking alternate treatment for Lainey.''

''Maybe, but I never had a chance to tell him. He came into Anita's office shouting about his contact downtown and how there was going to be a raid. Everything snowballed from there.''

''Roan was fascinated by what you had to say about this contact, though he and the Baton Rouge police knew Gower had to be paying off somebody. He could hardly have stayed in business so long any other way.''

''You think they'll find the man?''

"Maybe, but who knows? That's Roan's turf, or rather his friend's in Baton Rouge. Seems they'd had the center staked out for a while, but hadn't moved on it for lack of evidence. Speaking of which, I should apologize now for going behind your back with Roan on that setup. It wasn't because I thought I was right and you were wrong."

"What was it then?" she asked, her voice flat. "You thought I would tell Gower he was about to be raided? You thought I was in league with him? Or maybe that I kidnapped you in the first place because I wanted one of your kidneys for Lainey?"

"It crossed my mind," he said, his gaze on the lake.

"It crossed mine, too. Unfortunately I couldn't seem to go through with it."

"I figured that out."

"You did?" She looked at him with something close to disbelief.

"If you'd been willing to turn me over to Gower's scalpel, you'd have told him who I was that night he came to the camp. I expect the scar I'd be sporting on my back now would be lower down and to the side and shaped like a scimitar. Supposing I was alive at all."

"Don't," she said on a quick drawn breath as she looked away from him. "Drugging you was so incredibly irrational. I don't think I was myself when it happened, though that's no excuse. All I can say is that I'm sorry, so terribly sorry."

"I'm not."

She turned back to meet his gaze. It was as dark and still as the lake spread out before them, and had the same lavender reflections for the dying light. "Why not? Oh, I see, because of Lainey."

His expression didn't change for long seconds, then a wry smile tugged one corner of his mouth. "She called me Daddy. Did you hear?"

Janna gave a slow nod. "She was frightened. It didn't mean anything."

"It meant something to me, Janna. I'd like to be a father to her."

"Her father is dead." The words were bald, but she was in too much pain to be able to soften them.

"I know. And you don't want a replica. But there has to be another way."

"You can't have her."

He stared at her, the light in his eyes so intense they were like black-jet. Finally he said, "I don't want to take her away from you, Janna."

"Don't you?"

"I just want her to have her rightful place with all the other Benedict kids," he said with a slow shake of his head. "I want her to know where she comes from and how she got there. I want to give her roots, so she can grow up straight and strong and never worry that she wasn't wanted or wasn't loved by her father as much as by her mother."

Every word was like a blow to the sore center of her heart. It was so exactly what she'd always wanted for Lainey and never expected to gain, so precisely what her daughter needed. It was also the one thing that she'd never have because time and hope were running out, and soon would be gone entirely.

"That would be lovely," she said, her voice like the whisper of the evening breeze in the green lace of the cypress leaves. "If I could be sure Lainey was going to grow up."

"If?" A frown gathered between his brows. "Don't you know—of course you don't. Oh, God, Janna."

"What?"

"You understand so much, seem to know so nearly how I think and feel, that I thought you'd realize. Doc Watkins gave me the news an hour ago, while he was stitching up my back. He had it directly from Simon Hargrove at the hospital. Testing for antibodies between Lainey's blood and mine was negative. We're a match, as near to perfect as a parent and child can ever be, as perfect as if I had been Matt."

"You mean, you submitted to the tests?"

"Hell, I insisted on them, Janna!"

"And they are all okay, blood, tissue, everything."

"I can give her a kidney."

The magic in those few words. The sheer, unadulterated joy of them. And yet.

"But it's dangerous," she objected. "You might, that is, you could...die."

"It would be worth it."

"No, it wouldn't!"

She spun away from him and took a few hasty steps. Then she clasped her hands in front of her and bowed her head. She couldn't believe she'd said those words. Even less could she believe that she meant them. She did, though. God help her, she did.

Clay stepped close behind her. He put his hand on her shoulders and turned her gently to face him. "You're saying that you don't want to exchange my life for Lainey's?"

She shook her head, unable to speak for the hard knot in her throat.

"You're not? What is it then? You don't want my help? The Benedicts failed you once, so you don't want anything to do with them now? It wasn't Matt's fault that he wasn't there for you, Janna. It isn't mine that I'm not him."

"You don't understand," she whispered.

"Make me. Tell me what's wrong so I can set it right."

"Nothing's wrong. It's just that…that I can't stand to choose between you and Lainey."

"There is no choice. I've already made it. All you have to do is agree."

"But agreeing is a choice, too! Oh, Clay, you aren't Matt, no, but you're the one who matters. I hardly remember what your brother was like anymore. When I think of him, it's your face I see. The two of you have merged in my mind until it's as if he was only a shadow that looked something like you, that knowing him was a dream I had to live through so I could one day know you. You fill my life along with my Lainey, and I will die if I have to lose either of you."

He smiled, a slow, rich curving of his mouth with

gladness that rose to burn also in his eyes. "You won't," he said, the words a promise. "You will have us both for as long as you can stand us. I love you, Janna."

"Oh, Clay," she whispered.

"You are my mystery woman as well as Matt's. I love you because he did, and because you loved him and bore a daughter to remember him by. And I love you for all you are and have tried to be without help, without complaints, without apologies. I love you for your strength and your talent, and your stubborn, damned independence, and for so much more that I think it will take fifty long years or more of keeping you with me here at Grand Point to tell you."

"Maybe," she said with tears rising in her eyes, "but that will do for a starting place."

He caught her close then, and tasted the salty wetness of her eyes before he set his mouth to hers. She pressed into him, held tightly to him as she gave him her life and her breath. Until, suddenly, she stiffened.

"What is it?" His voice was thick as he spoke against her lips.

"Your back," she said. "Your stitches."

"You'd better get used to them," he said. "And to the scars."

"Maybe I'll kiss them and make them better."

"It's a starting place," he said, the words gentle, wickedly mocking. Then he kissed her again.

Epilogue

The wedding was beautiful, with an understated elegance designed to allay any possible resentment from those who had come expecting to see a show that would put the more modest weddings of Turn-Coupe residents to shame. It succeeded, too, at least among the guests who had no idea of the cost of such simplicity. Janna heard one woman telling another that she'd only come because she'd heard Roan was marrying a princess. "But if this is the best she can throw in the way of a wedding, I have to say I ain't impressed. Why Mary Lou Singer had eight bridesmaids, three flower girls and more flowers than was at the mayor's funeral, for Pete's sake, *besides* hiring white limos for the entire wedding party. This Victoria Molina-Vandergraff has only two matrons of honor to stand up with her, nothing but a few ferns and lilies to decorate the church and she and the sheriff are going away in that old purple Super Bird he's had since back in the seventies."

Every word the woman said was true, there was no denying it. But to Janna, the little Victorian chapel beside the lake was perfect. The bride was lovely in cream silk and baroque pearls, her groom stalwart and handsome in his tux, as was his son who acted as best man. The two matrons of honor, April and Regina, appeared cool and gracious in their pale green organza. The congregation, made up of so many extended family members that Janna would never recall them all, was quietly appreciative. The music was uplifting, the vows moving and the officiating reverend both eloquent and mercifully brief. And if Janna spent most of her time looking at Clay as he stood at the altar as a groomsman, she thought no one noticed.

She had no need to take notes on the proceedings for future reference. She and Clay had been married in a simple ceremony at Grand Point over four weeks before. He'd wanted no possibility of a slipup that would prevent her from belonging to the Benedict Clan all right and proper, he'd said. Janna tried to talk him out of it, mainly by rejecting the idea that anything might happen to him, but he'd insisted. She gave in, finally, since it was too tough arguing against him, much less against her own heart.

Truth to tell, she didn't at all regret missing a formal wedding with all its hectic preparation and huge crowd of Benedicts both large and small. The quiet exchange of vows with Clay, with only their closest family members present, had been moving beyond words and all that she required.

She did have one small pang of envy, however, and this concerned the honeymoon. Roan and Tory were leaving for Jackson Hole and two weeks of

mountain coolness and privacy. Janna and Clay, on
the other hand, had barely had two days of wedded
bliss together. On the Monday morning after their
Saturday wedding, both her groom and their junior
maid of honor had checked into a New Orleans medical center for surgery.

It was over. The transplant had been uneventful,
the recovery textbook perfect. Everyone who came
and went in the hospital room shared by Clay and
Lainey had been amazed at how fast the two of them
healed. They had assumed it was a family trait passed
from father to daughter and no one contradicted
them—certainly not Lainey who glowed every time
it was mentioned.

For her daughter, Janna thought, the secret of her
fast recovery was sheer happiness. That and, just possibly, a newly developed Benedict sense of compe-
tition.

Clay and Lainey had raced each other to see which
of them would sit up first, produce fluid from their
single kidney first, get rid of their assorted tubes and
catheters first, or be ready to go home first. They also
got a huge kick out of showing off their matching
scimitar-shaped scars, and had entertained the whole
hospital with the sight, not to mention every visitor
to darken the doors of Grand Point since their return.

Janna's main fear about the wedding today, in fact,
was that Lainey and Clay might provide a special
display at the reception. So far, they'd been good but
she put no reliance whatever in their staying that way.
Lainey was growing daily more lively and audacious,

and Clay aided and abetted her recklessly since he was certain that she was too quiet. Judging from the crowd of laughing, squealing Benedict offspring that skirted the edge of rowdiness as they flowed in and out among the guests like a school of baby barracuda, it seemed he might be right.

Lainey was running with the pack even now. It had taken some doing for Janna to convince herself it was okay. The main reason she was able to manage it was the realization that every adult Benedict kept a watchful eye on the kids, so they were not quite as unsupervised as it appeared. The rest of it was that Clay had directed Stephen, Regina's young son, to look after Lainey. The solemn responsibility with which the boy had accepted his assignment was clear indication of how Benedict men became engrained with their protective attitude toward women.

"So you're my new sister-in-law."

Janna turned so quickly at the deep-voiced comment that she sloshed a few drops of champagne from the glass she held. The spilled wine was forgotten as she looked at the man in front of her. Tall and broad, undeniably attractive in the classic Benedict mold she had come to recognize, he had the hard, sunburnished look of a man who spent his days under a desert sun and his nights exactly as he pleased. He was dressed in chinos and an open-necked dress shirt, with a jacket of tropical-weight linen as his only concession to the formality of the occasion. His dark brown hair had sun-bleached streaks and his eyes shaded from brown to green like the dark, rich, mint tea of the East.

"And you must be Wade," she said, putting out her hand.

He ignored the offer of a handshake. With a quick step forward, he slid his arm around her waist then bent his head and kissed her.

Janna stiffened and clutched a handful of his jacket, pushing at him as she dragged her lips free. In a furious undertone, she demanded, "What do you think you're doing?"

"Testing to see if you're the right one for my baby brother."

"Do it again," Clay said from behind Janna, "and your baby brother will knock you flat on your rear."

Wade Benedict lifted a brow as he met his brother's gaze. "You and what star fleet force, little brother?"

"I'll help him," Janna said, her voice cool as she pushed out of Wade's grasp. "If he needs backup, which I doubt."

Clay's brother looked from one of them to the other, then a slow smile crinkled the corners of his eyes and shifted the planes of his face into breath-stealing handsomeness. With a slow nod of his head, he said, "Yep. She's the one all right."

"I'm glad you approve," Clay said with irony. "From now on, you can do it from a safe distance."

Wade retreated a step. "Hands off, promise. But you can't blame me for wondering what you've got yourself into with a woman who hog-tied you, carted you off to the altar, then snatched a kidney for her daughter, all in less time than it takes for me to say it.''

''Matt's daughter.''

''Right. Speaking of which?'' He nodded, inquiringly, toward something he saw behind them.

Lainey, flushed and grinning, came to a skidding halt at Clay's side. She caught his hand, tugging at it, as she said, ''Come on. They want to see our scars.''

''Oh, honey, I don't think so,'' Janna began.

''I'd like to see, too,'' Wade said. ''Later, when we're all back at Grand Point. Do you know you look just like your mother?''

''Everybody says that,'' Lainey said in disgust as she gave him her attention. ''Who are you?''

Wade went to one knee in front of her. ''I'm your daddy's brother.''

Lainey stared at him in appraisal and total disregard for his obvious sex appeal. ''Which daddy?''

Ready amusement made emerald glints in Wade's eyes though his face remained serious. ''Both of them.''

''Oh. You weren't at the other wedding.''

''I was a bit busy. Sorry.''

Her smile was sunny. ''That's okay. Everybody else was there, Arty, Denise who let us stay at her camp, my new grandma, Uncle Adam, everybody. But I guess you're my uncle, too.''

''Right.''

''Good,'' she said with a decided nod. ''I like uncles. Mama says I have two of those, besides Clay who's an uncle and a daddy at the same time. And I've got lots of cousins.''

"Lots," Wade agreed dryly.

"And Stephen, who isn't a cousin, quite, though his little sister Courtney *is,* which is very weird. Jake is a cousin, too. He's Uncle Roan's son, and older than Stephen, but I like him anyway.''

"Right. But Roan isn't an uncle, just a cousin.''

"I know. It's just pretend, and that's why I don't count him. But he's older and the sheriff, and it isn't polite to call him Roan because I'm just a kid. So Mama says it's okay to call him Uncle Roan until I grow up. She says it's the…the…''

"The custom," Wade supplied in grave tones. "The old Southern way.''

"We've been talking about kinship," Janna said quickly by way of explanation.

"Something she'll need a lot of lessons in if she's going to be a part of this clan," he answered.

It was another validation, one of many over the past few days and weeks. Still, Janna could never hear enough of them. She felt her heart swell and the ache of tears in her throat. Reaching out, she took her husband's hand. He smiled, and there in front of God and everybody, especially his older brother, he kissed her.

It seemed that the reception would go on forever, that Roan and Tory were having too much fun to leave. Toward the end, the bride threw her bouquet for the cluster of unmarried females, and the groom snapped the garter so it flew back over his shoulder toward the gathered single guys. That bit of elasticized white satin, lace and ribbon went over their heads, however, and Wade, talking to the preacher nearby, put out a hand by reflex action and snatched it from the air. Laughter erupted immediately, however, as he looked with mock horror at what he'd caught and immediately let it fall to the ground.

Finally the couple hugged everyone then rattled away from the church dragging tin cans and old shoes behind their classic car. The crowd began to disperse. The last child was rounded up and buckled into a seat belt, the last "Y'all come!" shouted across the parking lot. Janna offered to stay behind and help the ladies of the church clear away the debris, but was shooed out the door.

She and Clay returned to Grand Point in one vehicle while Lainey rode with Wade who, by this time, had begun to figure high on her list of favorite people. It wasn't that surprising, perhaps; Janna was sure there were few females of any age who could resist Clay's brother once he'd made up his mind to charm them.

Wade would be at Grand Point for a while, or so it seemed. At least the pile of luggage that she stumbled over in the parlor as she entered the house ahead of Clay seemed to indicate it. While Clay carried the bags into the section of the big house that Wade claimed, Janna began to put on the automatic coffeemaker, that inevitable requirement for Benedict hospitality. She was still spooning grounds into the filter when she heard Wade and Lainey drive up.

"Mama, guess what?" her daughter called out as she came running into the house. "Uncle Wade says I might like to drink beer now."

"Beer?" She frowned at the man who followed her daughter.

"Sorry," he said at once, holding up both hands in a defensive gesture. "It was the only thing I could think of offhand that she might not like already."

"He says people who get transplants sometimes start liking the same things to eat or the same music or clothes that the person who gave it to them likes," her daughter said, her eyes wide. "And it's true, Mama. I like veggies now, also country music and going fishing, and taking pictures, and wearing jeans and T-shirts, all just like Daddy. Isn't that neat?"

"Very neat," she agreed, though it was it her private opinion that Lainey would adore practically anything so long as she could share it with Clay. The poor guy could hardly turn around without finding Lainey in his shadow.

"No beer, though," Clay said in stern tones as he walked into the kitchen from the bedroom wing, tucking his T-shirt into the jeans he'd already changed into after ditching his tux.

"Right," Janna agreed in a show of parental solidarity.

"Except," Clay amended with a thoughtful expression, "for maybe just a sip of two of brew to see if she really has developed a taste for it."

"Hopeless," Janna moaned. "You Benedicts are all hopeless."

"Not quite." He came close and put his arm around her as he murmured against her ear, "It's been ages since the surgery, and I'm feeling pretty hopeful about our interrupted honeymoon."

"Jeez," Wade said with a wry grimace. "If you two lovebirds are going to whisper sweet nothings, the kid and I are going to jump in the lake for a swim."

Janna glanced at Clay's brother, aware of the heat in her face. "You can swim, if you want. Lainey has to wade for another week or so."

"Right. Didn't I say that?" Wade asked in mock innocence.

It took several minutes, and a couple of trips back and forth for items Lainey considered essential, before the pair of them were ready for the outing. At last they were gone and quiet descended. Janna brought the coffee that had finished brewing and set it in front of Clay where he'd taken a seat on the sofa. He pulled her over against him and they sat in peaceful silence for long moments.

"Too bad your mother couldn't come for Roan's wedding," Janna said finally. "Or Adam."

"They had other things to do, I guess. Though one wedding a year is about all Adam can take."

He meant, she supposed, that they were lucky his mother and older brother had made it to see them married, much less Roan and Tory. "I'm glad Wade arrived in time."

"A coincidence. He really came to meet you."

"You think so? Then I'm even more glad. I like Wade."

Clay slanted her a wry glance. "Most women do."

"He's not nearly as handsome or a personable as his brother, of course."

"Adam's a lady-killer, too, I know."

She leaned back in the half-circle of his arm so she could see his face. "That's shameless fishing for a compliment."

"Ain't it, now? Though I think old Wade might be trying to steal the love of my life."

"Don't be ridiculous!"

"I meant Lainey," he answered with mischief glowing deep in the rich blue of his eyes.

That required retaliation, of course, which took some minutes and left them both flushed and breathless. Only the fear of being interrupted by the return of the swimmers prevented them from carrying it into the bedroom. In an effort at remaining presentable enough for company, they turned their attention to their coffee.

After a moment, Clay said, "Seriously, I think Wade would look after Lainey here at the house for a week or two. He's home between engineering projects and at loose ends. He told me earlier that if I ever intended to take you on a honeymoon, now's the time."

"Did you intend to?" she asked hopefully.

The look he gave her carried enough wattage to light up Turn-Coupe for a year. "I thought about it."

"So did I," she said, her voice not quite even.

"That's settled then. What about afterward?"

"Afterward?"

He took her hand, meshing their fingers, fitting their palms together. "You've put your work on hold these past few weeks while taking care of me and Lainey. One day soon we're going to be settled down here. I'll have to think about making a regular living now that I have a family. That means getting serious about marketing my nature photos, doing freelance stuff for *National Geographic,* getting the new book out on time, developing a line of notecards and calendars from some of my special prints, and so on. You don't have to do anything, if you'd rather not, but I thought you might be ready to go back to that line of fabrics that you were working on at the camp."

"I'd been thinking about it, to tell you the truth." It was funny that they really hadn't discussed this before now. There'd been so much else going on, of course, so much else to find out about each other.

"You'll need a studio," he said with a nod. "There's room for one next to mine, in the left wing there." He indicated the door that led into a hallway on the far side of the living room. "It's available until Wade or Adam decide they want to move back home for good. We may have inherited this place together, but I'm chief caretaker."

"That would be wonderful," she said, her voice soft. It was yet another example of how much he thought about her needs, how much he cared about her.

"One more thing."

"Yes?"

He disentangled himself and got up, pulling her to her feet beside him. "Come on. I have something to show you."

"What is it?" Janna glanced at him, puzzled by the intensity in his expression, as she allowed herself to be led toward the door.

"You'll see."

They descended the back steps and took the path made of old bricks that divided the backyard into squares. At a long flowerbed that lay between the walkway and the house, he stopped. Clasping her hand tightly, he gestured toward the low-growing vegetation that filled the bed in a luxuriant, dark green mass. "There it is."

The plants stirred no recognition, though they appeared to be perennial and bore some resemblance to common houseleek. "I don't understand."

"The Aphrodite's Cup."

It was the dye plant he'd told her about weeks ago, the one for which she'd searched high and low and given up as nonexistent. "You mean…it was here all along?"

He inclined his head in assent.

"And you knew it." She needed to be absolutely clear on that point.

"It's truly uncommon these days, a species seldom

found in nature anymore. But if you still want it, then here it is."

If she wanted it. The words, and especially the quiet assurance of his voice, were another way of saying that anything he had, everything he had, was hers. Her irritation that he had kept the plants from her until now drifted away on the gentle summer breeze. "Oh, Clay," she whispered. "Thank you."

"Don't thank me. I didn't find it."

The taut sound of his voice disturbed her. "Who did then?"

He met her gaze, his own troubled. "It was Matt. He found it the last time he was home, during the few days we had together just before he died. He brought in this handful of weeds, grinning over them because they reminded him of someone, he said, a woman who was interested in special dyes but would need more than just a sprig or two of these plants if she was to do anything with them. We planted them here by the back steps, he and I. Matt dug the bed for it. I hauled the compost and turned it into the soil while he rested. Together, we put the sprigs in the ground and watered them. He said when we were done that we had planted the Color of Love."

"Oh, Clay," she said over the tightness in her throat. "You could have told me before. It wouldn't have mattered."

"I know," he said simply. "That's why I can tell you now. Matt loved you, Janna. He'd never have left you to bring up Lainey alone, not if he'd had a choice."

It was proof that he understood he was no replica in her eyes. It was also a declaration of love finer than anything she'd ever known. "You're a rare man," she said, her smile trembling a little at the corners.

"No. Only one who loves you."

"Yes," she contradicted him, her voice growing stronger. "And because of it, we'll let the Color of Love stay just as rare, if it's all right with you. There will be other colors, other designs, other fabrics, but this one will remain ours alone. Aphrodite's Cup can grow here at Grand Point always, as a reminder. And one day I'll give a sprig of it to Lainey to grow at her home, and to all our other children."

"All of them?" he asked with a lifted brow, though the bright hope in his eyes belied the lightness of his words.

"All of them," she said firmly. Then she drew his arm around her waist and walked beside him back into the house.

Author's Note

Write what you know, authors have always been told. A recent fan letter alerted me to the fact that some readers may not realize that I've been doing just that with my Louisiana gentlemen series. Many of the place names given in the books are real—though not necessarily attached to the locations indicated. Chemin-a-Haut for instance, is the name of a state park in my section of Louisiana. I used it as the name for the house in *Luke* because I've always enjoyed the way the syllables whisper through the mind. So-called "dog-trot" openings were a special feature of many old Louisiana homes, and I included a house with that feature and name in *Roan* to counterbalance the Greek Revival splendor of the Benedict houses in *Kane* and *Luke*.

Along the Louisiana bank of the Mississippi River are several oxbow-shaped lakes that were formed when the river abandoned a watercourse, as described in the series. One of these is Horseshoe Lake where my family often fished when I was a child. However, the various descriptions of the lake in this series were taken from the interconnected Black and Saline Lakes, with their creeks and swamps, in central Louisiana where my mother and father had a fishing camp at one time. Regardless, neither Horseshoe Lake nor Black Lake have the fine old plantation homes built along their shorelines similar to those supplied for the Benedict clan around fictional Horseshoe Lake. This honor belongs to another oxbow lake known as False River that is located near Baton Rouge.

There is no Tunica Parish in Louisiana. However, the Tunica Indians once roamed the swamps and woodlands along the Mississippi River in the northern and central portions of the state. They were also resident in our sister state of Mississippi where there is a town called Tunica. As for the name Turn-Coupe, Louisiana has a Pointe Coupee Parish, an old French designation that means cut-off point. There is also the town of Cut-Off, a real place name on Louisiana road maps that came about, like Pointe Coupee, from having been "cut off," or displaced from the main flow of the Mississippi River, when the great waterway changed course during flood. Turn-Coupe is designed to be an amalgamated version of these two place names. The town itself is fictional as a matter of convenience, since that means I can make it just as it needs to be to fit my stories. It has its basis in reality, however, since many small communities in Louisiana, or across the South for that matter, share Turn-Coupe's blend of vices and virtues, dinginess and beauty, not-so-good-old-boys and true Southern gentlemen.

I've been asked many times if the men in my books, particularly my Louisiana gentlemen, really exist. They do and they don't. Though Kane, Luke, Roan and Clay are figments of my imagination, they are solidly based on the men I've known all my life: my dad and my brothers, the boys I went to school with, acquaintances made over the years, and especially my husband, Jerry Maxwell. The Benedict clan has its counterpart in my husband's family, a large one with four girls and four boys. When our children were small, the four brothers all built houses on land that had been deeded to them by their father, so we lived in a family enclave of grandparents, uncles, aunts and cousins not unlike that of the Benedict's in feeling. Because Maxwell is a Scots name, we referred to ourselves in aggregate as the Maxwell Clan. We've scattered since those days, and our families have grown exponentially, but we still reside in the same community where we have occasional clan gatherings and get along amazingly well. Family resemblance is easily traced, much like the Benedicts.

The background for the Benedict clan, on the other hand, is taken in part from the legends and stories of my own family. For instance, my great-great grandfather, Reddick Blake, married a Native American woman of the Choctaw nation and established a landholding with her in the 1830s in what was then the frontierlike backcountry of north-central Louisiana. It was another branch of my mother's family, however, that descended on the same isolated area a short time later in a party that included four brothers. They were only a jump or two ahead of the law, so the old folks say, due to the mysterious death of a sister's abusive husband. So it goes, in the odd way that a writer will often take a piece here, a piece there, and weave a story using strands of truth.

Speaking of truth, I should point out the Aphrodite's Cup is purely fictitious. The plant, its history and the blue color derived from it exist only in my mind.

The friendships that writers make often effect their work as well. I met Kathie Seidick, to whom this book is dedicated, on the online listserve for the Novelists, Inc. As a result of that meeting, she loaned me a copy of her book *Or You Can Let Him Go,* the story of her son's fight against renal disease and his eventual triumph over it with transplant surgery. The story in *Clay* would have been incomplete without this haunting addition. In token of Kathie's generosity, and as a result of the intensive research into renal disease required for this book, I've made a pledge to sign an organ donor card when I renew my driver's license. Since my blood type is O positive, I hope this will one day shorten the wait for transplant of two renal patients, children or adults, and perhaps even save a life. It's such a small thing compared to the good it can bring. It would give me immense pleasure to think that you, as a reader of this book, may sign a donor card as well.

Finally, although the characters in *Clay* had little time to cook, I can't leave out my usual recipe. This one came originally from the kitchen of a good friend and quilting buddy, Mary Rasberry. My family enjoys it, not least because it partakes of that fine Louisiana tradition, the sharing of great-tasting food between friends. Please accept it in the same spirit.

Baked Cabbage Jambalaya

1 head cabbage, chopped
1 lb. ground meat
1 lb. smoked sausage, cut into
bite-size pieces
1/4 c. cooking oil
1 c. raw rice, rinsed
1 large onion, chopped
2 ribs celery, minced
2 cloves garlic, minced
1 tsp. chili powder
1 can Ro-Tel tomatoes

Sauté the ground meat in oil. Season meat well with your favorite seasoning (such as salt and pepper or some other commercial spice blend). Add chopped onion, celery and smoked sausage. Cook until onion and celery are clear, about 10 minutes. Combine the meat and all the remaining ingredients and place in a large casserole dish. Cover and back at 275 degrees for 2 hours, stirring halfway through the cooking time.

The recipe makes a large amount, so is an excellent dish for church suppers and other covered dish events. It reheats well in the microwave but does not freeze well.

Warmest wishes for happy reading, and cooking, always,

Jennifer Blake
www.jenniferblake.com

International Bestselling Author

DIANA PALMER

When Texas Ranger Marc Brannon returns to the line of duty, a high-profile murder mystery pits him against the vibrant—and vulnerable—junior investigator from his past. Years ago, Josette Langley had made no secret of the fact that she was drawn to the rugged lawman. Yet Marc and Josette had parted on explosive terms when she made a shocking accusation and shattered both their lives. Now they are back together again—and this time a lot more is at stake than just their hearts....

The Texas Ranger

Available August 2001
wherever paperbacks are sold!

Visit us at www.mirabooks.com

MDP843

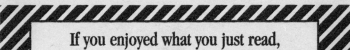

New York Times Bestselling Author

HEATHER GRAHAM

Slow Burn

Faced with the brutal murder of her husband, Spencer Huntington demands answers from the one man who should have them— ex-cop David Delgado. Her husband's best friend. Her former lover. Bound by a reluctant partnership, Spencer and David find their loyalties tested by desires they can't deny. Their search takes them from the glittering world of Miami high society to the dark, dangerous underbelly of the city—while around them swirl the desperate schemes of a killer driven to commit his final act of violence.

"An incredible storyteller!"
—*Los Angeles Daily News*

Available August 2001 wherever paperbacks are sold!

MHG864

JENNIFER BLAKE

66630	ROAN	___ $6.50 U.S.	___ $7.99 CAN.
66490	LUKE	___ $5.99 U.S.	___ $6.99 CAN.
66429	KANE	___ $5.99 U.S.	___ $6.99 CAN.
66419	SOUTHERN GENTLEMEN	___ $5.99 U.S.	___ $6.99 CAN.
66281	GARDEN OF SCANDAL	___ $5.99 U.S.	___ $6.99 CAN.

(limited quantities available)

TOTAL AMOUNT	$_____
POSTAGE & HANDLING	$_____
($1.00 for one book; 50¢ for each additional)	
APPLICABLE TAXES*	$_____
TOTAL PAYABLE	$_____
(check or money order—please do not send cash)	

To order, complete this form and send it, along with a check or money order for the total above, payable to MIRA Books®, to: **In the U.S.:** 3010 Walden Avenue, P.O. Box 9077, Buffalo, NY 14269-9077; **In Canada:** P.O. Box 636, Fort Erie, Ontario, L2A 5X3.

Name:_____
Address:_____ City:_____
State/Prov.:_____ Zip/Postal Code:_____
Account Number (if applicable):_____
075 CSAS

*New York residents remit applicable sales taxes.
　Canadian residents remit applicable GST and provincial taxes.

MIRA®